Elin Gregory

The Bones
of Our Fathers

Manifold Press

Published by Manifold Press

ISBN: 978-1-908312-61-7

Proof-reading and line editing: Hanne Lie

Editor: Fiona Pickles

Text: © Elin Gregory 2017
Cover image:
 Library © photogi | iStockphoto.com
 Maps © Nejron Photo | Shutterstock.com
 Table © namtipStudio | Shutterstock.com
 Coffee Mug © Andyd | iStockphoto.com
Cover design: © Michelle Peart 2017
E-book format: © Manifold Press 2017
Print format: © Julie Bozza 2017
Set in Adobe Caslon

For further details of Manifold Press titles both in print and forthcoming:
manifoldpress.co.uk

Dedication

As ever to my wonderful betas the fondest and most heartfelt of thank yous.

Also many thanks to the museum staff who have so generously shared their experiences and have provided so much inspiration for this book.

Please note that nobody in this book is based on anyone we know, okay?

Author's Note:

The town of Pemberland and its satellite villages, Escley, Brynglas and King's Norton, do not actually exist, more's the pity.

If they did, they would be about where Pontrilas is, just off the A465.

Chapter 1

"Oh dear God, just look at her."

Mal did and, although he'd be the first to admit that his interest was academic, he had to agree that Mrs Gaskell was gorgeous. Forever legs in tight jeans emphasised by extravagantly furry Ugg boots, a tailored blouse that clung to gravity defying breasts, masses of wavy blonde locks floating on the breeze like a shampoo advert and a pretty face currently obscured by the upmarket camera she was holding in French-manicured fingers. Just like a Sunday supplement advert for Chanel or Harvey Nicks, though he guessed in those she'd probably be taking photos of Petra, or Machu Picchu rather than a windy hillside in the Welsh Marches. She crouched and stooped, taking snaps of Mr Gaskell as he droned on about what an asset this development would be to the community, while his workforce looked on with hungry wistful expressions.

"Shouldn't be allowed."

Mal glanced over his shoulder at the speaker, a heavy-set man in a bright yellow hard hat who was staring at Mrs Gaskell as though he could eat her with a spoon.

"God, look at that arse."

"Oh, yeah, I am," muttered the younger, taller man beside him and Mal saw with utter shock that he wasn't looking at the girl. The young man caught Mal's eye and gave him a huge white grin. Mal looked away hurriedly, not quite able to believe it.

"Rob," the older man warned, "don't frighten the archaeologist. Christ, won't this windbag ever finish. I've got plant standing idle that should be working."

Mal had to agree. He had work to do as well but, instead, was standing ankle deep in wet grass, trying to stop an ill-fitting yellow plastic hat from sliding over his eyes and listening to one of the most boring pep-talks he had ever heard. But at least the view beyond Gaskell's brand new Jeep was nice. A wood-crested hill, gilded by the September sun and rimmed by the patchwork of smallish hedge-lined fields that seemed to be the local agricultural style, shouldered up into a blue sky filled with racing clouds. In the other direction, and Mal didn't think he could be blamed if his attention wandered, was the little town of Pemberland, Mal's new home, with its two churches, two chapels, many pubs and an honest-to-God market square with a big cross in the middle. Just to the left, Mal could see the slate roof of his new place of employment, once known as the Town Museum but recently rechristened The Pemberland Centre for Heritage and Culture. Names were important, Mal thought. 'Town Museum' told you exactly what you were going to get. 'Centre for Heritage and Culture' could mean anything.

"Sounds like he's running down now. Get ready to clap."

"Just a final word," Gaskell said, his hoarse whisky-voice only just carrying over the rush of wind and the shuffling of bored workers. "As we all know, the history of our town is never far from us. I want you all to be vigilant as you break ground. We don't want anything to be missed so keep your eyes peeled. Anything you find that might be of historical interest should be reported to Mr Glyn Havard," Mal glanced round and saw the older man behind him raise a hand in acknowledgement, "and he will liaise with Malcolm Bright, the new manager at the Pemberland Centre for Heritage and Culture." Conscious of the camera pointing in his direction Mal waved as well.

"If you don't want to liaise with him, Glyn, I will." The leer in the murmur was unmistakeable, followed by a grunt and a chuckle. It sounded to Mal as though Rob had been thumped.

"You're a godless heathen bound for hell."

"Says the man who was coveting his neighbour's ass."

Mal ducked his head so the brim of the hard hat covered his urge to laugh. He missed having someone to laugh with and, frankly, the thought of liaising with someone with such a saucy grin and such bright eyes was very appealing. It had been months since Mal had a good hard liaise.

"Oh, about bloody time too."

Gaskell produced a classy looking bottle, stripped off the foil and wire and passed it to the lady, swapping it for the camera. She posed with the bottle for a moment, pouting at the lens, then popped the cork. A froth of foam sprayed over her husband, the audience, and the nearest large machine. The last bit went all over her, gluing the blouse to her skin which shone pink through the fine fabric.

"God in Heaven," Mr Havard groaned. "How the hell am I going to keep everyone's minds on their jobs now? Apart from you, anyhow."

"Bet that's only Lambrini. If she's made my bloody digger all sticky …" Rob snarled and Malcolm couldn't help but laugh.

This was the sort of job Mal had been warned he might have to take when he got the job of curator at the museum – sorry, Heritage Centre. Once upon a time, when Local Government funds had flowed freely, there had been a County Archaeologist attached to the Planning department who kept an eye on all new developments. Now times had changed, the County Archaeologist post was long gone and anyone qualified could be sent along to peer down the holes. They had warned Mal about it at his interview. No museum work paid well, not at his level, but it was an interesting area and a fantastic, wildly mixed collection, and Malcolm had found himself a flat that was well within his means. It was a bit lonely sure enough but it was early days yet. He'd only been in town for a month and a half. This little extra job – just checking that the diggers and dozers didn't uncover anything archaeologically valuable – would be really handy money-wise, and could be fun socially, too.

As he walked down the hill to where he had left his bike, he glanced back at the gang of workmen, trying to pick out the younger of the two men – Rob. Had Mal imagined it or had Rob really been checking out Mal's arse? If he had, he didn't seem to be worried about being spotted.

Malcolm collected his bike and put on his cycle helmet before he cycled back to the museum. The good thing about Pemberland was that it was very compact with plenty of shortcuts. Avoiding the town centre, he pedalled hard along the road that cut behind the church and got off to use the pedestrian crossing. From there it wasn't worth getting back on his bike to go the rest of the way. He paused at the gates to the museum grounds to allow an ancient Mini to creep past and took the opportunity to admire the building as he pushed his bike up the gravelled drive. It was a gracious old pile, Georgian with a lovely balanced symmetrical design, some beautifully proportioned public rooms at the front and a rat's nest of tiny rooms at the back. Mal chained his bike to the rack and went up the newly built ramp to the lobby. It was a very imposing entrance with black and white tiled floors, and a marvellous wrought iron chandelier pendant from the moulded plaster ceiling. He had to admit that the effect was spoiled a little by shelves of stationery, and pocket-money toys and gifts, but nothing could conceal the perfect proportions of the room. To the right an archway formed the hallowed portal to the library, with the desk for checking books in and out narrowing the entrance. To the left was his own less hushed domain. Two young mums with buggies were chatting as their toddlers used one of the play areas and Mal made a mental note to obtain more crepe paper because they seemed to be using a lot. Straight ahead, tucked under the gracious sweep of the staircase, was the museum reception desk and tourist information centre, currently manned by what could have been a brilliantly hued tropical flower, or maybe a parrot, but was actually one of his few new friends.

"Yo, Mal!" The receptionist beckoned, her orange and blue hair bobbing. "Marcia's on the warpath. She says she's booked you for a meeting about lightbulbs this morning."

"Bugger." Malcolm took his messenger bag off his shoulder. "Look after this for me, Betty? I'll go and see what she wants."

Betty took the bag with a grin. "Brill, tell me about it when you get back. I'll make coffee. And save you a biscuit."

"Always amenable to bribery," Mal admitted and hurried into the library.

Bypassing the desk he peered along the stacks. As expected, Marcia Stenhouse, senior librarian and a major fly in Mal's soup, was holding court with her staff and a couple of customers at the far end of the library where there were comfortable chairs situated around a rack of newspapers and journals. She was tall, slender and poised, all the better to balance the meringue-white hair coiled on top of her head. She was an attractive woman with a killer smile, though Mal had never seen it directed his way.

One of the minions – Mal liked to think that he had colleagues but Marcia definitely had minions – saw him and nudged Marcia who hurried forward. "Mr. Bright," she said, "I expected you in here hours ago. Where on *airth* have you been?" As usual when in the grip of emotion, Marcia's Scottish accent was more pronounced.

"I'm sorry, Mrs Stenhouse, but I was called out to a meeting. It was for the council, for that new development up by Carew Hill. Betty said something about lightbulbs?"

"Oh," Marcia raised her eyebrows, "Mr Gaskell's Rifle Lane project. Well, for that I think you can be forgiven." With a gracious nod to the junior librarians and three elderly gentlemen with their *Telegraph*s, *Times*es, and *Daily Mail*s, Marcia caught Mal by the elbow. She marched him through the library and steered him past the reception desk where Betty shot him a look of utter sympathy. Marcia bestowed a gracious nod upon her and guided Mal back into the maze of what had been the servants' domain. She opened the door of a store room. Shared resources. Malcolm sighed.

Originally the museum had been the sole occupier of the building but times change and finances did too. It would save time and money, some moron had decided, if the museum and library were under the same roof and could share resources. In theory, at least. In effect it was just plain bloody annoying.

"What do you notice, Mr Bright?" Marcia gestured to the boxes stacked against the walls.

"Perhaps it would save time if you told me what I am supposed to be looking for?" Mal suggested

Marcia snorted. "The fluorescent tubes, Mr Bright. The little ones. We used the last of them a week ago and as you can see from their absence on the shelves, nobody has been bothered to order new ones."

Mal looked at the space on the shelf and asked, "Which of your staff was tasked with putting in the order for replacements?"

"My staff, Mr Bright, are not responsible for ordering resources for the maintenance of the building. Historically the museum staff have been in charge of the structure."

"Then which of my staff did you ask to put in the order?"

"You're missing my point, Mr Bright. It should not be necessary for me to have to ask. It should be done. There is a clear break-down in your system of monitoring, ordering and replenishing supplies. Good grief, you'll be allowing us to run out of lavatory paper next!"

Mal listened glumly, as she outlined a series of measures that he should put into place. Those girls at the museum reception desk, she suggested, could organise a spreadsheet. It surely wouldn't be more than a couple of days' work to inventory the stores. They would probably be glad of something to do since museum staff didn't have to work at the white hot pace of librarians.

"I will see what I can do," Mal promised.

He let Betty in on the plans at lunchtime when they took their sandwiches up to the little staff tea room on the second floor.

"'The whaite hot paice of librarrrrians.' Daft old besom. Also library stuff is on a different budget so – duh – no." Betty offered him a biscuit from the battered 'A Gift From Penzance' biscuit tin that had been at the museum, she said, since 1948. "So what's all the gen about Gaskell's latest folly then. You do know he's been trying to buy land all around the town? Making people offers they can't refuse and everything."

"No, I didn't." Mal shrugged. "What would I do without you, to fill me in on all the dirty laundry?"

"You're welcome," Betty said. "Gaskell bought those fields from old Beynon back when even older Beynon died and has been putting in for planning permission regularly ever since. Must be twenty years."

"I thought he'd come here more recently," Mal said. "And his missus. She created a bit of a stir by squirting champagne all over her shirt."

"Oh her?" Betty rolled her eyes. "Vanessa Pugh as was. You don't think that's natural, do you?"

Mal shot a pointed look at her multi-coloured hair and Betty grinned. "Not her hair, I mean …" She cupped her hands in front of her own plump chest. "Nuclear knockers. Gawd knows what's in there but I bet it has a half-life of its own."

"I didn't hear any complaints from the work force?"

"Well, you wouldn't, would you? It's hard to talk when you're hyper-ventilating."

"Not all of them." Mal smiled to himself and picked up his coffee cup. "But, yeah, most. She was putting on a good show."

"Hang on, what was that little smile for?" Betty moved the biscuit tin out of reach. "Come on, Mal. You can tell me."

"No, I can't." Mal lunged for the digestives. "Anyhow, it occurred to me that, while she was stooping and posing, perhaps the blokes weren't paying too much attention to what her old man was actually saying."

"Wouldn't be the first time." Betty nodded. "He keeps a firm hand on the purse strings, does our Mr Gaskell, when it comes to paying what he owes to his staff, but lets the pounds flow freely when it comes to treating his equals. You won't hear a word said against him up at the golf club. Coach and Horses public bar is another matter. Glyn Havard'll have to watch out that all his paperwork's in order."

"Oh, I met him." Mal beamed. It was so rarely that he knew the people whose names Betty dropped so casually into conversation. "He looks like the foreman or something."

"Just of the heavy plant guys."

"Plant?" Mal had heard Glyn Havard use the term but hadn't liked to betray his ignorance by asking what he meant.

"All the big diggers and bulldozers, tipper trucks and what not. He's got his own business – Havard Plant Hire – and works all over, providing specialist machines and the guys who drive them. Oh my God!" She slammed her hands down on the table making their mugs and Mal jump. "I know why you were smiling! You met Dirty Rob. Rob Escley?"

Mal knew his jaw had dropped and suspected his ears had gone red.

"You did! Oh jeez, Mal, what did he do?" Betty looked more delighted than appalled. "Only Rob could pull in the middle of a bloody field."

"He didn't do anything. And he absolutely didn't pull!" Mal said. "He just checked me out, that's all. Actually, it was rather nice."

"Oh God, I bet. There were wailing virgins from here to King's Norton the week he finally admitted which team he played for. Those eyes! That smile! Don't you let him give you any nonsense. And I can say that because he's family. Sort of. We were both in the same class all through school anyway."

"Warning noted and gratefully received," Mal said. "But anyway, it looks like the sort of job that won't put too much of a dent in my off-duty hours but will provide a nice little extra, so how about I take you out one night? My treat?"

Mal hadn't been out once since arriving in Pemberland and felt the need for a beer or two in a place that he didn't have to keep tidy himself.

"You absolutely can take me out," Betty said. "Tonight. I'll meet you under the cross at seven. Give me time to get my glad rags on. Curry then pool in the Coach?"

"If that's what you'd like," Mal said, grateful for the suggestion. "Should I book a table?"

"Oh no, bless your heart," Betty grinned at him. "The Coach doesn't take bookings. Bollocks, there's the phone. Who the fuck's that."

"Maybe one of us better answer it and find out?" Mal suggested and she swept off chuckling.

Chapter 2

The cross was a towering limestone and cast iron edifice in what had once been the market square but was now a bottleneck cursed by lorry drivers. Mal arrived there with a few minutes to spare, out of breath because he'd been held up at work by another round of recriminations from Marcia Stenhouse. He was in no mood for a lecture on punctuality so was relieved to see no sign of Betty's parrot hair.

He had four custodians, two of whom only worked weekends and so he rarely saw them. The museum was closed on Monday, giving him the place to himself, in theory, so he could catch up on paperwork though the librarians often demanded his time, but for the rest of the week he enjoyed the company of Betty and Sharon, who worked a complex pattern of mornings and afternoons that they swapped around between themselves. Sharon was older than Betty, with a teenaged daughter and a huge enthusiasm for local history. Betty looked pure art college though she had gone to Hereford Tech, then worked at her auntie's hairdressing salon, until they had fallen out over a matter of highlights. Betty had talked her way into the job at the museum in the hope of getting more young people to attend.

"Some pigging hope round here," she said. "If it doesn't run on batteries, the little tossers don't want to know."

She'd had him pegged as gay within the space of two hours' acquaintance and was refreshingly matter-of-fact about it.

"I'm sorry to say you won't find much in the way of nightlife round here," she'd said. "But there are some places that are more welcoming than others."

She'd reeled off a list but Mal had forgotten it. The Pemberland Centre for Heritage and Culture, once the Town Museum, was in the middle of a big readjustment. Not only had they lost a lot of space to the library but the previous curator had left in order to care for her ailing sister. With a mountain of paperwork, cataloguing and conservation projects, Mal felt he had earned a night out. All work and no play …

"There you are!" Betty appeared at his elbow and grabbed his arm.

"Let's go the long way round the square so I can show you off. You're not bad looking, in a geeky sort of way, and I want as many people as possible to see you."

"Betty," Mal fell into step with her as they circumnavigated a tub of tatty windblown petunias, "you aren't forgetting something are you?"

"That you don't do girls? Nope. But they don't know that, do they?" She tilted her head towards a Range Rover parked beside the old market hall and the three women, two in the car, one outside with a sit up and beg bicycle with an honest to God basket on the front, who were staring at them. Betty raised her hand and gave them a wave.

"Oh! That's Mrs Gaskell driving." Mal said, raising his hand when the three women waved back.

"Bella Farriner, on the bike, is Chair of the Ladies Circle, sort of an up-market version of the WI only they don't make jam and shit. In fact, I don't think they do anything much apart from wear hats and turn up at events. The other one in the car is Veronica Garth but she'll make you call her Ronnie. She's a hoot. Used to date Mick Jagger, or was it Keith Moon? Anyhow, she's more fun than the other two."

"Well, I expect they have their uses." Mal said. "Is it much further? Because it's coming on to rain."

"Oh my God, you're such a wimp. The Coach and Horses is just down here." Betty hurried him along the pavement to a street running off the square and down the hill. Another fifty yards or so and he spotted the stone arch of the entrance to a stable yard and a long rather low building beyond it. The timbered upper floor overhung the lower one by half a metre supported by heavily plastered beams. Above the door swung a battered sign with a shadowy picture that Mal quite couldn't make out.

"Here we go," Betty said reaching to open the door. "Mind your head, it's a bit low."

The Coach and Horses was definitely the oldest building Mal had been in since coming to Pemberland. Inside the beams were more obvious and the stone flagged floor was worn in dips and hollows from the passage of feet over time. Tudor, Mal guessed, at the very latest.

"It's not much," Betty said, "but they do the best curry in town."

Mal looked around at the mismatched tables and the wooden chairs whose legs had worn down against the stone floors, and the noticeboard scattered with posters and handwritten adverts. He took a breath, filling his lungs with the fumes of beer and lager and a brilliant dash of spice. It couldn't be more different from the plush yet sterile bars he had gone to in Bristol. This was real. Suddenly Mal wanted more than anything to be a 'local', to become a regular and get a welcoming grin from the barman, who would pull him his pint without having to ask his preference.

"It looks great," Mal said. "What do we do now?"

"Get us a table and I'll get menus," Betty suggested. "What do you drink? I know, I'll surprise you. No, you're not buying the first round. What is this? The fifties? You can put it down to me currying favour with the boss if you like. G'wan, go sit down."

The curry when it came, was spiced to a mild heat, filled with succulent pieces of lamb, and served on a bed of rice with puffy sweet-flavoured naan on the side. The beer was full bodied and dark. Mal sipped and ate, and sighed with happiness.

"I could get used to this," he said. "Is the rest of the menu as good?"

"Fish and chips to die for." Betty mopped up the last of her curry sauce with a scrap of naan. "And the steak pies are good or fabulous depending who makes them. One of the chefs is better than the other at pastry. But hey – it makes it interesting. Don't you like your beer?"

Mal drained his glass with a happy gulp and got out of his seat. Betty's glass was empty and he could take a hint. "It was great. Do you want another pint or are you ready for a gin?"

"For shame, trying to lead a girl astray. And you my boss 'n' all. Gin, please, and if you're still up for it we could go through to the snug for a game of pool."

They got their drinks and Betty led Mal through a door beside the bar – he had to duck to get under the lintel – across a quarry tiled corridor and into another bar.

"Oh look out, it's Peaches. Aye-aye, what can we do you for, darlin'?" The voice was familiar, and so was the bright grin.

"Piss off, Rob," Betty said. "Me an' my boss want the table when you're done. Hallo, Sion, Gary."

Other voices chimed in with greetings but Mal was exchanging measuring glances with Rob, who had swapped his hard hat, coveralls and high vis jacket for jeans and a long-sleeved tee that fitted in all the right places.

"Well, well," Rob said. "Didn't think I'd be seeing you again so soon, Mr Archaeologist."

Mal took him in with a sigh of appreciation. Outdoorsman tan, scruffy black curls, the sort of body you got from working bloody hard in the open air, with just a little hint of a beer belly from playing equally hard in the evenings. Or maybe he was relaxed because he knew he didn't have to try too hard? Either way, Betty was right, those eyes were wonderful. Almost as nice as the welcoming smile.

"Neither did I," Mal admitted. "Um, I'm Betty's boss, Malcolm Bright."

"Oh, so you're Captain Tightpants." Their hands met in a grip that went on for that extra moment that could mean something good. "Peaches has told us *all* about you."

"Shuddup, Rob." Betty gave him a shove. "I could tell a few home truths about you."

"Aww you wouldn't. So, Mal, let me and Sion finish our game then how's about you and Betty play us two?"

Mal's "If you like" clashed with Betty's "Not a chance". She set her glass down with a click and added, "Or, at least, we're not going to make it more interesting with a bet. Mal, trust me, never bet against anything with these three. They'll have the shirt off your back."

"That I'd like to see," Rob murmured then nodded to the other two men in the room. "Mal, this is Sion."

Sion was about five feet four, rectangular in build and none of it seemed to be fat. He had neatly cropped black hair and a warmth to his skin colour that made Mal wonder a bit at the Welsh name.

Sion reached across the corner of the pool table to shake Mal's hand. "Sion Thapa Rai," he said. "Da was in the Gurkhas till he met Mum. He's the chef here now. Welcome to Pemberland. I hope you're liking it."

"So far so good, thank you." Mal grinned at Sion. "Didn't I see you on the building site too?"

"Yeah, we both work for Gary's dad."

They all turned to the silent figure in the corner. "Hello, Gary?"

Gary eyed him for a second then shifted forward and began to stand. There was a continental shelf feel to the bulk of him. Rob was big but Gary was massive. His shoulders strained his plaid shirt and his thighs strained his jeans, Mal was sure that if he straightened up fully he'd strain the ceiling. His broad face showed signs of wear, a broken nose, a scar through one eyebrow, and his shaven head was adorned with a spider web tattoo. "'Lo," he said then he flushed a brilliant pink and muttered, "Hello, Betty."

"Hello, Gary," she said, reaching for a cue. "Come on then, boys, are you playing or not?"

At a bit of a loss, Mal rounded the table and stumbled over something that yielded under foot then darted away with a bass rumble.

"Dear God, what's that?" he asked, watching the enormous shaggy black beast sit by Gary's chair and lean against his knees. It gave him a reproachful stare then yawned to display teeth like a timber wolf

"Awww, did you tread on Morris?" Betty said. "You're lucky he didn't rip your leg off."

"It's a dog?"

"Sorta," Rob replied. He leaned over the table and lined up his shot, back arching just so. Mal was so entranced by the tight fit of Rob's jeans that he missed what Rob added.

Mal waited until the stripe thudded into the pocket before saying, "Sorry, I didn't catch that."

"I said …" Rob moved round the table and took his next shot. "Ahhh, bollocks. Your turn, Sion. I said that Morris is part Rottweiler and part husky, that we know about, but he's probably got a bit of pit pony in there too."

"N'awww. Don't be rude about Morris." Betty scowled at him.

"Morris is pedigree," Gary said. Both his hands buried in the black ruff around Morris's neck and Morris gave a low rumbling groan of bliss. "His mum *and* his dad."

"And that's more'n some can say," Sion said.

Gary turned to Betty and for a moment Mal thought he might speak again but he flushed and went back to stroking the massive beast leaning against his knees. He didn't take his eyes off Betty. Mal wondered if Betty knew she had an admirer, then gave himself a mental kick. This was Betty. Of course she knew, and was being kind and keeping her distance.

"So, um, what do you do, Gary?" he asked, just trying to make conversation.

"Security," Gary replied. "Me and Morris. Night-watchman sometimes. Sometimes I do bouncing."

"An' he can bounce 'em ever so far, can't you, Gazza?" Sion paused in lining up his shot to give Gary a proud smile. "Best bouncer in the business."

"Wouldn't need to bounce if twats like you didn't start fights," Gary said sadly. "But sometimes it's fun." He gestured to his throat. "I like black tie best. People tip."

"You've got a tux?" Betty looked at Gary directly for the first time. "Now, that I've got to see."

Gary went pink again. "Next time I got to wear it I'll let you know."

Rob's yowl of disgust drew Mal's attention back to the table which was now devoid of spots.

"You got magnets in your balls or something," Rob accused, glaring at Sion.

"Yep, s'why I jingle when I walk."

The banter was familiar, throwing Mal back in memory to his student days so he made the 'bah-dum-chhhh' sound of a punchline rim-shot and held up a hand so Sion could high five it. Sion did, grinning at Rob with a cocky lift of the eyebrows.

"I bet you're just as bad, Mal." Rob grinned. "Are you good at ball games?"

There were a number of answers Mal could have given to that but he opted for taking the question at face value. "Oh God, no, I'm rubbish," he admitted. "But with loads of practice I might improve. Are Betty and I playing you two, or are you having a go, Gary?"

"I'm banned," Gary said. He grinned and shrugged. "I ripped the baize. Twice. Don't know my own strength, see."

"I'll play you at darts, just as soon as I've seen off these tossers," Betty promised, chalking her cue.

"Like to see you do it, Peaches," Rob said.

And they almost did. Mal had enjoyed pool in his previous local and hadn't quite forgotten how to set up a shot and Betty played with a ruthless dash that suggested a lot of very serious practice. They lost but not by much and Sion challenged Mal to another go while Betty fulfilled her promise to Gary, and Rob went in search of a basket of chips.

"What?" He patted his belly when he noticed Betty giving it a critical stare. "I worked hard today. I earned it. But for that you're not having one. I'll share with Mal though. Want a chip, Malcolm?"

"Don't mind if I do," Mal said reaching for the basket – and wasn't completely surprised when Rob moved it so he'd have to come a bit closer to get one.

"Here you go," Rob said, taking one of the salty ketchuppy morsels. He offered it to Mal's lips and when Mal hesitated he grinned and ate it himself. "Playin' hard to get. I like that in a man."

"No, you don't," Betty scoffed and threw a double top.

Mal couldn't remember the last time he'd enjoyed an evening so much. Rob's frank appreciation, and that it was ignored by the others apart from a few gibes at Rob's expense, had filled Mal with a sense of confidence he didn't normally enjoy and he played his pool with a flair that surprised him and made Betty nod approvingly. He had even held his own when the banter became more general.

"I'm not letting you upset Betty," he'd said after an innocent question about her 'Peaches' nickname prompted a story about a house party when they were sixteen and Betty's karaoke performance after a pint of peach-flavoured schnapps.

"Knight in shinin' armour, is it?" Sion said.

"No, I have to work with her tomorrow. Besides, don't some of the rest of you have nicknames? Dirty Rob, isn't it?"

There was one of those tense and silent moments. It can't have lasted more than a second, but it felt much longer and quite a lot happened. Rob's lips thinned, Sion glared at Betty who flushed a very ugly pink, and Morris emitted an anxious whine. Mal realised he had said absolutely the wrong thing.

"I – um – was called Rainbow in school," he said. "Rainbow Brite? Like the cartoon."

"We used to watch that." Gary grinned. "Didn't we, Rob?"

"Dammit, Gary!" Rob's tone was aggrieved but his lips were easing into a smile. "Never out me as a Rainbow Brite fan, lapsed, when I'm trying to impress an attractive bloke."

There was no doubt who Rob was referring to but Mal didn't even take a moment to bask in the glow. "I'm sure it worked. Sion, *do* you feel impressed?"

Sion let out a hoot of laughter and this time he offered his hand to high five.

Betty rolled her eyes. "That's it, boss. I think you've had enough."

Since it was closing time and they all had empty glasses anyway, Mal took her arm without arguing and offered to walk her home.

"We'll do that," Rob offered once they were on the pavement. "Wouldn't want to take you out of your way. Not on a first date anyhow."

"First date?"

"Hell, yeah. We're doing this again. We play pool every Thursday."

"Darts night Tuesdays," Sion added.

"Dominoes Wednesdays." Gary had the last of Rob's chips in a napkin and was sharing them with his dog.

"And the rest of the time they just drink," Betty warned Mal.

"Yeah, right, but the point is," Rob said, reaching out and giving Mal a gentle poke in the lapel of his jacket, "the point is that you're welcome to join us."

They took their leave, moving off along the pavement with Gary and the hulking Morris bringing up the rear. Mal smiled as he heard Rob grunt and Betty laugh. Mal suspected she had elbowed him.

Then he too went home and didn't think he should be blamed if his last thought before sleep was of Rob's strong hands around the pool cue and how they might feel up close and personal.

Chapter 3

The fun and companionship of that Thursday evening sustained Mal over the hard work of Friday and the comparative loneliness of the weekend. He had plenty to keep himself busy – a huge backlog of paperwork to get through and he had all the normal housekeeping chores to attend to. His flat was, to put it mildly, in need of some TLC. His previous home had been a nearly-new two bed apartment, high spec throughout, whose bland appearance had been outweighed by the amazing view of Bristol Docks, and that he was sharing it with someone he had thought he loved. The rent for this one cost him less than half of the one in Bristol and its scruffy nineteen seventies wallpaper and swirly patterned carpets were bearable now he was no longer being nagged. It had the potential to be lovely – huge Georgian windows and little cast iron fireplaces appealed to Mal's inner-curator – but for now its biggest advantage was that it only took five minutes to walk to work. As Mal pushed the vacuum-cleaner around he imagined the fireplace opened up, some moody lighting and a long couch to stretch out on – with someone, perhaps. That was a nice idea. The bathroom wasn't too bad. As Mal scrubbed the limescale off the shower-head it occurred to him that the shower cubicle was probably big enough for two as long as they stood close together. From there it was barely a step at all to imagine who the other person could be. Rob, of course. Mal sighed and closed his eyes contemplating that muscular arse and broad shoulders. He'd have to be careful, he decided. It wouldn't do to get his hopes up as well as his inconvenient and insistent cock. Just because Rob flirted it didn't mean he was prepared to carry through.

Monday and Tuesday passed with all the routine annoyances and Wednesday was shaping up to be more of the same until Betty arrived.

"What the heck happened to you?" he demanded, eyeing her pale face and red rimmed eyes with alarm. "Are you ill?"

"It's not catching." Betty turned the kettle on, wincing at the click. "Darts last night. Coach and Horses vs the Dog in King's Norton. We won."

"I'd hate to see you when you've lost," Mal said.

Betty snorted. "Just don't ask me to do anything technical, okay?"

"How about I look after the desk and you look through my emails?" he suggested, but she just gave him a narrow-eyed look so he left her with coffee and a duster to flick around the shop and went up to his office.

Five hundred emails since last night. His predecessor, an older lady, had a finger in every professional pie going and had subscribed to every professional journal's newsletter. Mal hadn't been there long enough yet to know which he could safely unsubscribe from. Then there was the ever-present spam. Invitations to conferences, offers of racking, coffee machines, health insurance, and a Mercedes for 'only' £300 a month. And so much stuff from the council. Why on earth would Mal need to know about lunch hour Pilates classes at a venue thirty miles away? Or that the car park at the Shire Hall was being resurfaced and inaccessible. *Click, double-click, delete. Click, double-click, delete.* There was a nice rhythm to it.

By ten he had got rid of everything superfluous and could settle down to deal with the things that actually needed his attention. A solid hour's typing then he fired off all the emails together and turned off the computer. Now for some proper *museum* work.

He called down to reception to let Betty know that he'd be up in the stores. In the foot well of his desk there was a wooden box printed on the side with the name of a Hereford business – 'Cranston, Seedsman, King's Acre'. It was an interesting object, and from the number hand-printed on the edge had been catalogued sometime in 1998, but since then it had been filled with several disintegrating Tesco bags holding a collection of brass and pewter candlesticks.

"They came in a few years back," Betty explained, "and we put them in the box for safe-keeping and – well, you know how it is."

Mal did. Also, the box was bloody heavy. He dragged it out from under the desk, wincing at the dust behind it, and went up into the attic to find a safe spot for it in the stores.

This was the part of the job he liked best. Deciding whether to catalogue the items as one collection or separate them out into 'local businesses' and 'domestic lighting'. Handling the objects, checking their condition, assessing them for inclusion in potential future exhibitions, packing them carefully into acid free cardboard boxes nested in wonderful crinkly tissue paper. It was a luscious sensory experience plus it also fed his imagination. The brass and pewter columns were satisfyingly heavy in his latex-gloved hands. Most were simple shapes but one pair bore the patinated glow of frequent handling and had broad flanged tops still spotted with wax. When he held them up to his face he could smell the faint tang of beeswax under the sharper scent of burning. The candlesticks' stems fitted his palms, inviting caresses. Whose hands had caused the subtle patterns of wear, whose fingers had fitted the candles into the sockets, or had struck flint against steel and coaxed the wick into light? What sights had the brightening candle flames revealed? The pages of a book, a letter with the crabbed writing of a lawyer imparting serious news, or perhaps that yellow flicker had warmed the bare skin of a lover. Mal sighed as he covered the box with a final layer of tissue and fitted the lid. Job done. He picked up a 2B pencil and copied the numbers of the items onto the outside of the box and made a little space for it at the end of the 'lighting' shelf, beside a scatter of small loose objects that he'd probably get around to boxing eventually. There was just so much to do. For the moment he stood the snuffers and wick trimmers on a sheet of tissue in the Cranston box and made a note of their catalogue numbers in the notepad app on his phone.

His phone bleeped making him jump. "Hello," he answered cautiously – not that many people had his mobile number. "Who's that?"

"No need to panic." Betty sounded as though she had been giggling. "Remind me to set you up with individual ring tones. There's a gentleman here with some flints he's picked up."

"Ooh." Mal enjoyed flints as much as he enjoyed candlesticks. "I'll be right down."

"It's lunchtime," Betty pointed out, "and I have to pop out for a bit. How about I send him up to your office?"

"Cool. Have a good lunch."

As Mal trotted down the narrow stairs from the attic to the lower landing it suddenly occurred to him who might have been making Betty giggle and who she might trust enough to let them loose on the upper corridors of the museum. So he wasn't altogether surprised to glimpse a yellow hard hat through the wrought iron of the bannisters.

"Hey." Mal leaned over the rail and grinned as Rob looked up at him.

"Didn't think I'd see you again so soon. No pool table, but I can make you a coffee."

Rob gave him a beaming smile. "Tea and you're on," he said, and followed Mal into the little room they had set aside as a staff kitchen.

Mal took a couple of mugs down from the cupboard and turned on the kettle. "I think I thanked you all for last Thursday, didn't I? It was good fun."

"Yeah," Rob's grin sounded in his voice but Mal turned to look at him anyway just for the pleasure of it. Rob had taken off his hard hat and put it on the window sill and was leaning against the edge of the window, hands in his pockets and looking out over the patch of grass and shrubs that was all the museum could afford of a garden these days. With his high vis jacket and coveralls undone to show a bright segment of printed tee shirt – Mal could see the '-oun-arm-lu' of 'Young Farmer's Club' and a bit of a bull logo – and with long legs in rigger boots crossed casually at the ankle, he looked both wildly out of place and very much at home. Mal really envied his ease. Here was a man who knew exactly what he wanted and was confident of getting it.

And what he wants right now – apart from tea – is me! Mal found that a very satisfying thought.

The kettle whistled and Mal poured the boiling water into the mugs, soaking the special pyramidal bags that Sharon insisted made much better tea than any other variety. Mal stooped to open the fridge.

"Milk?" Malcolm asked. "Sugar?" Rob had stopped looking out of the window and was watching Mal. Mal could feel it.

"I never say no to a bit of sugar. Bit o' milk too. Just enough to take the edge off."

Mal grinned and made the tea, then turned and offered Rob his mug.

"Thanks," Rob said then lifted the mug a bit to read the printing on the side. "*Museum Curators do it Meticulously*? Oh. My. God. I hope that's true."

Mal snorted. "It's part of the job to keep the paperwork in good order."

"That's not what I meant and you know it."

Mal just smiled his agreement. "Come through to my office," he suggested. Rob followed, his boots sounding heavy even on the threadbare carpet.

"Blimey," Rob muttered as Mal opened the door. "Bit of a mess, innit?"

"Inherited, I assure you. My predecessor had some health problems the last few years of her tenure and everything got a bit out of control." Mal went to the desk to put his mug down. The only other chair in the room was burdened with yet another box – this one contained two rebate planes, a chisel, a sheaf of papers rolled and secured with a perished rubber band and a couple of zip lock bags of Roman grey ware pottery sherds – so he shoved it into the foot well where the candlesticks had been. By the time he had straightened up Rob was in the chair, ankle cocked on one knee with his mug balanced on the other. "I believe you've got something to show me?"

"Oh hell yes. And I brought you some stuff I found to look at too."

Mal couldn't help but laugh. "You're shameless!"

Rob shrugged. "Saves time, doesn't it? I like the look of you. If you didn't like the look of me you'd'a told me to fuck off by now." He grinned and offered Mal a jiffy bag with a scrawl in Biro on the front. "Betty's been after me to bring these in for a while but I never got round to it before."

"Oh?" Mal eyed the bag feeling the familiar flutter of excitement. There could be anything in there. Could he be blamed for prolonging the moment? "And why would that be?"

"Because the previous curator was a nice enough old lady in her own way but I didn't want to rip her clothes off with my teeth."

Mal took a deep breath. "Fair enough," he said. "Though you don't actually have to rip. I'm quite capable of taking my own clothes off for the right person."

"Where's the fun in that? Come on, take these off me quick before I do something the council might object to."

Mal took the bag, enjoying the brush of Rob's fingers against his. *Bloody council. Bloody 'no bonking on the premises' rules.* "Thank you," he said. "I've only just got this job and I wouldn't like to lose it."

"Betty told me to mind my Ps and Qs, though what she thinks I'd do to you in a space this crowded I have no idea, especially since I was rather hoping you might come out on a date with me. Bloody woman's got no sense of proportion. So what do you think then?"

While Rob was talking Mal had seated himself at the desk and opened the bag. He was pleased to see that the scrawl of letters and numbers was an address and an OS map reference, which was always handy. He peered inside then gently tipped the slightly muddy bits and pieces out. "Did you find these all in one place?" he asked.

"No, I meant about coming on a date with me?"

Struck by an uncomfortable sense of déjà vu, Mal sat back in his chair and stared at Rob. Rob stared back with a broad grin.

"That was a trick question, wasn't it?" Mal asked. "If I mentioned the bag you'd claim you were talking about a date. If I mentioned a date you'd probably claim to have been asking what I thought of Betty's sense of proportion. If I mentioned Betty you'd point out that I should be looking at the flints. Most of which look as though they came off someone's drive, by the way."

"Oh my God, you're good." Rob shook his head admiringly. "The wonders of a university education."

"No, I learned about never being able to find the right answer from an ex. He was the sort who used to like to keep people on the wrong foot so he could manipulate them. Not an admirable character trait." Mal turned over the pile of stone chips, sorting them and setting some aside. "Hmm, a few of these are rather good but as for some of the others – are you having a laugh?"

He glanced up and was a little surprised to see that Rob's smile had gone and he was looking down at his mug. "No, I'm not," Rob said. "I'm sorry."

"No need to apologise." Mal tried to smile but suspected that he looked a bit strained. The memories of his last few months in Bristol had kept him awake more than one night. "It wasn't a pleasant experience – one I don't want to repeat. You've been straight with me so I thought I'd be straight with you."

Rob looked up again. "If either of us were straight, neither of us would be here working our way to finding out if you're coming out with me. I'll even let you choose where to go. I've got a tie – somewhere."

That sounded promising. "Not if, when. But you'll need to tell me what the options are."

Rob began to talk, a cheerful babble of distances, facilities and reminiscences, while Mal inspected the scraps of stone that littered his blotter. Rob's voice was deep but hit occasional high notes as he moved from disgust to laughter or indifference. His accent was the mild mixture common to the area, Herefordshire's soft country burr tinged with the lilt of Welsh, as seemed right to Mal for this border country. The pieces were a mixture too – some clearly picked up from the same source, probably the drive of a house. In fact Mal thought he knew which house. He had cycled past one with just such virulent alien yellow flint chips on his way back from the development. But others were of great antiquity and he set them in order with care.

"So the Red Lion's very plush," Rob continued. "But they have absolutely no sense of humour and I probably wouldn't get away with feeling you up under the table in there not like in the White Horse. Also the Lion might still enforce that ban. It wasn't as though me and Sion did much but Phil Rother and his mates was right out of order."

"Phil Rother?" Mal grinned. "Still got all his teeth?"

"Yeah, fuck him. Well, I wouldn't, but you know what I mean. Honest," Rob sighed, "it's the twenty-first century. You'd think we'd be over the whole eighties gay panic shit but the small-minded, tiny-dicked morons are always with us."

"I'll have to watch out for him then."

"Probably not." Rob considered Mal for a moment then flapped a hand at him. "You talk posh, work in an office and I bet you got a string of letters after your name. He'll leave you alone. Also he's built like a brick shithouse so he'd look like a bully if he had a go at you. But he's Gary's boss so feels he can throw his weight about a bit with us. You'll meet him. He's doing the security for Gaskell Developments."

"I'll not look forward to it," Mal assured him. "I've met a few homophobes and there's really no doing anything about them."

"Nah, punching him in the gob didn't work. He just stands out of reach now and slags us off from a distance."

"Nasty, so we won't go to the Lion then. But the White Horse is all right for some fun, the Coach is great but your mates might interfere, and the Carpenter's Arms has a good kitchen but the barman doesn't know his stout from his lager. I guess we'd best go to the White Horse then."

"Good choice." Rob grinned. "When? I'd love to say tonight but I've got to take some stuff over to Leominster for Glyn and won't be back 'til late."

"That's okay. I've got a meeting at County Hall first thing tomorrow and will need my wits about me. I'm free Friday," Mal offered.

"Another good choice," Rob grinned. "What's the verdict on the stones and stuff, then?"

"Well, these," Mal pushed the yellow stones to the edge of his blotter, "are very interesting. I suspect of foreign origin and I know exactly where they came from – the drive of that run-down nineteen-thirties semi in Ross Road. Remember when I said you were shameless? Well, you are."

Rob chuckled then nodded to the other little pile. "It's a fair cop. Didn't want to make it too easy for you, did I? But what about those others?"

"These are the real thing. Did they all come from the same spot?"

"Yeah, found 'em years ago. I looked it up on the map as best I could and wrote down the reference. It's from the field above the development. Gaskell wanted to buy it too but Old Beynon wouldn't let it go." Rob got out of his chair uninvited and came to lean on Mal's shoulder. "Tell me what I'm looking at, then."

"Well, you obviously already know that flint isn't natural to this area so it's of interest."

"I never missed an episode of *Time Team*, if that's what you mean." Rob reached past him and turned over the biggest chunk. "What's that?"

"That's part of a core. Probably discarded because there was a fault in the flint and it broke along the fault. See the long strips on the sides? That's where the flint worker, the knapper, struck off flakes to work up into blades. Look." Mal picked up a narrow fragment and held it against the core. "They were making things like this. Knife blades. Or they would set a series of them into wood and make things like sickles."

"So Stone Age, then?"

"Yes, some of them. The really tiny ones are what's called Mesolithic – Middle Stone Age – but most are a bit later than that." Mal picked up the best piece of the lot, in a pale cloudy grey flint almost translucent along the edges where the chipping was finest. He tested the edge with a fingertip and smiled to see the little indentations of the serrated edge on his skin. "See this arrowhead. One of the barbs has been broken off but otherwise it's perfect. They were making them like that during the Bronze Age, about three to four thousand years ago. Absolutely lovely."

"So it's an old break, not a new one?" Rob asked. "I thought I'd done it.

Spent some time looking for the other bit."

"You can tell from the edge. A fresh break is as sharp as a razor. That had been in the soil for a while. These rounded ones are scrapers." Mal picked one up between thumb and forefinger and demonstrated its use, roughing up the edge of his blotter. "Here, take my magnifying glass. If you look at the edge along here you can see a little bit of polish. That shows it has actually been used. And this almost triangular bit, I think, is a chisel point arrowhead."

"For birds," Rob said. He was inspecting the scraper minutely, turning the little object between gentle if work roughened fingers, handling it so delicately that Mal had to swallow hard. What would those hands feel like on his skin? "I saw a programme about them once. That's so cool to think we had people making tools right up there on the hill above the town, way before the Romans."

"Not just making tools," Mal said. "Scrapers were disposable. Like Stanley knife blades. Nobody bothers to sharpen those. You just get another. So I'd expect to see a few scrapers about casually discarded. But these other pieces, the blades and arrowheads, are finely worked and they look to me as though they may have been broken deliberately. Maybe, at one time, there was something up on the hill that people visited and left a token."

"There's a spring," Rob suggested. "I'll take you to see it if you like. It's on private land but Dai Beynon won't mind. He's a good lad is Dai."

"Another friend?"

"Oh aye. People used to go up to the spring and leave stuff there. If you know where to look you can still see bits and pieces, ribbon and stuff, on the trees."

"Wow, genuine folk tradition?"

"We could ask him," Rob suggested. "He's often in the Horse, Fridays. Pick you up at yours, seven o'clock?"

"Cool. I'll just write down my address for you."

Rob shook his head. "Mr Archaeologist, you're in Pemberland now. Everybody knows where you live."

Chapter 4

Betty's eyebrows climbed when she got back from lunch and Mal told her about the date.

"He's taking you to the Horse? Oooh, they do a good dinner there, and if it's Friday you'll meet – um – an interesting bunch of people."

Mal tried to get her to elaborate but she laughed and shook her head.

"You'll see when you get there. And you'll have fun. Rob'll show you a good time," she said. "Just don't let him break your heart."

The sentiment was repeated that evening when he took a phone call from Zoë, his sister. After the usual exchanges about health, professions – she was in midwifery training and had a fund of stories that made Mal cringe – and the welfare of their mutual acquaintances, she added the usual, "So, are you … seeing anyone yet?"

Mal grinned, delighted to be able to say, "As a matter of fact I have a date on Friday."

"A proper date? Oh my God, really?"

"No need to sound so shocked. Yes, a proper date." Mal heard Zoë draw breath so added, "Before you ask, he's nothing like Oliver."

"Are you sure?"

"Absolutely. He's definitely a beer and darts bloke, not the least bit 'I'd play polo only I'm allergic to horses'."

"Oooh, does he have a flat cap and a whippet? Are you going to ask him to keep it on in bed?"

"The whippet?" Mal waited until she'd finished cackling. "No, I don't think he has a flat cap. The only head gear I've ever seen him in is a yellow hard hat – he works on a building site – and now you come to mention it, that's not a bad idea."

"You're so bad." Zoë sighed. "But I hope you have fun and I hope you – well, don't get involved too fast."

Mal had no plans at all to get so enthralled that his heart was in danger but appreciated the idea of the date very much and wanted to do Rob some credit. On Friday, when five o'clock came and Betty looked him over, critically, and said, "You're not wearing that, are you?" Mal took heed and hurried home.

Clothes shopping in Pemberland offered a choice between tough practicality and OMG expensive but he had been able to fit in a trip to Marks & Spencer after his County Hall meeting. After a shower he changed into his new shirt. It was a fine, silky cotton mix checked in brown and cream, and he matched it with dark brown jeans and a blazer that he wore so infrequently that he was shocked to discover that it felt a little tight. *Too many Hob-nobs*, he told himself, turning sideways to his mirror and sucking his belly in.

At five to seven he was ready, cash and phone in pockets, bedroom tidy – not that he was counting chickens but hey, a gentleman was always prepared – when he heard a soft wheezy burping sound. It happened again and he realised it was a doorbell.

"I didn't know I had one of those," he muttered as he locked the flat. He ran down the stairs to the lobby where he parked his bike and opened the street door.

"Well, don't you scrub up nice?" Rob's smile was warm and his blazer fitted a bit better than Mal's.

"So do you. Are we going to walk?"

"No, it's a mile or so out of town. I brought the car."

A battered Toyota was idling at the kerb and Mal grinned as Rob opened the door for him.

"Whoa, the inside of this car doesn't really match the outside."

"I'm saving up to have the dents knocked out and a respray. Cylinder head's new, so is the gearbox. Should get another hundred thousand out of her easy. You ready for a night of debauchery?"

"Where are you taking me? Gomorrah?"

"Naaah, the White Horse at Escley, *twinned* with Gomorrah."

Mal chuckled. "And is there a local village that should be twinned with the other one?"

"Yep." Rob grinned. "But the council won't let them put up a sign."

It took longer to drive through Pemberland than it did to reach the pub. It was on a cross roads embellished by an old cast iron finger post with signs for places Mal had only seen in old museum correspondence. Straight ahead was King's Norton, to the left was Brynglas, and to the right was Escley, a scatter of houses and a church tower just visible.

"So this is Escley," Mal said. "Tell me, were you named after it or was it named after you?"

"Hah, it after me of course." Rob laughed as he indicated to turn off the road. "Actually we've just been here forever. Dad used to say we had been Lords of the Manor but I reckon we were just local peasants. Nice though, to feel so at home."

Rob parked on the gravel to one side of a large building very much in the local style. Another leftover from a bygone age, like the Coach and Horses, but this one was painted proudly black and white and still had the graduated stone slabs on the roof instead of tile. It also had a massive door with enormous hand-forged hinges that looked like it would stop a tank.

"Built back when they really knew how to build," Rob muttered. "Not like these modern places. Breeze block and plaster held together with spit and hope."

"And you a builder, for shame." Mal tried a gentle tease, hoping not to give offence.

"Me? Not on your life!" Rob locked the car doors and began to lead the way to the bar. "Heavy plant boy, me. We prepare the ground and let someone else do the fiddly stuff."

Rob heaved the huge door open and light, sound, and a powerfully enticing smell of food and beer spilled out. Inside the décor was less twee olde worlde than Mal expected. The solid vernacular architecture had a modern overlay that looked warm and welcoming and was definitely aimed at locals. In addition to a noticeboard similar to the one in the Coach and Horses, there was a boot scraper by the threshold that looked as though it had been used recently and, just inside the lobby, a ceramic bowl of water labelled 'Ci' and a couple of mats thick with tufts of dog hair offered a resting place for the farmers' best friends. Mal smiled and followed Rob into the bar.

Warmth and noise were Mal's first impressions, followed by how busy it was. The place was packed with groups and couples and the conversation almost drowned out the strains of a recent pop hit playing quietly over the sound system.

"What would you like to drink?" Rob asked. "The beer's really good, or there's lager. Local cider, but I'd go steady with that."

"Oh, beer, definitely beer," Mal said with a grin.

"Ah, cheap date, that's what I like to hear." Rob gave him a nudge and hailed the barmaid. "Evening, Mary. Got a new customer for you. Mal, this is Mary Swan, owner manager of this esteemed establishment. Mary, this is Mal Bright, the new curator at the museum."

"Really?" Mary paused in polishing glasses and offered him her hand. She was stocky with a pleasantly pink face under neatly coiffed brown hair. "I'm pleased to meet you, Mr Bright. I might just pay a visit. Last time I went nothing at all had changed for – ooh must've been twenty years. Even some of the dust was the same."

Mal held back on a comment that might have been professionally unethical and shook her hand. "Pleased to be here, and I hope you won't mind if my visits are a bit more frequent."

"Bless you, no. Now, shall I serve you here or are you going round to the little bar until your table's ready. It won't be long."

"We'll go round," Rob said. "Mal's got to meet them some time. Thanks, Mary."

"Who have I got to meet and should I be scared?" Mal asked as they edged through the crowded bar.

"The Friday Night Irregulars," Rob explained. "Informal gay bar, very informal, but it's nice to have a bit of space of our own."

They stepped to one side to allow a young couple with a tray of lager to pass, followed by a tall well-dressed man in his forties with little gold specs and a receding hairline. He paused and shot them both a small self-contained smile, and said, "Good evening, Rob, and Mr Bright, isn't it?"

Mal had thought he was familiar and smiled. "Mal, please. Yes, that's right. Um – we met before didn't we? Mr Farriner?"

"Yes, when you brought the lease for your flat round to my office."

"Oh, yes, of course." They shook hands. "It's a pleasure to meet you again."

"Indeed. Welcome to Pemberland and it's Leo, please. Mr Farriner, locally, is my uncle. Are you two eating here tonight?" Leo dropped his voice to a whisper. "I can recommend the steak and kidney pie."

"I hoped it would be on the menu," Rob said. "Fantastic. We're waiting for our table. Why not join us for a drink?"

"Oh – um – that's kind but I wouldn't want to intrude." Leo's pale cheeks had flushed. Mal thought he looked pleased at the invitation, but also a little uncomfortable. "Unfortunately I'm expected at home. Enjoy your meal. Goodnight, Rob. Goodnight, Mal."

"Ah well," Rob sighed as Leo hurried away. "There's a man who doesn't relax enough."

"Difficult wife?"

"Nope, golden retriever. Come on, there's another bar round here."

They turned to the right into another seating area separated from the rest by a framework of massive beams. One wall was taken up by a large fireplace, another had a curtained window, and the other had another bit of bar and two doorways, one labelled 'Staff only, no admittance' and the other 'Dining room'. Mal heard a whoop and "Rob, darling … oooh who's that?"

"Jeez, Harry, give us time to get a drink in," Rob said.

Mal was served with his pint by a dark haired and broad shouldered young man who was almost as attractive as Rob. "Name's Tom," he said, offering a hand. "And I know you're Mal Bright. News travels fast round here. Welcome to Pemberland."

Mal thanked him and took an appreciative sip while Rob asked after someone called Julie.

"Kids have got stomach flu or something," Tom said, handing Rob his pint. "I told her not to worry about coming in to work 'til they're better. Your table should be ready. I'll just go and check."

Rob nodded. "Thanks, Tom."

"Julie?" Mal asked. "Your sister?"

"Sis-in-law," Rob said. "I'll tell you in a bit. For now come and say hello to the lads."

Mal had been aware that the three men seated around a table near the fire had been paying him some attention, so was prepared for the barrage of appraising stares.

"Aye aye." The dapper elderly man with a natty waxed moustache nodded a greeting to Mal. "Come on Rob, introduce us."

Rob made no attempt at formality. He rattled off the names – Dai Beynon, Harry Farriner – a little too fast for Mal to put the names to faces apart from the last one.

"And finally, Major Godfrey-Merrick," Rob said, indicating the man with the moustache. "Signals, served in Northern Ireland, Belize, Kosovo aaaand … help me out here, Merrick, you've been all over."

"That'll do to be going on with." Merrick grinned, extending his hand to shake. "Very pleased to meet you, Mal. Please won't you join us."

"Maybe another time?" Mal said. "There's a table in the dining room with our name on it."

Merrick twirled his moustache. "An actual date. Have fun, my dears."

The dining room of the White Horse was small, with only a dozen tables, but had the same comfortable atmosphere as the bars, and the food smelled terrific. A teenaged waitress grinned and said, "Hello there, Rob," and showed them to a table.

For the first few minutes they settled with their pints, accepted the menus and requested a jug of water.

"I've heard a rumour," Rob whispered to the waitress, "that there's steak and kidney pie tonight."

"The rumour would be right," she whispered. "Do you both want some?"

"Sounds good to me," Mal admitted. "With chips, please."

"Only way to eat it," Rob agreed. He waited until the girl had gone then Mal felt the nudge of a toe against his ankle. "So, can we get back to flirting, now we've got some peace?"

"Flirting? Absolutely. Though I'd quite like to know a bit more about you."

"Hey, what you see is what you get." Rob grinned. "I'd like to know a bit more about you too. Maybe we could take turns?"

"Taking turns can be a lot of fun in a lot of ways," Mal said, and they both raised their glasses in agreement.

"Shall I kick off?" Mal asked. "Mum and Dad were head and deputy heads in different schools until they retired, now they – I dunno – holiday a lot, I suppose. I've got a younger sister, Zoë, tried teaching, decided she didn't like kids *en masse* so swapped to nursing and now she's training for midwifery."

"Wow, could you get more white collar?"

"I wouldn't have described midwifery as white collar." Mal grinned. "Not the way Zoë talks about it. Just be glad she's not here while we're eating."

"Some of the guys do that on the building sites. Injuries I have seen, that type of thing. I tell you, nothing puts you off your burger faster than – ooh boy, here come our pies!"

By mutual agreement they stopped talking to treat the pies with the respect they deserved. Crumbly pastry, melting chunks of meat, rich gravy and chips to die for, plus a dollop of Savoy cabbage that tasted nothing at all like any cabbage Mal had eaten before.

"What have they done to this?" Mal asked after his first mouthful.

"White Horse secret." Rob grinned. "Wait until you try the chips."

Mal did and they were brilliant but once the edge was off their appetites he said, "I've told you about my family. Your turn to tell me about yours. Are they retired too?"

Rob rolled his eyes. "Gotta have a job in order to retire, haven't you? No, that's not fair. Mum does her best, fruit picking in the season and stuff, but Dad's got a bad back." Mal could hear the quote marks. "Had it as long as I can remember. I've got two brothers. Keith is the oldest. He buggered off to join the army when he was seventeen. Haven't heard from him for a while so I'm not sure what he's doing. And Kevin's about five years younger than me and is bloody useless. He's married to Julie and they have twin girls. Julie deserves better but the apple doesn't fall far from the tree with the Escleys."

Mal frowned at the bitterness in Rob's voice and reached across the table to touch his hand. "I wouldn't have said that. It looks to me as though the work you do is pretty hard."

"Yeah, well," Rob flushed and turned his hand to grip Mal's, "Gary is my best mate and I spent a lot of time there when I was a kid. The Havards are like family. I learned everything I needed to know about work from Glyn."

"I like Glyn," Mal said. "He seems – genuine."

"Pure diamond that man, and Helen, his missus, even more so." Rob grinned, gave Mal's hand a squeeze then let go again to pick up his fork. "And she could give Mary Berry some pointers in the kitchen."

"Did you diss the blessed Mary?" Mal demanded, in mock horror.

"You haven't tasted Helen Havard's fairy cakes, you poor soul."

While they ate the rest of their main course they talked about the town and villages, how the place was so tangled up with the border that it was hard to tell whether it was English or Welsh.

"The border runs somewhere between Brynglas and King's Norton," Rob said. "There's this bulge on the map but just there it runs through woodland and we've no idea where it is actually on the ground. So every year just after Easter we have an inter-village football match to establish who gets the woodland for that year."

Mal beamed at the thought of another genuine ancient tradition alive and literally kicking in the twenty-first century. "What does the county council think of that?"

"Who cares? I think we dropped a couple of years during the world wars because there weren't enough men left for the match and the women are usually too sensible to join in. Apparently they didn't play in 1350 either. Not enough people fit enough after the Black Death to field a full team."

Mal stared at him. "You're joking"

"Not really. We take our traditions seriously. Look in your archives. There should be photos and stuff."

"From 1350."

"No, you div! Are you going to eat that chip? No? Give it here then."

Mal offered the chip on his fork and bit off a chuckle as Rob licked the tip of it. "Are you teasing?" he asked.

"Why, yes I am, how kind of you to notice." Rob bit the chip off the fork and chewed thoughtfully. "Are you up for pudding?"

There had been a meaningful pause there that Mal found corny but delightful. "I absolutely am up for pudding. What do you recommend?"

They had a lemon mousse, light and astringent, and while they were scraping out the bowls Rob asked, "So, is this where we establish whether I'm just taking you home and dropping you at your door or you're going to say 'want to come up for coffee?' and I say 'don't mind if I do' and we see where the night takes us?"

That was a line that Mal had heard before and had found quite resistible. Mal smiled at Rob and put his spoon down. "I make it a rule not to drink coffee after nine," he said. Rob's face fell, just a little, so Mal added, "Unless there's something I need to stay awake for."

"You rat bag." Rob chuckled and his toe brushed Mal's ankle again. "I think I can promise you something at least."

They went Dutch on the bill, paying in cash and telling the waitress to keep the change, then retraced their steps through the bar.

"There you are." Major Godfrey-Merrick smiled and pulled out a chair. "Now you can come and join the Irregulars."

The table was littered with glasses and plates so it looked as though they'd had a good time, and while it would be nice to get to know some other locals, Mal had other things on his mind.

"I'd love to," Mal said. "Honestly, but I have to get back. Things to see to."

"I just bet you have, darling," one of the Irregulars drawled, his cut glass RP accent at odds with a scruffy appearance. Good looking though, with silver rings in both ears, a mop of dark curls shading long-lashed bedroom eyes and a sinful mouth. He grinned at Mal, tip of tongue showing between sharp white teeth then said, "Rob's good at giving things a seeing-to."

"Shut up, Harry!" So this one must be Dai Beynon, the owner of the field where Rob had found the flints. He had black eyes, deep set and intense, in a narrow weather-tanned face. Close cropped curls lay flat against his skull in the shape of the cap that lay on the table. If Mal had heard right and the other was a Farriner, he couldn't be more different from Leo.

"It'll be museum business, no doubt. I visited your museum once," Dai said. "Those stuffed animals gave me the 'eebie jeebies."

"You trash talking my badger, Dai?" Rob wagged a finger. "Been my favourite since I was three. Never seen such a cheerful lopsided beast ever."

"But it's got moth holes."

"One man's 'oh dear God' is another man's 'hello old pal' and yeah, we've got things to see to."

There was a general chuckle and Major Godfrey-Merrick waved them away. "Get along with you then. Hope to see you soon, Mal."

After a quick round of farewells they hurried to the door, Mal snorting with laughter as Harry chanted, "Have fun stuffing the badger."

"They mean well," Rob said as they stepped out into the cold evening air. "Damn, it's starting to rain."

"Last week of September," Mal pointed out and they hurried to the car.

The journey back to Mal's flat seemed a lot longer than the journey out had been. Mal spent it pondering over the difference between this and previous encounters in clubs and bars – sometimes little more than a meeting of eyes to acknowledge mutual lust. They had been satisfying but hadn't touched his heart. Rob's polite but unashamed intent was a novelty. They knew where they stood and Mal had every intention of enjoying it. Just the thought of being alone with Rob, being able to touch and explore, was making him light headed.

Rob parked by the church rather than in the street outside Mal's door and they ambled down the street together, close but not quite touching. Pemberland on a Friday evening – Mal was surprised to see it was only nine-thirty – was busy with people but they made it to Mal's flat without anyone hailing either of them.

"Keys," Mal said. "Always in the last pocket you pat." Rob chuckled and touched him properly for the first time that evening, a gentle sweep of hand from shoulder to hip followed by a pat on a back pocket. His fingers flexed as the door opened then Mal stepped inside and Rob followed.

Upstairs, Rob looked around the cramped and tatty flat, at the mismatched chair and couch, the tiny TV and the boxes and boxes of books that Mal intended to shelve properly once he'd got some shelves. Rob said, "This is nice. Really cosy," as though he meant it, then stepped forward and hooked a fingertip into the collar of Mal's shirt, stroking down into the hollow of his throat. "Is it as nice in the bedroom?"

Mal grinned. "No. The carpet looks as though it was laid in the seventies."

"As long ago as that? Poor thing," Rob said, and stepped closer still, leaning in for a kiss.

Mal had wondered whether he'd be one of those 'go straight for the tonsils' men or a bit more tentative. In fact Rob was one of the ones who liked to take his time and explore a bit, which was great because Mal preferred that too. Gentle pressure increasing as Mal kissed back, a hand low on his back, the other cupping his jaw. Mal took a good hold of Rob's waist and without breaking their contact began to edge back towards the bedroom door. Rob grunted his approval and took his hand off Mal's face to feel for the doorknob, then they were through the doorway and edging into the small space between the wall and the side of the bed.

"Damn," Rob breathed, his lips still against Mal's, "you're a bloody fine kisser, Mal Bright."

"Could say the same about you, Rob Escley." Mal dived in for another taste and hoicked Rob's shirt out at one side and ran his hand up over firm, hairy muscle to find and tweak a nipple. Rob snorted a little laugh and let himself topple sideways onto the mattress, taking Mal with him. An energetic few minutes later they had shrugged out of most of their clothes and were kissing again while Mal fished down the front of Rob's boxers. "Nice," he said then tugged the fabric down to mid-thigh. There was enough light from the street-lamps to see that Rob, bared from collarbones to knees, was an impressive sight. Mal hadn't expected the ripped physique one saw in magazines, but Rob was attractively bulky and a touch on his belly proved there was solid muscle beneath the curve of furred skin.

Rob must have been able to guess what Mal was thinking. He chuckled and grabbed Mal's wrist. "Haven't got any abs," he said. "Unless you count it as just the one big one."

"Nothing wrong with that," Mal said, then slid his hand lower. "Sometimes just one big one is everything you need."

Rob sucked in a breath. "Full working order. Want me to show you?"

Mal chuckled and took a tighter grip. "Thought you'd never ask."

Chapter 5

Saturday morning, at ridiculous o'clock, Mal was woken by the delicious sweep of a hand down his spine. It was still dark but enough light was coming from the living room for Mal to be able to see that Rob was fully dressed.

"Morning." Rob grinned at him. "You take some waking."

"Sleeping's what I'm best at," Mal mumbled, but turned over and propped up a little to peer at his watch. "What time is it?"

"Nearly six. Didn't want to go without saying goodbye. I've got to be over the other side of Hereford by ten and got to pick up the small excavator from Glyn's first. I'll be digging out the footings for an extension for the rest of the weekend."

Mal made a disappointed grumble. "Pity," he said. "I had plans for this morning."

"Did you now?" Rob put his hands on the pillow, one either side of Mal's head. "Any reason why those plans have to be cancelled? Could they just be postponed?"

It had been a brilliant evening and Mal felt like a limp noodle. The possibility of feeling this way again, the sooner the better, wasn't one to turn down.

"Postponed works for me," he said, and had just enough time to smile before Rob leaned down and kissed him.

When Mal awoke for the second time it was to a wrecked bed and the powerfully pleasant scent of warm men, beer and sex. He buried his face in Rob's pillow with a groan, gave it a hard squeeze then sat up to get on with his day.

Firstly a text because, while he knew he'd spoken to Rob, he couldn't remember the details and was worried he hadn't been clear enough about how much he'd enjoyed their evening and night. Not that he was smitten, of course, but they'd had fun and he'd be delighted to do it again and he wanted Rob to be sure of that. His phone was charging on the bedside table and it bleeped as soon as he picked it up and turned it on. Two new messages. The first was from the bank suggesting he might like some insurance but the second was from Rob. *"Can u do W/day? U choose where."* Followed by a smiley face.

Mal grinned. "Wednesday," he said as he keyed in his response, "will be fine!"

The rest of the weekend would have been an anti-climax if it hadn't been for the texted pictures from Rob showing everything from the little excavator and the astonishing garden he was working in, to his room at a guest house and the lavish breakfast on Sunday morning. Mal responded as best he could, showing the heap of bedding he was feeding into the washing machine and the moth-eaten badger in the museum, snapped when he popped in on Saturday afternoon.

His weekend custodians had worked together for years and had been friends and confidantes of the previous curator, and they both still treated him with extreme suspicion. He tried to be amused that they seemed to view him as though he was some kind of dangerous beast who might ravage them in the tea room. Soon after he had arrived, Betty had recounted to him their reactions, doing all the voices and actions, and he had almost cried laughing as she had deepened her voice as Gillian and barked "They have appointed a *man?*" then clasped her hands to her bosom as Melilot and intoned "Oh the Lord preserve us!" in a silvery fairy-like whisper.

Actually the two ladies were very efficient and welcoming custodians, so Mal made sure the biscuit tin was filled and that the supplies of tea were topped up, and he hoped that they would eventually decide that he was harmless.

On Tuesday morning he opened his email and spent an efficient twenty minutes getting rid of the rubbish, then began to open the more important ones. He didn't get down to one with *Visit* in the subject line until 10.15 and cursed as he read it:

"I'd like to take the opportunity to welcome you to the community on behalf of our sector of the council and will be in your area for an hour on Tuesday morning. If I don't hear otherwise I'll assume that it's all right for me to pop in just after ten.

"Yours

"Lionel Pugh, Cllr i/c Culture."

On the one level Mal was delighted to see that the museum was counted as culture, while on another he looked around his chaotic office and groaned.

Grabbing the phone he called down to Betty and warned her of the impending visit.

"He's already here," she murmured. "Marcia collared him as he came in through the doors so you've got a few minutes yet. Just move the box of veterinary specimens. They're enough to turn your stomach. I'll ring up to let you know when he's on his way."

Mal thanked her then took a deep breath. If one couldn't be tidy at the very least one needed to look busy.

By the time the good councillor was ready to come up, Mal had fetched a trolley from the stores and had loaded it with half a dozen boxes, including the hideous bottled tapeworm and the foetal sheep, had draped a dust sheet over them, and had parked it all on the landing.

"Hello?" Pugh peered around the corner from the stairs and gave Mal a wary smile.

"You've made some changes," he said. "Last time I came up here it was boxes all the way."

"We've been having a rationalise," Mal admitted. "Loads of stuff to sort through, still, of course. Can I offer you coffee, or tea?"

"No thanks, just a fleeting visit this time. I wanted to introduce myself properly though I expect you remember me from your interview." Pugh was solidly built and tall, with dark hair combed over a bald patch. He sported a golf club tie, a fancy waistcoat with a blazer and a tasteful diamond pinkie ring. Mal remembered him very well.

They shook hands and Mal invited him into the office, apologising for the boxes he had arranged on the floor. "I'm at the stage of making it look worse before it gets better," he explained. "This is turning out to be a steep learning curve. I know best practice and the most common documentation systems, but we have methods here that are completely new to me and, of course, I don't know the history of the town yet."

"I could help you out there." Pugh grinned. "The Pughs have been serving the community hereabouts for centuries."

"I wondered." Mal nodded to a box of legal briefs, neatly folded and tied with faded red tape. "It's a name that I've seen regularly. Along with the Havards, Beynons, Escleys, Farriners and Derrys. But then it's such a lovely town that I suppose people are loathe to move away."

"You'd think," Pugh said. "But honestly there's not much for the kids to do. And, of course, housing is a big problem."

Mal made an encouraging sound while thinking, *Ah, I wonder if this is the point?*

"I understand you've been seconded," Pugh rolled the word around in his mouth with relish, "to supervise the treatment of archaeological remains – if any – discovered on the new development up along Rifles Lane? I'm just keen to help out any way I can. I've done a lot of study of the area and am almost one hundred per cent certain that the site is clear. Just plough land, you know, so ideal for new housing. Widening Rifles Lane will be a boon, too, because it will open up another whole tranche of land along the slope that's inaccessible at the moment."

"I see." Mal didn't really. From what he had seen, the town was shrinking rather than growing. Rob had said as much on Friday night. Kids moving away to find work and it wasn't as though the town was touristy enough to attract the young-retired, downsizing crowd. "I suppose that area's on the side of town closest to the A465. Good access for housing but also just the place for a business park?"

Pugh nodded. "Nothing has been finalised, of course, but it's a good site, and would lead to more jobs and more opportunities for locals."

"Well, I don't think anyone wants to put too much of a stopper on that," Mal agreed, "but, you know, if there is something ancient there, we need to know and make it safe. If it's a big site we wouldn't even have to excavate it, as long as we could ensure it wouldn't be damaged. Cover it up and preserve it is what happens in ninety percent of cases. It's just if something is vulnerable that it has to be moved."

Pugh frowned. "Well, I'll count on you to hurry it up as far as you can. The bottom end of the site runs right along where we think the old road to Hereford lies and that has Roman foundations so might bear a look, but I think they are going to be making a start along the lane and it's essential that is cleared quickly so the lorries and trades can get in without having to go through the town."

"I'll have a word with Glyn Havard," Mal promised. "He seems reasonable."

"He does what he can with what he has," Pugh said grudgingly. "Though some of his staff could be better."

Having spent the best part of thirty-six hours exchanging daft pictures with one of the staff and being well aware why someone like Pugh might disapprove of Rob Escley, Mal merely smiled and repeated his promise to do what he could with what he had as well.

Pugh gave him an approving nod. "Glad to hear it," he said. "I know that there has been some opposition – there always is to change – but we need it desperately. Oh dear, is that the time. I've got a planning meeting at County Hall in three quarters of an hour."

"You might just make it." Mal got up and opened the door for him then accompanied him down to reception.

"Well, it was a pleasure to do business with you," Pugh said, shaking his hand on the doormat, then hurrying out into the chilly morning.

Mal watched him get into a Jag a few years too young to be considered retro, then turned back to find Betty watching him with raised eyebrows.

"Business?" she said. "I'd be careful if I was you, Mal."

"Nonsense!" Marcia Stenhouse cut in before Mal could reply. "Councillor Pugh is a good friend of mine and a colleague of my husband's. I know that you may feel that the council has been clipping the museum's wings but you must see it's for the best." She gestured to the high ceiling and sweeping staircase. "It was by far cheaper to move the library here and it gives you the opportunity to get a few extra visitors when our many customers come in to renew their books."

"And I'm sure we're all very grateful for that," Mal said. "Was there anything you wanted, Marcia?"

After an hour shifting some boxes of books from the store room to the main body of the library – recorded in a message to Rob who responded with a photo of Sion drinking tea – Mal wiped the sweat from his forehead and returned to the desk. Sharon, his other weekday custodian was there, dusting the shop shelves. She waved her feather duster at him, and smiled.

"Betty said she's making you tea." She dropped her voice to a pantomime whisper. "Said you'd need it after the morning you've had with Marcia."

"It was my other visitor that gave me food for thought," Mal muttered and Sharon beamed.

"Councillor Pugh, wasn't it? Such a nice man, Mal, and does so much for the community. Get him on your side and you'll be able to do a lot for the museum."

"Oh yes, I bet."

Mal repeated that sentiment to Betty who hooted with laughter.

"Pugh does a lot for the town, yes, but he also does a lot for himself. You do realise that it's his daughter, Vanessa, who is married to Selwyn Gaskell? And he and Gaskell regularly make up a golf-four with Sandy Stenhouse, Marcia's hubby, who's something in Planning and Melton from the Highways division?" She grinned at him. "What goes around comes around."

Mal frowned, uneasy at the thought that he might be expected to ignore important finds at the request of powerful men. "Have you and Sharon got things to do?"

"Sharon's going to carry on with the monthly sales figures, in between gassing to whoever comes in, and I thought I'd make the most of you and I both being here and have a bash at some of the boxes in your office. Try to match up things with paperwork, for a start. Then I can file and you can catalogue?"

"That would be brilliant. There's a box in the corner – the one under the stuffed owl – and I'm sure that's not just old correspondence. Last time I looked in a box like that I found eighty quid in loose change. Every little helps. Oh and the veterinary samples are on the trolley by my office door."

"Ewwww tape worm." Betty shuddered. "Let's finish our tea first."

Chapter 6

Mal's encounter with Councillor Pugh preyed on his mind for the rest of the day, so much so that he woke early Wednesday morning, sweating, from a nightmare about being in charge of a runaway bulldozer that was destroying Stonehenge.

"This is ridiculous," he said to his reflection in the mirror above the bathroom sink. "Bite the bullet and go to see Glyn Havard. The worst that can happen is he'll think you're over anxious." Also it would be good to see Rob in person, instead of on his phone.

He checked in at the museum first to make sure that Betty had plenty to keep her occupied, then set out. He strode through the town centre, pushing his bike so he'd have a nice freewheel back to the office, and looking at the streets and buildings with new eyes. The conversations with Rob and with Councillor Pugh came back to him and he was a little shocked to see the shabbiness behind the bright planted tubs and the sale signs in so many shop doorways. There were empty properties too. Not many but some were quite big buildings with rooms above and parking behind. Good places for retail but, he supposed, expensive to fit out since so many incorporated listed features. He paused a moment to peer through the dusty bottle glass windows of a shop that had obviously been closed for some time. A hand lettered sign above the door said 'Antiques and Gifts' but the sign was an antique in its own right as was some of the yellowing mail on the floor. Through the layers of grimy cobwebs he could just make out a massive stone fireplace, a section of beams with the plaster fill knocked out and the exciting curve of a spiral staircase. Between them they narrowed the width of the shop to a bottleneck. It would be a listed building and the very features that made it so exciting would make it hard to adapt to modern shop fittings. That, he assumed, explained why the shop had been empty for so long.

"Jacobean," he sighed. "Such a pity."

He took the turn off Escley Street into the narrow lane that, Pugh had told him, probably lay along the line of the old Roman road. Straight as a die, it led across the back of the town paralleling the main road and then up onto the side of Carew Hill. Mal decided that when he got back to the museum he'd try to find time to drag out some of the old maps and see if he could find any evidence. Romans were popular. People had heard of Romans. An exhibition would be nice. He grinned, wondering what Rob might look like in a brief tunic, or possibly even armour, then heard the rumble of engines up ahead and put the exciting visual image out of his mind.

In the past week the construction company had cleared a lot of ground. A patch of hedge had been removed and a wide gateway suitable for vehicles to turn in had been constructed. A large truck had reversed into the gap to dump a load of hard core into the quagmire of mud and a small digger was scooping and spreading it. As Mal approached he heard a shrill whistle and saw Sion at the wheel of the truck giving him a wave.

"You'll not get through there," he warned once Mal was close enough to hear him. "Another fifty yards though and there's a stile and a bit of fence where you can chain up your bike. You looking for Rob?"

Sion's smile was friendly but there was a glint in his eye that made Mal wonder what had been said. Then he decided he didn't care. Sion seemed quite accepting of Rob's overt admiration for Mal, so Mal would assume that if he was thinking about them it was without ill will.

"Not right this minute," he said. "Though I might be later. I was looking for Glyn. Is he on site?"

"Up by the Portakabins," Sion waved vaguely towards the woods-crested hill. "He's getting the stores fixed and the Portaloos installed. Follow the line of the hedge and you can't miss them."

"Thanks." Mal pushed the bike past the front of the lorry and along to the stile. It was easy enough to clamber over, and lift the bike over too, then he propped it against the fence and headed uphill. The Portakabins glowed an eye-aching yellow against the soft greens and ochres of the fields and clashed with the rich red of the raw earth. Mal filled his lungs with the damp air, regretting the tang of diesel and exhaust. This had been a beautiful place, well drained, sunlit, and sheltered from the prevailing winds. Good farmland. On the one hand, it was a tragedy that such quiet fields should be paved over, on the other, people needed somewhere to live.

On a flatter patch at the top of the field, a section had been cordoned off with barriers of Harris fencing buttressed with scaffolding poles. Hard core had already been spread over the mud and tamped down, and a dozen Portakabins were ranked with their backs to the hill to form the third and fourth walls of the compound. Pallets laden with supplies dotted the area and there was another huge mound of hard core and another of smaller gravel. It looked to Mal as though the construction crew had put in a good week's work. Close to the largest of the Portakabins was a pickup with Havard Plant Hire emblazoned on the doors and back. Mal picked his way across the rutted ground towards an open door and the sound of familiar voices.

"Hi," he called, not wanting to eavesdrop. "Glyn?"

A man in navy trousers and a sweater with fabric patches at elbows and shoulders, and enormous, muddy combat boots stepped out into the yard and gave him a glare. He had cropped light brown hair and a surly cast to an otherwise quite handsome face set on a thick neck and muscular shoulders. "What?" he said. "Can't you read?"

His gesture took in the No Unauthorised Entry sign.

"Yes, thank you," Mal said, still approaching. "I am authorised and I need to speak to Glyn Havard. If you would be so kind as to ask him if I can have a few minutes of his time."

"Ah, so you're the museum bloke." He gave Mal the type of measuring glance that started fights in pubs. "He's in there, you can ask him yourself."

He brushed past, giving Mal a chance to read Rother Security on the shoulder patch, professionally embroidered in red thread. To Mal's surprise, and suppressed hilarity, the man was also wearing a police style utility belt with slots for radio, nightstick, cuffs and gun – though the holster, he was relieved to see, was empty.

"Dear lord," Mal said as he entered the Portakabin, squinting until his eyes adjusted to the comparative darkness. Glyn Havard was standing by a table blocking in the man sitting behind it. "I assume I just met Phil Rother? I thought for a moment I was going to be frisked."

"Phwoaaar, can I, Glyn? I'll wear rubber gloves and everything." Rob, of course. He grinned at Mal, but Mal could see how tightly he was gripping his mug and the tension around his mouth and eyes.

"Jesus Christ, will you shut up a moment." Glyn rubbed his forehead leaving a muddy smear. "Hi, Mal. Your timing's perfect. Thank you. Laughing boy here was twisting our security guy's tail and I thought I was going to have a fight on my hands."

Rob made a 'who me' face at Glyn. "Not my fault if he's a fucking bigot, is it? Not my fault if he comes up to me and more or less asks for a smack in the mouth."

"No, but we have to work with the wanker and he could make our lives really difficult." Glyn stepped away to let Rob out from behind the table. "You just keep your gob shut and make Mr Bright a cuppa or something."

"I can do that. So what's your poison, Mr Bright?" Rob asked as politely as if he and Mal hadn't been getting sweaty together just a few days ago. He draped a tattered tea towel over one elbow and said, "Personally, sir, I'd advise against it. The coffee hasn't travelled well and the milk's getting a bit vintage."

"I've not long had a cup, thanks," Mal said, and took a seat at the table. "Have you got a minute, Glyn? There's something I want to check with you."

"Ah," Glyn grinned, "right. I thought … No, of course I've a minute. I could do with a cuppa. Vintage milk is traditional in builders' tea. So what's up then?"

"I had a visitor yesterday morning," Mal began, and gave them a quick précis of the conversation he'd had with Pugh. "There was just something about the way he was talking that made me wonder if he knew something I didn't. Have either of you heard about any remains up here?"

Glyn and Rob exchanged wary glances. "Archaeological remains, no."

"Oh God, not human remains?"

"Only the once," Rob said. "Years ago. And that was a sad accident, so no, not that either."

"Right enough," Glyn said. "And I don't think you need to worry about old Pugh, either. He's a good soul, even if he does seem to have been a bit heavy handed."

Mal scowled at the scarred table top. "Well, I expect he is but I've heard a few other things and it struck me that when you have local councillors and people from planning and highways accepting favours from developers who are related by marriage to the councillor there might be more to it than a bunch of new houses. For instance, why hire an expert and then ask him to skimp on doing his job? Why hire anyone at all? Why pick someone whose job could be at risk if they don't comply?"

"It isn't, it is?" Rob stared at him. "I mean, Pugh can't sack you if you find stuff, can he?" He plonked down in a chair beside Mal, sideways so his arm could lie along the back of Mal's chair.

"No, he can't," Mal said, smiling as he felt the sweep of Rob's thumb against his shoulder blade, "but, as you said about Rother, I have to work with him. Our budget's likely to be cut again, and during my first week I had a visit from some people from County Hall to see if some of the rooms on the upper floors of the museum could be repurposed into offices. I don't want to have to lose any more space, or people."

There was a short silence. Rob's pinched look had come back and his fingers worked against the back of Mal's shoulder as though he wanted to put his arm round him properly. It occurred to Mal that if he had been one of Rob's straight friends he probably would have offered the easy comfort of a hug, but in this macho environment even in front of Glyn he felt he shouldn't offer the same contact to Mal. Glyn just seemed to be mulling over what Mal had said and formulating a reply. It took a moment or two and when he spoke it seemed to be a non sequitur.

"You come from Cheltenham, don't you?"

"Originally, but I've been living in Bristol for years. Why?"

"Big cities and small towns," Glyn shrugged. "They work a bit differently. Look, in Bristol if you wanted – I dunno – a lawyer, a solicitor, to handle a little bit of legal business, you'd get out the Yellow Pages and look down the list, or ask around and see if you got any recommendations. Round here we have a choice of two firms. There's Collins, very good, very dynamic. He does a lot of work for local businesses, kind of mini-corporate, and lets his partners do the routine conveyancing and such. If you prefer old school you can go to Lockhart Farriner who deal with the farmers and estates, and still use typewriters for all I know, they are that dry and dusty. My point is that there's not much competition. If you want to open a shop on the High Street, Collins is your boy. If you're in dispute over straying sheep ruining a crop of beet you go see Leo Farriner. In some places they'd call that a monopoly, but round here that's just how it is."

"If you look at the plans for the houses on this site," Rob added, "you'll see the name Pugh at the bottom. Councillor Pugh's youngest, and Gaskell's brother-in-law, works for the company that drew up the plans."

Glyn nodded. "If you kick up a shine in the town centre because your team won and you celebrated hard and it seems like a great idea to climb up the cross, Police Constable Farriner, lawyer Farriner's nephew, will come and ask you to get down."

"He was ever so polite about it, though," Rob said without a trace of shame. "And if you try and break into this place to nick a few breeze blocks you'll get caught by Gary Havard, Glyn's son, who works for Rother Security, poor sod."

"Silly bastard," Glyn grumbled.

"I see," Mal said. "I think. So it's just – people doing jobs for people, not because they hope to gain anything from it but because they are the only option?"

"Well, I wouldn't put it like that," Glyn said. "We all get paid. And I reckon that maybe Pugh father and son being involved with this development was a good thing."

"Gaskell wanted to build forty detached 'executive dwellings'," Rob rolled his eyes, "with double garages and big gardens, which is all right if you can afford that kind of thing but what we're really short of are starter homes for youngsters so they don't all have to go off to Hereford or Gloucester or Newport to live because there's bugger all they can afford round here."

"Pugh made sure that those plans were turned down." Glyn raised his mug to the absent councillor. "Each time they were submitted, with minor tweaks and inducements, they were turned down again, until Gaskell took on a new architect who re-jigged the site so Gaskell can have some of his fancy houses but also a load of really eco-friendly little places with patches of garden and hard standing for cars. We *need* those."

"S'the only way I'm ever going to get a place of my own," Rob said. "I'd love to live in a lovely old house like Old Court or the Grange but as soon as those come on the market they get bought up by downsizing retirees from Birmingham and Coventry who've got pots of money to spend. An' I don't want to move away. This is home. Since they sold off all the council houses, what's available for rent is either rough as heck or really nice but more expensive than a mortgage. No, a new little two bed house with a place to park and a view of next door's washing is the best I can hope for and I'm grateful to Pugh, father and son, that there's a chance for it."

Overcome with a wave of guilt, Mal turned to Rob and put his hand over the one still kneading his shoulder. "I'm sorry, Rob," he said.

"That's all right, you div." Rob grinned at him and turned his hand under Mal's palm to give his fingers a squeeze. "You don't know. You haven't been here five minutes yet. Just don't slag off anyone until you've found out whether you are talking to their auntie or whatever."

"True enough," Glyn said. "With the older families we're all related. Hell, I think Rob's, what? My second cousin twice removed?"

"And once bound over to keep the peace," Rob added. "Yeah, it's complicated but there were these three sisters and one was my great-granny and another was Glyn's granny. Or something. You'd need to ask Aunty Lillian. She knows everything about everyone."

"Lillian? My landlady? Right, I'll pick my moment," Mal said, "preferably when there's no pressing business."

"Ah that's our Lil, right enough," Glyn agreed. "She could talk the hump off a camel."

Rob laughed. "Too true. An' don't you worry about archaeology. When we start the next phase of breaking ground I'll be doing the digger work and there's nobody as good as me at going to just the right depth." The cocky self-confidence in Rob's expression was one of the sexiest things Mal had ever seen. "If there's anything down there, I've got you on speed dial."

Reassured, Mal made his way back to the museum, but not before checking up with Rob about their Wednesday evening date.

"You're in my diary," Rob said. "Any preferences?"

"I really fancy a curry," Mal said.

"Coach it is then. Meet you by the cross? Half past seven?"

They were both a bit early, which Mal could only think was a good sign. Tonight Rob looked freshly washed and glowing with health, though his rugby shirt and jeans had seen better days. Mal liked that. He felt it showed they were getting comfortable with each other and he really liked the beaming smile with which Rob greeted him.

"Sorry 'bout the scruff." Rob glanced down at an oil stain on the jeans. "I didn't get a chance to do laundry this weekend."

"Don't apologise. How could you when you were away?" Mal peered at the faded rose embroidery on the white shirt. "Isn't that the England strip?"

"Yeah, got it in Oxfam," Rob said. "Saving up, see. Means I'm often working weekends and some evenings. Means I'm not free as often as I'd like to be."

Mal smiled. "I'm quite often working too, only I'm lucky and can do mine from home. Which means I'm pretty flexible."

"Are you now?" Rob's smile was blinding. "That I've got to see."

"Rob! Hey, Rob!"

The shout wiped the smile from Rob's face. "Oh fuck. Won't be a moment, Mal." He turned and took a couple of paces back the way they had come to meet two men who were hurrying towards him. From the open car doors, Mal assumed they had just got out of a battered VW Golf that was idling at the kerb. One of the men was a bit younger and smaller than Rob but like enough to be family, so Mal wasn't surprised to hear the long-suffering tone in Rob's voice when he said, "What do you want, Kev?" Mal had used that tone often enough with Zoë.

"That's nice, innit." Kev rolled his eyes. "Just sayin' hello." He was smartly dressed, his hair was gelled but he was grimy and gave off a sharp acrid smell of cider.

"Yeah, right. Are the kids any better?"

"We took 'em over to Julie's dad and mum's. Our place isn't the best right now. Bloody landlord." The man with Kev muttered something and Kev nodded. "Yeah, so, right. I don't reckon it's fair to expect Mr and Mrs Skidmore to look after Paige and Kimberley without me giving them something towards their keep. So I was wondering …"

"No," Rob said. "I'll drop by myself."

"Ah Rob, come on. It's just 'til payday."

"You, working? First I heard of it. Mum'll be so pleased."

"You leave Mum out of it. I've got an interview, garage in Kington, didn't want to tell her in case it doesn't work out. Go on, just a couple of hundred."

"A couple of – no, fuck off."

"You tight wanker. It's not as though you can't afford it." Kev looked at Mal for the first time. "You can't be spending it all on your nancy boyfriend."

"He's Dirty Rob's boyfriend?" The other man sneered.

"Rumour has it, Dazza."

"Then why's he checking my cock out? He bored with yours already, Rob? He looking for something better." Dazza grabbed his crotch and Kev whooped with laughter.

Mal just managed to grab Rob's arm, but it took quite a lot of strength to hold him back.

"Oh please," Mal said. "I've got more self-respect than that. Not if yours was the last hole on the planet."

Dazza scowled and let go of his trousers. Behind them the other man began to get out of his car and Rob shook Mal off.

"Forty quid." Rob shoved the notes towards Kev. "It's all I've got on me and it should be enough to buy what you need. Now. Go on. Fuck off the lot of you."

"Thank you very kindly." Kev grinned at Mal. "I'm sorry if you haven't got enough left to buy your little petunia a small wait wain. But my need's greater than yours."

Rob and Mal stood there, waiting until Kev and Dazza got back into the car, then it accelerated away. The ear-splitting blast of its horn might have made Mal jump if he hadn't been expecting it.

Rob didn't say a word. His lips were tight with fury, his face flushed. Mal moved a little closer and wished that they were in a place where he could take Rob's hand, or his arm or just do anything to take that furious and hurt look off his face.

"And I don't even like white wine," he murmured and moved until his shoulder touched Rob's. Rob twitched as though he had forgotten Mal was there, then let out a long breath.

"Fuck," he said again. "You can choose your friends. Sorry about that, Mal."

"Brother Kevin, I take it?"

"Tosser. I shouldn't let him wind me up like that but … Fuck." Rob looked both ways along the road and Mal noticed just how many people had stopped to stare and the hushed comments they were exchanging. Small towns being what they were, Mal was certain that the brothers' argument would soon be common knowledge.

"You know, Mal, I'm not sure I'm in the mood for the pub after all," Rob said.

Mal didn't for one moment believe it was anything to do with the lost money. "Okay … but we could swing by the chippy? I've got some beer in my fridge? Changed my sheets Monday?"

"Beer and chips and clean – *ish* – sheets?" Rob glanced at him sidelong then smiled. "Sounds perfect."

Chapter 7

Beer chips and clean – `ish` – sheets restored Rob's good humour and Mal coaxed him to spend the night. That was Wednesday. On Friday Rob stayed again, this time by arrangement and brought his laundry to take advantage of Mal's washer-dryer. Mal had pointed out that it made better sense than sitting in the town's grimy little launderette, and had been touched when Rob turned up with his own washing powder and fabric conditioner.

"I like to pay my way," Rob said, and they went out and had their postponed curry while the first load was in.

On Monday Rob turned up at the museum with two hot pasties, two cans of Coke and two Mars Bars.

"Builders' lunch," he said. "If you're man enough for it."

They ate in the museum garden, enjoying the sunshine and chatting about nothing in particular. Later in the afternoon Mal realised that he had been staring into space rather than writing a funding request. He also had a silly smile on his face.

"Dammit." Mal sat back in his chair and examined his feelings. There it was – a warm bubble of happiness deep in his chest because he knew he'd be seeing Rob tonight and Rob had agreed that keeping a spare shirt, plus socks and underwear, at Mal's was just common sense and, yes, he'd love to.

"I've only known him a month." Mal checked the calendar. "Less, twenty-seven days. I can't possibly be … I really can't have …"

Zoë disagreed when he spoke to her on Wednesday evening. "Rob sounds dreamy and if he's making you happy then go for it. And it's not as though he's your rebound squeeze."

"No, he certainly isn't." Mal laughed.

"No, I figured you probably got bloody Oliver out of your system during your attempt to shag your way around Bristol."

"I did *not* –"

"Oh, yes you did. Well, a little bit. But no harm done and at least you had a bit of fun. Are you having fun now?"

"Er …" Mal considered. "Yes, I am."

"Have you set up a unique ringtone for him and do you feel all warm and glowy when you hear it?"

"What am I? Fourteen?" Mal demanded. "How would I go about doing that then?"

Thursday morning Mal had forgotten all about his conversation with Zoë. Sharon was telling him about a phone call from an estate agent about a mangle that was the museum's if Mal wanted it and if he could dismantle and transport it.

"Did he say how big it was?" he asked.

"Well, he was a bit cagey on that point," Sharon admitted. "It's in a massive old house in Brynglas that they are doing up. My sister's boy did some plumbing work up there and he said that the cellar is all still set up for servants, lovely stuff in there, and there's a laundry with a massive mangle in it. I bet that's the one."

"Oh God, I don't think I'd get that on my bike would I?"

"You're going to have to get a car," Sharon warned. "You're going to freeze on that bike this winter."

Mal sighed. "I suppose. It's been five or six years since I last drove regularly. Might have to brush up my skills again."

"You could get young Rob to take you out," Sharon suggested. "What on earth's that noise?"

"It's – um – a song." Mal clawed his phone from his pocket before the lyrics could start. "Excuse me."

He picked up Sharon's neatly written messages and headed for his office, answering the phone as he walked. "Hi Rob," he said. "How's it going? Are we still on for tonight?"

"Yeah, serpently are." Rob sounded breathless and was shouting over the roar of an engine. "But look, you got to get up here now, Mal. I found something and, well, you got to come see it. Get up here, quick."

Mal put the papers down and began to shrug back into his coat. "What is it, Rob?"

"I dunno, not for sure. There's a stone box and … look you have to see it. I'll stop anyone from interfering with it. Glyn's trying to get Gaskell's man to call you but he's just saying it's a lump of sandstone and I should just dig it out and get on with it."

"Oh, he did, did he? You stand your ground. I'll be there in ten minutes."

"I will," Rob promised. Mal finished the call and ran for his bike.

Mal took the fastest route he knew to the development site, cutting through alleyways and darting along the maze of narrow access roads into shops' back yards. Access to large scale maps was a huge boon. Always ahead, he could see how the green hillside was being scarred with the strips of what would be roadways and the flat squares of mud that would be foundations. But his attention was fixed on the cluster of vehicles, amongst which Rob's digger stood like a giraffe amongst wildebeest. The hard core had been laid in the gateway and Mal cycled across it, wincing at the judder of his wheels on the rough ground, then took to the grass and pushed hard up the slope. He left his bike against the tracks of the digger and hurried into the knot of men.

"It's just a few stones." The man in the expensive Barbour and pristine wellies looked flustered. "Unless you open up this part of the site we can't widen High Rifles Lane. And that will mean we have to bring in everything along Ross Road and that means time lost, and that means money lost."

"We have a duty of care for anything we discover in these fields." Glyn sounded harassed too. "It's in the bloody contract, for God's sake."

"Yes, it is," Mal shouted, pushing through the crowd.

"And here's our archaeologist," Glyn said with as much pride as if he'd pulled Mal out of a hat. "Just in time. Thanks for coming. Mal, this is Mark Berkley, site manager for Gaskell Developments. Mr Berkley, this is Malcolm Bright, the archaeology expert retained by the county council to ensure that everything at this development is carried out in as professional a manner as possible."

Berkley gave Mal a terse nod. "Good, perhaps you could get on with it?"

"Absolutely. I can tell you whether it's a bunch of stones or if it's something you need to take care of." Mal looked around the site. "I'm assuming that there's other work the men could be carrying on with so the rest of the day doesn't have to be a dead loss?"

"Dead right," Glyn waved to the crowd of men. "We can make a start on laying that hardcore on the next road down. Get to it, lads. Rob, show him what we found."

Mal had spotted Rob by the bucket of the digger, hard hat shading a red face, and wondered if he got into trouble for calling him. He smiled at him and went across to the bucket. "So what have you got for me?" he asked and decided that he had been right in his guess when Rob didn't even manage to crack a joke.

"I was scared to move any more earth in case it all fell in," Rob said, words spilling out in an excited rush. "We have to clear this area to make the lane wider. The earth was built up a bit along the edge of the lane. I thought it was just run off from the field above, or maybe an old tree stump that had grassed over, but there's this edge of stone. I spotted it and did another sweep and look." His voice was reverent, his eyes fixed on the find, enthralled.

Mal stooped to inspect the stone. It was a slab of the local sandstone, two inches thick, scarred white at one end by the bucket of the digger where a corner had been chipped off and lifted slightly to show a void beneath. The next stroke of the digger's blade had skimmed the top of it, leaving just a thin layer of earth caking the surface. Mal had believed Rob's confidence in his skill but hadn't realised that the huge machine was capable of such precision work. There was a large shovel set against the swell of earth that Mal assumed had been used to delineate the visible edges of the slab. It was massive.

"My God, Rob." Mal dropped to squat on his heels and rake through the disturbed earth with his fingers. Rob dropped down too and they looked at each other over the stone and mud with growing excitement.

"I hope that's all right." Glyn had come back after shooing his workforce back to their machines. He pointed to the shovel. "Berkley was yelling at Rob for stopping work so I thought I'd settle the matter by finding out how far back it went. Not the best stone work I've ever seen but that didn't get there by accident."

"Is it what I think it is?" Rob asked, leaning to peer into the darkness beneath the slab.

Mal took a deep breath and blew it out. "Yes, Rob," he said. "Oh God, yes. Glyn, I'm sorry. This needs to be treated with kid gloves."

Within the hour Gaskell was on site. So was Rother. Councillor Pugh arrived ten minutes later. Mal wasn't sure what they thought they could do to hurry him up. He wasn't prepared to cut corners with what they had found.

"But I've seen it on TV," Gaskell protested. "Three days. Nice and quick. You can do that, can't you?"

"That's TV," Mal said, searching for a number on his phone. "On TV, they don't show the teams who went in to prepare the sites. They don't show that they have twenty or so volunteers there to do the grunt work. They keep them out of shot. Apparently it's really gutting to make an exciting discovery only to have the camera crews make you cover it up again so one of the more photogenic helpers can pretend to find it right there in front of the camera. This is real life and it could be a huge find. You don't want the publicity you'll get if we rush and bugger it up."

Gaskell had been trying to get a word in but at the mention of publicity he closed his mouth and frowned, thoughtful.

Rother was less restrained. "Publicity? Who cares. You've got a job to do. Get on with it."

"Which is what I was doing before someone called this meeting." Mal glanced at the councillor, who was also looking thoughtful. "Councillor Pugh, this is most probably a Bronze Age barrow burial. Normally barrows are quite obvious but it seems this one has been partly cut through by the lane and the build-up of soil along the line of the hedge hid the rest of it. At the moment we have no idea what's in the cist – the stone box. Since it doesn't appear to have been disturbed I would hope the grave goods are intact."

"You mean stuff like Tooting Carmen?" Gaskell's voice had hit a high note.

Mal took a moment to work it out. "No, not exactly like Tutankhamun. It's a completely different culture. But there should be bones and often these people were buried with some of their belongings. I'd expect a pot and a few flints at least." He fished around for an idea that might inspire some interest. "And the other thing to bear in mind for people like Councillor Pugh, and Glyn Havard, and Rob Escley who made the discovery, is that this is one of the family. It could be your great, great plus a few dozen other greats grandmother in there. So surely it's worth treating her with some respect?"

"When you put it like that ..." Pugh nodded. "Gaskell, I think we should show Mr Bright every consideration."

"Dr Bright," Mal said. It wasn't often he played the PhD card but he thought it might be necessary here. "And thank you. I have a list of what needs doing before you shut the site up tonight, one of which is to ring the police. Standard procedure when dealing with human remains. And I need to get some kit from the museum so I can make a preliminary investigation."

"I'll give you a lift," Pugh promised. "You can put your bike in the back."

Mal hurried to fetch his bike. He wasn't particularly surprised to find Rob, still hovering protectively over the stone. Nor was he surprised at the sly grin.

"Are you really a Doctor?" Rob asked. "Because, if you are, I've got something you can examine later?"

"Is it your dick?" Mal whispered. "Because I feel like celebrating?"

"Now you come to mention it …" Rob chuckled. "See you in the Coach, about eight?"

"Not the White Horse?"

"The White Horse is for Fridays. Go get your stuff. I'll make sure nobody fiddles with this while you're gone."

Mal's kit filled the boot of Pugh's Jag, shedding dried mud and a scatter of sand grains on the pristine interior but Pugh either didn't mind or didn't care. He seemed almost as excited as Rob had been. Mal asked Pugh to stop briefly outside his flat while he changed into clothes more suitable for rolling around in the mud and also took a moment to make the bed and push some laundry out of sight because he had high hopes he might be doing a bit more rolling around later tonight with Rob after the pub.

Then Pugh took him back to the building site. "I wish I could stay and watch," Pugh said, "but I need to get back to my meeting. They thought I'd gone crazy rushing out like that. You will keep me posted, won't you?"

Mal promised him that he would, then two of Glyn's men helped him carry the measuring rods, the camera bag and the tool kit, up the hill. Sion was one of the volunteers. "Glad you're back," he said. "Berkley had another go at Rob and Rob's being a right stroppy sod."

"I don't blame him. He did absolutely the right thing," Mal said.

"It's a bit more'n that." Sion grinned at him. "I think what you said about it being his great-great-lots-more-greats granny really struck home."

Mal pondered that as they approached the huge yellow digger, and made a mental note to ask Rob if the Escleys of Escley had been in the area as long as it sounded. But first he had some work to do.

First of all, barriers. Mal paced off a section that should cover the whole of the area of the barrow and his excited volunteers brought Heras panels, stands and cable ties to fence it off.

"I've got a spare padlock and chain," Glyn said. "Two keys, so if you have one and I have the other it'll be quite secure. Have you checked the weather forecast?"

They put up a gazebo too, complete with zip-on sides, in case of rain. Mal knew it wouldn't be long until the local press arrived and thought that since he'd got his own way over doing the excavation properly, it wouldn't hurt to put on a bit of a show on Gaskell's behalf.

Once that was done he was able to get down to business. He had already photographed the area in which they were working and the slight swell in the ground, which was all that remained of the barrow. Now he laid down the red and white striped ranging rods, aligning them with the cardinal points of the compass and took more photos from every angle. Partly this was for an accurate record but it was also partly to impress upon Gaskell and Berkley that there was to be no rushing him, and partly to reassure the police constable, who had come along to supervise, that this was archaeology and not a murder victim.

"You're sure?" he kept asking as Mal explained how, to an archaeologist or forensic scientist, there was nothing harder to hide than a hole in the ground. It took a while to convince him then he went off to one side and, from the bleeping that followed, played Tetris on his phone.

Gaskell and Berkley were made of sterner stuff but after half an hour of being chivvied out of Mal's way, they got bored and went off to, as Gaskell put it, 'plan their strategy'.

Mal set the camera aside for the moment to clear some of the mud away from around the stone lid. It was trowel work, quick and satisfying even with frequent stops for more photos, and he was soon able to see the slabs that formed the top of the cist in their entirety. They were a lot wider than he had thought they would be and he realised he'd be unlikely to be able to move them alone. Luckily Sion and Rob were still close by and each man fitted a hand into the overlap of the lid with the supporting stone and stood ready to lift on Mal's word. He held up a length of two by one. "Just lift the first one a couple of inches," he asked, "so I can slip this in to support the lid. I want to get more pictures. If we can document the whole process it could be good publicity for the site." *And for the museum*, went without saying.

"Ready, Rob?" Sion grinned at Mal. "On three then – one, two, three."

The stone lifted smoothly, just a little soil tumbling into the void below, and Mal slotted the piece of wood in about a foot. "Lovely," he said and took a penlight from his pocket. "Want the first look, boys?"

"Hell yeah," Rob said, and Sion grinned at him and shouldered into the space between Rob and Mal.

"Hang on," the policeman hurried across. "I'd better see, too, then I can go and write my report. It's cold up here."

Mal turned on the little torch and directed the beam into the gap. He smiled to hear two indrawn breaths. It was such a thrill to be the first to see something that had been hidden in the ground for centuries. He remembered his first time well. The dry earth under his knees, sun on his back, the grit on his tongue as a breeze laden with the scent of thyme and seaweed blew dust across the rocky Aegean peninsula. Then he had moved some more dust and had been looking into the face of a man long dead, just bones but broad-browed and strong-jawed. Moved, Mal had murmured, "Hello, brother."

It was a long moment before Rob or Sion stirred.

"Oh wow," Rob whispered, his voice a little shaky. "Hello, you. Pleased to meetcha."

"Mal," Sion looked across at him, eyes wide. "You got to see this."

They moved aside to let Mal tilt his head and peer under the stone. "Oh. Oh, yes," he said. "You don't see something like that every day."

Chapter 8

By 2 p.m., Mal had all the photos he could wish for safely on his camera. The press had come and had taken some photos of their own, but just of the slabs, Mal had sworn Rob and Sion to secrecy over what lay beneath. Then the coroner had turned up with the same morose policeman in tow.

"I'm no expert, obviously." The coroner was a lady in her fifties with a strong Welsh accent, a mop of iron grey curls and a cheery grin. She put her hands on her knees and stooped to peer under the slab of stone. "But if you assure me that it's an antique interment I see no reason why you shouldn't proceed along normal archaeological lines. Will the site be secure? Then carry on and – oh, this is all so exciting. I'd love another look when you've uncovered a bit more. Professional interest and all that."

Rob found a spot in the Portakabins where Mal could store his ranging rods and other kit.

"Most amazing thing I ever saw," he said. "Oh, Mal. Come here."

The memory of kissing Rob in the darkest corner of a Portakabin ensured that Mal was still grinning like a monkey when he got back to the museum.

"Well, don't you look pleased with yourself," Betty said when he came in.

"We got you a sandwich." Sharon offered him a paper bag. "And some pop and a Mars bar."

"I reckoned you might need the sugar to keep the excitement going. So – how was it?"

Mal looked from his two expectant custodians to the customers browsing the bookshelves in the library and poking at the items in the tiny museum shop. "Can I tell you later?" he said. "I need a better look at my photos and to check a few things first. But it's a great find. Something very … unusual. I – um – just don't want to jump the gun."

Betty pouted at him. "I don't want your steenking secrets," she said. "I'll ask Rob. He'll tell me."

"Rob doesn't know what I know," Mal said. "But thanks for my lunch."

Betty snatched the bag out of reach for a moment more then let him have it.

Mal hurried up to his office and put his lunch on the desk. First things first. Card reader, SD card, cable, USB port, download. He took off his jacket and cycle helmet while he waited for the download to finish, dashed to the loo, then went back to his desk and grabbed his lunch. Just to be perfectly safe he copied all the pictures to a data stick and again to County Hall's servers, glaring at the message that it would take fifty minutes. So much for ultrafast broadband.

Once sure he had enough backups, he felt able to settle down to pore over the pictures. The series of photos weren't professional quality but they were clear and sharp: the digger, with the hill in the background, the torn up earth, the scarred edge of the slab, Rob grinning at him – he saved that one to his personal folder – Rob and Sion stooping to lift the slab, and finally a series of the contents of the cist.

It hadn't been easy getting good photos through the little gap that was all he had allowed himself to open but what he had was enough to make his heart thump with excitement. There was a bed of fine silt – water always filtered in over the years despite the close fit of the stones – and so the two sets of bones were partially buried. But enough of them were visible for Mal to see how they had merged as the bodies had flattened in decomposition. There were the expected pots, two large finely made beakers, and what were probably the weapons and other belongings of the dead. A tiny glint that Mal magnified turned out to be a piece of amber, a pale scatter of spheres, bone beads. But it was the bones that caught his attention. He scowled at them, willing them to disentangle so he could see clearly how they had been laid out. Surely they should be less mingled? Surely their apparent placement was an accident?

"This is so good." Mal sat back in his chair, already imagining a refurbishment of the large room at the back of the building where they currently had an uninspiring exhibition of Victorian porcelain. It could be the 'Early Times' room. They had plenty of Neolithic and a few Iron Age finds and this wonderful cist and its contents could form the kernel of the Bronze Age exhibit. There was even, if he remembered correctly, a view of Carew Hill from the window – a window that could cause all kinds of problems for delicate organic material if he didn't filter the light properly. For that he'd need sponsorship, of course. Maybe a grant? But this could catch the imagination if what he suspected was true, and could put the museum on the map.

Mal let out a breath and opened his email. His old mentor during his studies at Bristol University was an expert on the Bronze Age, in Britain as well as in Greece. Mal hastily hammered out a general 'hope you are well' message then added a plea for advice and a trimmed and resized photo. He ended with:

The site is being developed. I'm under some pressure to excavate as fast as possible. I can't just make safe because the area is going to be dug out for a road widening. I just need to know if I'm seeing what I think I'm seeing and I can make a case for this being a find of national importance worthy of a proper excavation instead of a rescue style one. I'd really appreciate a quick reply as they have a burly bloke with a bulldozer – yeah, I know, not your thing but, oh my God, you should see him – standing by.

Mal ate his sandwich, going over the photos again, and was only just starting on his Mars Bar when the reply popped up in the corner of his screen.

Jesus Christ. Don't do anything until I'm there. I'll be with you first thing tomorrow morning. Book me a room at the hostelry with the prettiest bar staff.

"So, no doubts then," Mal said with relish and picked up the phone to give the Red Lion a ring.

The evening at the Coach and Horses was as uproarious as any Mal had enjoyed in college. Rob and Sion both seemed wired at having been part of the discovery, Betty and Gary seemed a little jealous but otherwise enthralled as Mal showed them the photos he had printed off.

"Ewww," Betty shivered. "I don't much like seeing skeletons. A bit too much of a reminder."

"Yeah, an' I got to be out there with 'em from midnight on." Gary grimaced and took a sip of the orange juice he had insisted on having since he couldn't drink when going on duty.

"But you were out there last night, too," Rob pointed out.

"I didn't know they were there then."

"Just keep Morris away from them," Mal suggested and laughed as Morris, hearing his name, looked up with lifted ears. "No, Morris, I have nothing for you. You ate half Betty's curry as it is."

"It'll make him fart." Gary gazed at his dog with a fond smile. "Good job we're gonna be out in the open air."

Morris looked back at him, tongue lolling in a doggy grin, then his ears flattened and he stood up.

"Oh fuck," Rob muttered as the door opened. "Grab him, someone."

Mal and Gary almost banged heads as they both lunged for Morris's collar. Mal assumed that the grab was because the huge dog might make a break for it, but Gary's expression was grim.

Morris growled a huge rumbling snarl as Phil Rother, still in his uniform, came into the snug bar. His face was red and he seemed a little unsteady on his feet.

"Oh Christ." He blew out his cheeks. "There was a poetry reading in the Castle, fucking folk music in the Red Lion and the Lamb's got a hen night in. Isn't there anywhere a *man* can get a quiet drink in this town."

"Good evening, Mr Rother," Rob called. "Did you miss the memo? The meeting of the Association of Bigoted Homophobic Knobheads was cancelled, sorry."

There was one of those silences, during which the two elderly men who had been enjoying a quiet round of darts, abandoned their pints and their arrows, and slipped past Rother into the other bar. Rother grinned.

"That so, Dirty Rob?"

Mal straightened up, feeling he should try and do something to break the tension in the room. He did, but not quite the way he intended.

"Mr Museum," Rother beamed. "I didn't see you there but I can't say I'm surprised."

"I am," Mal said. "I was under the impression that Gaskell's site was going to be guarded tonight – until midnight by you, unless I read the schedule in Havard's office incorrectly. Can you assure me that the site is being adequately supervised? By someone who hasn't been drinking?" He shot a pointed glance to the orange juice by Gary's place-mat.

Rother flushed and took a pace towards their table.

"Don't you dare, Philip Rother." Betty was white with fury. "Don't you fucking dare!"

"Now, now." A quiet voice from the doorway caused another tense silence. The man who entered gave Rother a reproachful glance then turned an equally reproving gaze on Rob. "Betty, are you all right? I heard raised voices."

He didn't look like much of a saviour – medium sized, narrow built, unremarkable, and he was dressed almost identically to Rother, except that his shoulder flashes were white. Then the radio on his belt emitted a loud buzz and a female voice made some kind of reference to sheep on the Ross Road. Mal relaxed. The police had arrived, it seemed.

"We're fine, Brian love." Betty beamed at him. "Night off, is it?"

Brian nodded and hefted a plastic bag bulky with the corners of takeaway containers. "Just picking up a korma. First night off for – oh God, ages. So I really don't want any trouble. Not from any of you lot."

The mild gaze of one of the most beautiful pairs of grey eyes Mal had ever seen tracked impartially around the room then fixed on him. "Hello?" The smile lit up his unremarkable face. "I don't know you, do I?"

"Hi." Mal got up to offer his hand. "Malcolm Bright from the museum. We were just talking about security."

Brian shook his hand gravely and there was something in the way he held it and the warming in those amazing eyes that made Mal's gaydar give the world's smallest ping.

"PC Brian Farriner," the policemen said. "I went to school with most of this lot and could tell you some stories, Mr Bright."

"Dr Bright," Rother chanted but Brian just smiled.

"Doctor then," he said. "Nice to have met you. Oh, are these the photos from the site? Bellamy was up on your site with the coroner and was telling me about it when he got back to the station. Can I see?"

"'Course you can, Mal was just telling us about them." Rob leaned to grab a chair from another table and everyone moved up to let the law in.

"Sorry, lovely," Brian said to Morris as he moved him gently aside. "No, you can't have my supper." He put the bag on the table and reached for the first photo. Unlike PC Bellamy, Brian seemed as excited as any of them to see the photos and asked a few questions that suggested to Mal that his interest in history went well beyond watching the Discovery Channel. Given such an appreciative audience it was easy for Mal to slip into lecture mode and keep it up until Rother had gone. Everyone breathed a discreet sigh of relief.

"Can I stop now?" Mal asked and Brian laughed.

"I was interested, honestly," he said. "But I must admit it was a good way to shut Rother up."

"Git," Rob muttered.

"Yeah," Betty's lips were still pinched. "If you hadn't been here, Brian –"

"Well, I was," Brian pointed out. "And I don't think he'd have hit Doctor Bright. But he would have said more stuff. Rob, you have to keep your temper when he's around."

"I'm sorry," Mal said, "but isn't there something we can do about him? From the moment he came into the room he seemed to be set on starting trouble."

"Would have done too if you hadn't been here, Brian," Rob said. "The only reason I can think he didn't start swinging straight away was that he'd spotted Mal, here."

"But that's ridiculous," Mal said. "In front of so many witnesses?"

There was another uncomfortable silence then Rob sucked in a deep breath. "Something you need to know, Mal. Rother can get away with it. Always has. He's hated Betty since she turned him down, then laid him out with a cricket bat when he put his hand up her gym skirt."

"Too damn right I did, cheeky bastard," Betty growled. "But – but I really wouldn't want to be alone with him and he bloody knows it. And he bullies Gary because Gary wants to keep his job and because he knows that if he started something Morris would join in and Rother would make him have Morris put down. Everyone knows that Rother is the only one Morris *ever* growls at, but Morris looks so bloody scary the court would think he *must* be vicious."

Gary reached out to apply a gentle pat to her hand, covering it completely. "Won't let that happen, will we, Betty?" He turned to face Mal again, his heavy features troubled. "Rob's been bound over to keep the peace. Still got a few months to go on the sentence."

"Yeah," Sion scowled. "But Rother was having a go at me about Dad, and Rob got between us and Rother tried to take Rob apart in the car park of the Castle but someone's car got damaged and Rob got into trouble for it!"

Rob nodded, his eyes smouldering with fury. "I can't afford to be up before the beak again."

"You're doing very well," Brian put in. "And we daren't let Sion fight Rother because he wouldn't know when to stop. A cricket bat would be the least of it." He and Sion exchanged grins. "So we try our best to keep Rother away, don't we?"

"Yeah, but if he's going to make a habit of coming in here, where are *we* supposed to go?" Sion snarled. "We had to stop going in the Castle when he started to drink there. This is Dad's pub, and I could ask him to ban Rother but that wouldn't go down well with the publican's association. They seem welcoming enough but Dad's – well he's Dad. But more than that, they've never seen Rother behaving like that."

"I have," Mal said. "Do you think they'd take my word?"

"Well, yeah," Rob said, "except when he's fighting an Escley. Everyone knows they are bad news, see."

He didn't explain any further but everyone seemed very sympathetic. Mal made another mental note to ask Rob about it when they had some peace to talk. That wasn't long coming. Brian wanted his supper, he said, and some quality time catching up on recorded episodes of NCIS and Criminal Minds, and soon after he had taken his leave the group broke up. Sion went through to help in the bar. Betty expressed an interest in an early night and graciously accepted Gary and Morris's offer of an escort home. Rob just slipped a finger into Mal's palm and gave him a tickle with a lift of his eyebrows.

"Another pint?" he asked. "Or do you want an early night too?"

"Early night?" Mal grinned at him. "I thought we were going to play doctors?"

Back to Mal's place was a hasty five minute walk. Out of clothing and into bed took even less time but after that there was no rush and it was close to eleven before Mal collapsed, burying his face against Rob's furry pecs, and allowed gravity, and the copious amounts of natural lubrication smearing their bellies, to slide him off to rest along Rob's side. He tucked his bony feet under Rob's sturdier ones and let out a deep sigh of satisfaction.

"Well, Doc? What's the verdict?" Rob muttered. Mal could hear the smile.

"You'll live," Mal said.

"Cool." Rob stretched and yawned. When he drew his arm back in again he hauled Mal even closer and nuzzled the top of his head. "I'd invite myself to stay, but I got to be up really early."

"How early?" Mal asked, lifting his head to look at Rob. He couldn't deny that the thought of having Rob here all night was very appealing. Mal had always been a cuddler and the discovery that Rob was one too pleased him no end.

"*Early* early," Rob said. "Five-ish." He ruffled his knuckles through Mal's sweaty hair. "Can I invite myself to stay another time?"

"No," Mal said. "I invite you, and your rain check will be good 'til whenever."

"Rain check." Rob snorted. "Don't get those in rugby. If you're too much of a wuss to get wet while supporting your team and miss a match, that's your problem." He nudged Mal until Mal moved enough to kiss, then Rob pushed him onto his back and sat up.

"Nice dinner, nice couple of pints, even better fuck. I love Thursdays."

So do I, Mal thought as he watched Rob get up and swagger to the bathroom. *Or rather any day I get to spend time with you.*

Mal contemplated going after Rob to suggest they share the shower but it was only sensible to let him leave. It was getting late and Mal didn't like the idea of Rob using heavy machinery on not enough sleep. The building trade could be very dangerous. Far more so than curating, where a mishap with a stapler was about the worst that could happen. The thought of those huge pieces of metal grinding together and what they could do to a hand, or any of Rob really, made Mal feel ill. In fact the thought of anything nasty happening to Rob was very upsetting.

In the bathroom the loo flushed. Mal called over the rush of the water. "I'll see you tomorrow anyway. Got to get to the site early to plan the excavation." Rob grunted a reply but Mal couldn't catch what he said. "Are you free Friday? If so maybe you'd like to stay over then?"

"Yeah." Rob put his head round the bathroom door and grinned at him. "I would." He bowled over arm and a wadded-up towel flew across the room to land on Mal's chest. Rob grinned again and popped back into the bathroom.

"Thanks." Mal dabbed at his chest and belly and spread the damp towel demurely over his loins.

"There's so much to do," he added. "Harvey Biddulph is coming up tomorrow."

"Oh, I know him." Rob popped out of the bathroom again. "He's on the telly. The one who flails around like a heron in a hurricane."

"Yeah, that's the one. He taught me in Uni. He's coming to look at the burial and advise on the safest way to retrieve it. I know what I'd do, but it's always good to have some outside input. And then," Mal grinned at Rob as he sat on the bed, "we need to decide the best way to exhibit it."

"Exhibit?" Rob stared at him. "But surely you're just going to move it?"

"Where to?" Mal asked. "That whole area is going to be torn up over the next few years. If Gaskell has his way, anyhow. I don't really want to see that but if there's new houses then there needs to be a new school and better roads, and more jobs would be nice, wouldn't they? Maybe then all the kids won't go off to Birmingham and Hereford to find work and homes. More jobs might mean more locals can stay local and fewer incomers, like me, come in and upset the balance."

"Well, yeah, I know all that. I told you all that." Rob fished under the bed for his boxers, pulled them on then sat down again to pull on socks and jeans. "But they put that – whatever – cist there for a reason and, okay, we need to keep it safe while the work is going on, but it should go back. They shouldn't be put on show. If you died you wouldn't want to be displayed like a – like an old *pot* or something. Those are people."

"Yes, they are people." Mal frowned. "But that's what makes it so important to be able to see them. By putting the burial on display we can show that people just like us have been here for years and years and they loved and valued the same things we do, even if they show it in different ways. They wouldn't be displayed like a freak show but with care and respect."

"Still not right, not for people just like us." Rob was scowling now, a hot angry look in his eyes that brought Mal up short.

"Okay," Mal said. "But what should we do with them, then? I can only get funding for a proper excavation by making promises. There have to be visible results. There has to be some kind of payoff for the sponsors. Otherwise, it will be rescue, pure and simple, just get them out of the ground and shifted and box them up somewhere on a shelf."

"You can't do that!" Rob was aghast. "They need to go back. I remember when they widened the road by the chapel they had to – what do they call it – disinter some bodies, and move the headstones. But they reburied them in a special plot and made sure the families knew what happened to them."

"But that's different," Mal said. "Those were probably recent burials with family members still living."

"Oh, bollocks! Of course there are family members still living. Because if people have been here for years and years, then it's people like me and Gary and Glyn, and old Pugh, and the Farriners. They *are* our great great granddads and grandmas. They are family. And you look after your family. And you certainly shouldn't make a fucking exhibition of them." Rob had been pulling clothes on with sharp angry tugs and scooped up boots and jacket and headed for the door. "You're not local, Mal! There's stuff about this place you don't know. Like – like you don't know why it's called Rifle Lane for a start, you ignorant bloody *sais*. If you can't understand how important family is then, yeah, you are a fucking incomer and you are upsetting the fucking balance. And, no, I don't want to cash in any fucking rain checks. Stupid idea." He was still grumbling as the bedroom door slammed behind him and Mal stared at the magnolia painted plywood with his mouth open.

Rob had gone and, apparently, wouldn't be coming back. That was so unexpected, so sharp and so shocking that Mal couldn't cope with it. He turned his mind away from the raw ache of it and fixed on something puzzling but less painful.

"Syce?" he asked. "I'm a Hindustani groom? What the fuck?" Then, slowly and sadly, he made his way to the bathroom.

Chapter 9

Next morning at the Rifle Lane site, Mal arrived with a heavy heart and a thumping head. But he had to paste on a smile because his old friend and mentor Harvey was with him and he was one of the most cheerful and upbeat people Mal knew. Harvey Biddulph had been a university lecturer coming up to retirement when the sickness of a cast member of a well-loved TV show about historical matters led to him being called in as a temporary replacement. His brand of cheerful enthusiasm and occasional passionate flailing made him such a favourite that he was invited to take part regularly, whenever the programme featured any of his specialist subjects. He had a great expertise in the study of the Bronze Age – the first great flowering of human civilisation, as he called it – and really Mal couldn't have been more delighted that Harvey was not only prepared to help but had dropped everything to come immediately.

"Such a beautiful spot," Harvey said. "It's a pity about the development but what can you do? People need places to live. Odd to think that the population of Gwent now is approximately the same as the whole of England in the Neolithic era."

"Really?" Mal asked as Harvey parked his car. "Are you sure?"

"Nope." Harvey grinned and got out of the car, his mass of white hair glinting like salt as the wind caught it. "Estimates vary but it makes a good sound-bite for people to remember. Oh, smell that air! You're so lucky to have found a nice place here, my boy. Bristol is a lovely city but hardly fragrant."

Harvey made gentle fun of Mal all the way up the hill to where the gazebo now stood in lonely splendour. Mal looked for Rob and his digger and found them in the far corner. The backhoe part with its narrow bucket was in play, probably digging trenches for utilities. That sharp pang of sorrow hit him again so he turned away and led Harvey into the shelter of the canvas roof.

They spread tarps, then borrowed a passing workman who was delighted to meet even such a minor TV celebrity as Harvey, and quite willing to show off his strength by lifting the top stones off the cist for them.

"Thank you," Harvey said, polite but already peering into the darkness of the hole. "Mal, get that light set up. Oh now, yes." He lowered his lanky body to lie full length beside the cist, head and shoulders over the edge as he shone his torch onto the remains. "Thank you for calling me in."

Mal turned on the powerful battery-powered light and shone it down into the pit, then took a position prone on the other side. His trowel made a gentle pass over the damp silt, easing it away from the bones while Harvey muttered instructions. He had a small, handheld video camera and was following Mal's hands with the lens. This was new but Mal assumed it was a technique Harvey had picked up from his TV show. It would certainly save time, but Mal ensured Harvey both took stills and kept an old fashioned paper record too, just in case.

"Good, hold it there." Harvey tweaked the focus on the camera. "Can you take a little off the pelvis? I just want to be sure."

"Here?" Mal swapped his trowel for one of his brushes to ease the silt away a millimetre at a time. He knew what Harvey was looking for and smiled when the bowl of the pelvis became obvious.

"Excellent." Harvey settled more comfortably, recording with one hand and making occasional notes with the other. "So we have the remains of two individuals of extremely robust build. Mal, can you measure those long bones? Our estimates are going to be rough as a badger's chuff, obviously, but we can do it properly once we get the poor souls back to the lab."

Mal extended his steel tape along the closest femur, making sure the measurements were in shot, then leaned to do another. He did the sums in his head. Whoever they had been, they hadn't been tall by modern standards but for the time period were impressive.

"Oh, very nice. So we have two robust individuals between five feet five and seven in height. Nothing gracile about these two, is there? Going by the strength of the jaws, supra-orbital bulges and the narrow sciatic notches, two males. These males have been placed in the grave facing each other touching at forehead and knees. From the way the arm bones have fallen I'd say they were embracing, wouldn't you, Doctor Bright?"

Very well aware that he was being recorded and that he, as a simple curator of a small museum, had very little academic clout, Mal stifled the impulse to punch the air and said, "I'd think it would be foolhardy to make any assumptions until we have a chance to excavate more fully. However, from the mingled hand bones under Subject One's humerus, it's possible that the hands were either one on top of the other or were perhaps even meshed together."

"Holding hands, in fact," Harvey added. "My thoughts too. Also visible are two very fine examples of Beaker ware pots, from the decoration made by the same potter. There are – one two three – er – seven white bone beads visible. One large round bead of cloudy yellow amber. What's that, Mal? Just expose it a little – brush not trowel. Thanks. Two small jet beads. A piece of white bone approx ten centimetres in length and half that in width, pierced at the corners. I can only see one flint – a piece of broken blade – but I would expect more. There's some green staining on Subject Two's sternum. Make a note to check for evidence of bronze pins. Ditto staining on Subject One's femur. Mal, I bet we've got at least one sword in there. Oh frabjous day! Ending recording at – um – nine forty two."

Mal glanced up, surprised, but Harvey was propping himself up and frowning at the burial site.

"That's enough for now," he said. "Let's cover these two up and get back to the museum. You've got some decisions to make and need to have a long hard think about them."

"I do?" Mal stared at him, getting up as well. "Well, of course I do. But in what way do you mean?"

"Let's talk about it at the museum, preferably over some coffee. You do have proper coffee, don't you?"

"Not the type you mean," Mal admitted, "but I'll see what I can do."

Harvey gathered up his kit and hurried back to the car to make a phone call while Mal went in search of someone to help him ease the stone lid back onto the cist. The man who had helped before was out of sight and Mal didn't want to disturb the team working further down the hill around Rob's digger. He watched the huge machine for a few moments, replaying last night's argument in his mind and feeling confused, regretful and frustrated, then turned away and looked elsewhere.

In the end Glyn Havard came and found him.

"You look a bit lost, Mal," he said. "Anything I can do to help?"

He may have meant professionally but he had sympathetic cast to his expression that made Mal certain that he was referring to Rob.

"As it happens …" Mal said and as he led him back to the gazebo confirmed that, yes, Glyn had heard all about his and Rob's falling out.

"I'm sorry," Glyn said once they'd put the site to rights and covered everything with weighted down tarps. "That's Rob's problem, see. He makes all these jokes, acts daft and folks think he is daft, but he's not. I've known him since he was a tiddler, Gary's best friend in and out of our house at all hours. Half the time he spent the nights, at least once his old man started drinking, then when his mam got too ill to do it he went back to look after the old sod. He deserved better, he really did. And his mam's family are worse. They never bothered with him."

"So he takes family really seriously," Mal said. "Oh, hell. And what am I supposed to do with this excavation? It needs doing properly otherwise it will be damaged and there's no way we can re-bury it up here. You know as well as I do that this whole hillside is scheduled for development. There wouldn't be a safe place to put it, even if – God knows, Glyn, the museum could do with something a bit exciting to exhibit. And this – this is one of the most exciting things I've seen for a long time."

"More exciting than Rob?" Glyn asked. "No, that wasn't a fair question. Look, there's nothing more pointless than advice, but if I were you I'd give him a day or two to calm down." Glyn put his hand on Mal's shoulder and gave him a little shake. "It probably wouldn't have happened if it hadn't been for the pub earlier."

"You mean that we'd been drinking?" Mal asked, appalled at the comment about Rob's father.

"No." Glyn's mouth formed a grim line. "I mean that Rob's Mam was a Rother, and they never forgave her for marrying an Escley."

Mal mulled all that over as he returned to the car, then on the way back to the museum. He had been warned that local family politics was a minefield but hadn't expected the results to hit so close to home. Clearly he needed advice, but right now Harvey and his professional responsibilities came first.

"Penny for 'em," Harvey said as they got out of the car. "I've often seen you looking thoughtful, Mal, but not usually this miserable."

"Sorry, just a relationship hiccup," Mal said.

"The burly bulldozer." Harvey nodded. "I hope it works out. But for now I think we'd better get inside. It looks as though it might rain."

Once inside the museum, Mal introduced Harvey to his custodians. Betty, with her coat on ready to leave, caught Mal's eye and rolled her own as they listened to Harvey flirting with Sharon who had just come on duty.

"You'd think they were fifteen," she whispered to Mal. "He'll be offering to show her his collection of Pokémon in a minute."

"Harvey doesn't do Pokémons, he does etchings," Mal replied. "And I dunno. I think a bit of admiration might do Sharon some good."

"Yeah, you're never too old to make a fool of yourself over a pretty face. Speaking of which are you going to have a haircut? You're getting a bit bohemian over the collar."

"All right, I'll make an appointment."

"I could come round after work," Betty offered.

"I'll be taking Harvey out tonight, got to catch up with him. He doesn't mind me looking bohemian."

They both looked at Harvey who was beaming at Sharon and running a hand through his own wild mane.

"Yeah I can see that." Betty grinned. "All right, Tuesday is Lil's late night. We could use the salon, do a proper hair job on you. Laters, boss."

Wondering what, for Betty, constituted a 'proper hair job', Mal made tea for Sharon as well as himself and Harvey and then found a comfortable place for them to sit up in the stores rather than in the cramped and littered office.

Harvey leaned back in his chair and looked around the room. "You've got a lot of sorting out to do," he said. "This place is both loved and neglected. I imagine your records are a disgrace."

"Oddly enough, no, they aren't. We've got a catalogue, a bit patchy on detail, but if someone comes in and asks to see the item their gran donated in 1967, we can find it. But, yes, the record does tend to consist of date and donor's name and address and a simple description like 'frock, pink, poss. Vict.' which isn't that informative. It was easier to find stuff before they boxed it up."

"And precious little environmental control? I bet it's freezing up here during the winter."

"And hot in the summer – but not too damp, thank God. We have dehumidifiers just in case, but it tends to hang around the fifty five percent mark fairly naturally unless it's very wet outside. It's not a bad building."

"But the exhibits need work?"

"Haven't been updated since the seventies," Mal admitted. "And we have hardly any money in the kitty. If this new find is as interesting as I hope it will be, I could get some heavy duty grants to do the place up a bit, might even be able to afford a couple of new cases. Honest, Harvey, the prices are extortionate."

"The phrase 'conservation grade' in any description automatically doubles the price of the item," Harvey said. "But still, it would be worth doing. You just need to decide how you are going to sell the exhibit to possible sponsors."

"Apart from the obvious?" Mal raised his eyebrows. "Harvey, this is an amazing find. Firstly, it's almost unique in that they didn't normally bury two cadavers in the same cist. Not unless the cist was reused. From the way the bones lie it's obvious they were interred at the same time and deliberately placed in a position that suggests intimacy but not – not mocking, not derisory. The implication is that they were a couple."

"Yes." Harvey nodded and made a 'come on, what's the next step' motion with both hands.

"Distinct 'couple' burials are incredibly rare. I can only think of half a dozen outside the Andronovo culture."

"Siberia," Harvey said, nodding. "Terribly cold, Siberia."

"Yes, quite. So that is a selling point. Something unusual, something unique, right here on our doorstep." Mal took a deep breath. "It shows that humankind has always sought and found someone to love. Love has always been a powerful motivator and we can see it there in those two sad piles of bones. That struck me very strongly. The more of the bones we exposed the clearer it became that they had been positioned that way deliberately. And the fact that they seem to be two male skeletons is even more incredible. Men like me have always been here, Harvey, and there have been times we were treated with honour instead of having to hide, dissemble and apologise."

Harvey smiled. "That's true. And that's a good, a very good point to make, but is your notoriously conservative local authority going to buy it?"

"They better fucking had," Mal said. "Because once that cist has been properly excavated and we've got all the facts and figures and are sure of what we've got, there's no way in hell I'm going to try and explain it away as an anomaly, or that the two skeletons were disturbed after burial. We know what's there. And there's no way I'm going to hide and dissemble and apologise for that!"

"I didn't think so." Harvey sat up a bit and grinned. "Well, for what it's worth I'll have your back. And you'll need it because, my boy, I think you might have a fight on your hands."

They talked all afternoon. Mal gave Harvey a tour of the museum, poking around back room and storage areas that Mal had barely had a chance to look over. They took a tablet, a portable light, temperature and humidity monitor and a tape measure and quickly narrowed down the options for storage until the new exhibition area was ready.

At quarter to five Harvey rubbed his stomach and said, "Well, I think I'll go and check into my hotel. Join me for dinner? My treat."

Mal thought bitterly of the simple entry in his calendar – R – that he had forgotten to delete, and agreed.

"I'll buy the wine," he promised. And that was fair enough because he drank most of it.

Mal and his mentor had always got along well together and it was great fun to catch up with him, even more so since Harvey had a fund of stories to do with his new career in TV. Mal enjoyed both the meal and the company, especially since it did a little to take his mind off how much he was missing Rob.

"Congratulations," he said, when Harvey told him that the TV company had renewed his contract for another series. "You're very good at explaining things in ways that don't sound too technical. Like that wildly inaccurate claim about the population of Gwent."

Harvey laughed. "If you think that was inaccurate you ought to hear some of the other tosh in the script. I don't suppose it can last," he said, "but I'm coming up for retirement at the university, if I want it. It's tempting to get my golden handshake and concentrate on the telly and my writing. I'd like to do another couple of books. There's some fascinating stuff coming out of Russia."

"Not in Ukraine." Mal wagged a finger. "Too dangerous. Wait until they've resolved their differences before you go off and try to dig up Scythian gold."

"'Harvey Biddulph, Tomb Raider' has a bit of a ring, doesn't it?" Harvey grinned.

"It really does. Whereas 'Malcolm Bright, Manager of the Pemberland Centre for Culture and Heritage' –"

"Heritage and Culture!"

"Why so it is. I blame the wine. As I was saying, Malcolm Bright, blah-di-blah, is so bloody *bland*." Mal shook his head. "It's time-sheets and policy meetings and who forgot to order light bulbs. Whereas you – you're all about exciting races against bad weather, mounting guard against night hawks –"

"Scum of the earth!"

"Indeed, and I bet you have any number of young lovelies hanging on your words since your celebrity rank went up a few notches."

"Youth is over-rated." Harvey shook his head. "At my time of life a pair of pert knockers has far less appeal than the ability to balance an account, cook a pie, proof-read a paper and carry on a sensible conversation."

"There you go! How about my custodian, Sharon?" Mal grinned. "All the above, a lovely lady and you can write anywhere, can't you?"

Harvey sat back in his chair. "My goodness, Malcolm," he said. "Are you setting up as a procurer?"

"No." Mal sighed. "I'd just like it if *someone* had a happy relationship. It might rub off on me."

Chapter 10

That mood of melancholy stayed with Mal all the following weekend. The site had been made safe and Harvey felt that getting the opinion of a respected osteo-archaeologist might be a good idea so, first thing Saturday morning, they took a sheaf of Mal's photos and headed off to Bristol to see Harvey's colleague.

Mal didn't get home until nearly nine on Saturday evening. He was tired and still a little head-achy from the wine, but he had the confirmation he needed to be able to say with confidence that both skeletons were male. Sunday, he spent doing his usual chores. As he filled the washing machine he wondered where Rob was. Had he found somewhere else, someone else to spend time with? Mal just hoped Rob wasn't feeling as miserable as he was.

By Monday afternoon he was so fed up that he rang Zoë to talk it over. He got short shrift.

"I'm due in work in half an hour, so I haven't got time to listen. And why are you telling me, anyway?" she demanded. "If being without Rob is making you sound that pathetic you need to go and tell *him* you can't do without him."

"I'm not pathetic," Mal protested. "And I can manage without him … I just don't want to."

"Well, tell him you're sorry. Grovel. Promise not to do it again."

"It's not that kind of problem. Not like putting an empty milk bottle back in the fridge or forgetting to buy loo paper."

"God, Oliver really worked you over, didn't he, the bastard. Go to Rob, throw yourself on his mercy and offer to compromise or something. But whatever else you do, drop the self-pity. It doesn't suit you."

That was pretty sound advice when Mal looked at it dispassionately. But there was a time and a place for everything and giving Rob some space for a day or two had been good advice too.

Tuesday morning Harvey was back again, packed for a long stay. He inspected Mal's spare room, snorted at the stacks of boxes and turned his nose up in the nicest possible way at the somewhat saggy spare bed.

"Thanks all the same, dear boy," he said, "but I think I'll try and negotiate a good deal with one of the hotels."

Then Mal and Harvey made a proper start on clearing the burial site. They could easily have got in some volunteers, but Mal knew that the more people involved the more likely it was that the press might get hold of some cause for speculation. So he worked in silence and assumed that Harvey had picked up his mood, because he was unusually quiet too

All went well until lunchtime when Harvey demanded a break. He looked a bit pink in the face, something Mal had put down to the biting October wind, but on the way back to the car to fetch the soup and rolls Mal had made up that morning, Mal noticed that Harvey was sweating.

"You know," he said, "you really need to get out more often if this is too much for you."

Harvey rolled his eyes at him. "Not at all. I just think I might have a bit of a cold coming. Throat feels a bit scratchy. One of my students was sneezing all over the place, last week. I hope I didn't pick it up."

"Oh dear." Mal pondered the contents of his backpack. "I have some paracetamol, but I think you might be better off with Lemsip. Shall I go and get you some? It won't take long."

"If you could, dear boy, I'd be most grateful."

But by three o'clock Harvey was light-headed and his temperature was through the roof. Mal took him back to his hotel, shopped for suitable 'invalid' supplies and then left him to sleep. Harvey was robust and healthy, despite his age, and very fond of pointing out that seventy was the new fifty. To see him brought so low by a cold was very worrying.

But Mal had appointments of his own to consider and, at five thirty, headed down the stairs from his flat to get his hair cut.

A bell on the front door jingled as Mal stepped inside. At the front of the salon was a waiting area with arm chairs and a coffee table and a reception desk surely built in the seventies with a ruched white vinyl front. Beyond the screen made from IKEA shelving was an area with white sinks and mirrors, ranks of the old-fashioned beehive hair-dryers, wheelie carts laden with strange devices, and everywhere pictures of pouting, big-eyed women with perfect hair. Mal wrinkled his nose at the scent of chemicals partially masked by perfume.

A skinny boy with black shoulder-length hair and copious eyeliner paused in sweeping the floor.

"Are you Mal?" he asked. "They're expecting you. Lillian?" he called.

"Back here, Mal." Mal's landlady appeared in a doorway at the back of the room. Petite and classily dressed, her height was increased considerably by a sweeping up-do in a pleasant shade of lavender that clashed with Betty's multi-coloured mop.

She peered over Lillian's shoulder. "We got a treat for you, Mal. Terry agreed to stay on."

Mal hadn't seen Lillian's staff so was expecting someone similar to her skinny gothy sweeper-upper. He was a bit shocked when he saw the barber – a man almost as big as Gary, whose black tee-shirt barely contained an impressive set of muscles.

"Hey," Terry rumbled, raising a hand like a shovel. "Pleased to meet you. Come on in."

In the room at the back of the salon the tiles changed from blue and white to glossy black vinyl and the two chairs looked more suitable for a nineteen-thirties dentist than a barber. Mal grinned at the pile of *Autocar*, *PC Gamer* and *Classic Bike* magazines on the little table by a line of austere bentwood chairs. This room smelled too, but it didn't make Mal's sinuses twitch. It smelled, somehow, of masculinity. Soap, Mal thought one of the expensive woodsy ones, aftershave of several different types, boot polish, dog and maybe just a hint of socks.

"Do you like it?" Lillian asked. "Since Cyril's down by the market closed, the closest place for a haircut in a proper barber shop is Abergavenny. I poached Terry from them."

"Handier for me," Terry said. "I don't live far and the blokes prefer to have a place of their own, silly sods. 'Ow you going to meet girls if you don't go where girls are. Siddown."

He spun the chair towards Mal who seated himself and put his hands on the arms, tightening his grip as Terry spun him back to face the mirror.

"I love it," Mal said. "Not that I don't like the rest of the set up too, Lillian, but this has a very welcoming feel. Oh, is that an original Brylcreem steel?"

The rectangular advert looked good against the stark white of the wall. Red and black again, and rugby players with muddy knees and glossy hair.

Mal read the tag line of the advert – *Get ahead from any position* – and grinned.

"Picked it up in a salvage yard," Terry replied. "So what'll it be?"

"Well, he's a museum curator," Lillian pointed out, "so he'll need to look tidy. Professional."

"But the last thing he needs is a high and tight," Betty stated. "He hasn't got the face for it."

"What on earth is a high and tight?" Mal asked.

"Something you really don't want," Terry said. "It'd make you look like a stormtrooper."

"He's got some nice length coming." Lillian tilted her head. "Have you considered growing it out? Oh I do miss the seventies. All those lovely flowing locks."

"Don't interfere, ladies," Terry said. He put a big hand on top of Mal's head, scrunching up the hair there between his fingers. "It's fine. Bet it goes flat when you're hot."

Lillian leaned in for a feel as well. "Nice hair. Oh, there's the bell. This must be my client. Don't worry, Mal. Terry and Bet will take good care of you."

Lillian ambled back into the main room and Mal heard her call a greeting, then Terry nudged his shoulder.

"Let's do this," Terry said. "I'll soon have you looking a million quid. First thing, lean forward. You'll be needing that jacket off."

Mal did as he was told. For a start he was in the abode of experts. He wouldn't tolerate being told how to go about things in the storerooms and labs of a museum so why should he object to following direction here? Then there was the calm way Terry met his eyes in the mirror and gave him a nod, man to man, to reassure him that nothing awful would happen no matter how much Lillian might seem to be stuck in the days of feather cuts and flares or Betty advocate a complete makeover involving, as a first step, an application of bleach. Then there was Terry himself, with his build of a prop forward slightly gone to seed, messy black curls and neatly trimmed beard framing a wry smile. And finally Mal had to admit that he had a little bit of a thing for men who were just a tad bossy in bed. Not that he was looking at Terry in that way, of course, but the strong confidence with which Terry handled him, tilting his head forward to scoop out the locks of hair that were under the collar of his sweater, was undeniably pleasant.

"Your neck's stiff," Terry grumbled. "Relax, man, you're not getting the Jason Statham look."

"Mal's got worries, haven't you?" Betty said.

"Nothing I can't handle," Mal said. "I've just been spending a lot of time thinking about that burial and how to handle its disposal. And Harvey's not well. I had to take him back to his hotel this afternoon."

"There's flu about," Betty said. "Isn't there, Terry?"

"Stomach flu as well as the cold type. The twins went down with it and now Mam's ailing too," Terry said. "Nasty. Right, Mal, you hold still."

The sweep of the comb followed by the precise clip of scissors was almost hypnotising. Mal closed his eyes for a moment, enjoying the peace. But Betty was there so it couldn't last.

"I saw Rob today," she said. "He asked after you, and I didn't know what to say because I didn't know what was going on."

Mal's heart sank. He had intended to ask Betty's advice on how to mend fences with Rob but maybe over a quiet drink somewhere. Certainly not in front of strangers. "Oh yes?" He tried to keep his voice indifferent. "He's working on the new road system, isn't he? I could see his digger making trenches. It's astonishing the progress they have made already."

"Rob Escley?" Terry's steady snip snip snip didn't falter. "Good lad with a digger, Rob."

"Yeah, well, he's not looking so good right now." Betty glared at Mal. "As you probably know."

Mal glared back. "How would I know? I haven't seen him."

"He did come up to see you while you were at the dig today but apparently you completely ignored him."

Terry's scissors did stop then. "Bloody Nora, Bet," he said. "What business is it of yours?"

"Well, duh, Mal's my boss and Rob's one of my best mates, and they are both miserable as fuck at the moment. Of course it's my business."

"Excuse me," Mal raised both hands causing the drape around his torso to billow and bits of hair to fly everywhere. "Betty, I don't think this is the place to discuss this."

"Best place ever," Betty said. "And where else would we? You've been up at High Rifles most of the time and God knows where you were at the weekend. Did you have your phone off? How d'you know Rob wasn't trying to call you?"

Terry sighed. "Betty, we know you mean well but Mal's differences with Rob are their business and nobody else's. Also, there are places where casually outing someone like that can earn them a thumping. You're safe enough with me, Mal," Terry growled. "Play for the same team, don't I? But yeah, Bet. Best not to talk out of turn."

Betty flushed, her eyes glinting. "I'll just keep my opinions to myself then, shall I?" she snapped and got up and walked out without waiting for a reply.

Mal and Terry exchanged mutual stares of resignation in the mirror.

"Sorry about that," Mal said. "I know she means well."

Terry nodded and picked up his comb. It was fascinating to watch those big hands manipulate the bright steel of the scissors and the cloudy black-brown of the comb. Fake tortoiseshell, very nineteen fifties. Very soothing. Mal felt the tension begin to leave his shoulders again and relaxed back into the firm embrace of the chair.

"Always been into everything, our Bet." Terry's voice was a bass rumble of calm. "She used to work here. Bloody good with a pair of scissors. Then she and Lil had a falling-out over – what was it now? Highlights or something. Anyhow Bet walked out and got a job up at the museum instead. Reckoned she'd brighten the place up a bit."

"She certainly does that." Mal sighed. "And the museum needs it too. It's so – oh my God – so beige! The museum is desperately in need of some TLC, just like my hair, and I can't do that without something to inspire the council. The dig and the burial could make a terrific exhibit if it was funded properly. A nationally important find to exhibit might get them to loosen the purse strings a bit."

"Yeah, it would do that, all right." Terry glanced up to catch Mal's eye in the mirror again. He looked calm and wholly sympathetic.

"But Rob looks at it another way. A way that, to my shame, I hadn't considered. He doesn't like the idea of family members being on display."

Terry's mouth drew down a bit. "They are important things, you know, family, and community. 'Specially important to blokes like us who might not ever have a family of their own. I've got cousins and second cousins all around the local villages – Escley, Brynglas, King's Norton. After a bit you'll get your eye in and will be able to see. We all got a look, if you know what I mean."

Mal raised his eyebrows. "I don't see the resemblance between say Councillor Pugh and Rob or Glyn Havard and Phil Rother."

Terry grimaced at the last name. "It's there. It's like we all looked the same once but as time went by one family kept the eyes and another has the jawline and someone else has the little whippet build. Lots of us have the hair," he grinned and gestured to his own dark curliness, "and some have the attitude. Or any combination. And there's a few quiet out of the way places where there'll be a family who has got all of it and they tend to be bloody weirdos. If you don't mind me saying, you've got a bit of the look yourself. Just here."

Terry's big hand framed the set of Mal's jaw and ear, and Mal laughed.

"Weirdo ears? Well, my mum's family came from this area a couple of generations back. Bright is Herefordshire and I think my maternal great grandmother was a Powell, or was that my paternal great grandmother? Yes, I think my mum's grandma was a Derry but that's probably Irish."

"No, it isn't. Can't get much more local than Derry. Derry comes from Welsh. Means oak tree. We've got Derry neighbours in Brynglas."

"Really?" Mal grinned. "I'll have to look them up. You seem to know a lot about it. Have you done local history?"

"Not me, but there was a Women's Institute project a few years back and my mum was part of it. Let's just say she really enjoyed it and liked to talk about it – a lot. Now, my name – Skidmore – is a version of Scudamore and that's from Welsh *ysgwydd mawr* which means 'big shoulders'." Mal chuckled as he took in Terry's considerable width. "Yeah, it runs in the family. The Skidmores, Derrys and Beynons aren't in Domesday cuz Duke William's men didn't chance coming here to ask their questions."

"Good grief." Mal smiled. "So this was a wild and lawless place, then?"

"Still is, sometimes, but we take care of our own." Terry met his eyes in the mirror again. "Like young Rob. He takes stuff seriously, does Rob, for all his talk. And he could do with someone to look after him a bit. Someone who understands that without much to hang onto, you hang onto anything you can."

Since the scissors were nowhere near his ears, Mal nodded. "I'll talk to him," he promised. "Try to make him understand."

"You could try understanding, too," Terry said. "Now hold still while I do the back of your neck."

The purr of clippers, cold against his nape, put paid to further conversation, which left Mal time to think. Terry seemed sympathetic, but there had been a clear warning that Rob revered family and that his own family had let him down. It would explain Rob's difficulty in getting his washing done. Mal had taken it for granted that Rob had been joking when he admired Mal's poky and poorly furnished flat. It hadn't occurred to Mal that perhaps Rob's home was less comfortable.

Terry snipped a bit more, combed, gave him a vigorous scalp massage then took a plastic tube off the shelf, squeezed a little clear gel from it and combed it into Mal's hair.

"It only takes five minutes to style," Terry said. "Don't even have to wait for your hair to dry. Squeeze out a bit about as long as the end of your finger, rub it through your hair, comb it into shape and bingo. But a word to the wise." Terry grinned at Mal in the mirror. "Never ever mistake this tube for the lube. Bloody stuff stings."

Their laughter brought Betty back in, somewhat cautiously, to see if Mal was done. She seemed a bit subdued but soon cheered up when Mal asked her opinion.

"Yeah, what do you think, Bet?" Terry added. "Best in the business, Bet was, until she and Lil got into hair-pulling."

"I heard that, Terry Skidmore," Lil shouted from the other room. "It's all lies, Mal."

"No, it isn't," Betty whispered. "Now let's have a look. Turn round? And again. Gawd, Ter, that looks nice. Really nice."

"I'm astonished," Mal said. "Although I know I've got less hair, I seem to have more. Thanks, Terry, it's a really good job. Can I get some of that stuff you put on it?"

"You can." Terry took a boxed tube from a shelf and slapped it into Mal's palm. "That's on the house. Entry level hair care. You'll be back for more and it'll cost ya."

He grinned at Mal and suggested he settle up with Lillian on the way out. "I got to sweep up. Hey, Betty, we think Mal might be related to the Derrys."

"Oh my God!" Betty stared at him. "Yes! I thought there was something when you came for interview. Aunty Lillian!" She darted out into the salon to spread the word and Mal thanked Terry then followed her.

It took a while to get away because Lillian seemed to have an exhaustive memory for family history and seemed to be related to half the county. By the time they had shared the tail end of the coffee in the pot and established that yes there had been a Derry around the turn of the nineteenth century who had married a man called Bright from over near Leominster, it was getting on for 8 p.m. and Mal was feeling the need for some peace and quiet. More specifically the peace he had found with Rob's steady heartbeat under his ear. Some hopes now, he supposed, but – heck, family *was* important and maybe he saw that a little more clearly now. Surely he and Rob could find some common ground?

Betty was of two minds about it when Mal asked her where he might find Rob.

"It's Tuesday so he's probably at the Coach, unless he's working for Glyn," she said. "Look, Mal, Rob's a great friend and I love him dearly but he's got baggage. If you've upset him it's probably best to keep away. And – well, you're a museum curator. You could do better, you know."

"I don't want to," he said. "And if you're his friend why are you trying to put me off?"

"Because if you were that easily put off you wouldn't be right for him, would you?" Betty poked his arm. "If you're going to see him you'd best get down there before closing time."

"I had." Mal poked her in return. "Thanks, Betty. Who knew that a hair cut would take so long?"

"All the best ones do," Betty said with a grin. "See you tomorrow."

Chapter 11

It wasn't too far to the pub – along to the clock, around the corner and another fifty yards. The closer Mal got to the pub the less certain he was about the sense in walking into the bar that was so very much home to Rob and his mates. On the doorstep, he paused and took his phone from his pocket. He stared at it for a moment trying to decide – call or text, or was either being a total wuss and a coward. If what Betty had said was true, and why would she lie about it, Rob had tried to speak to him today but he had been head down in a hole concentrating on what he was doing. Mal knew how intensely he focused when working on delicate items and wasn't surprised that he hadn't noticed any watchers, but Rob might not realise that so no wonder he'd been hurt by it. Yes, it was definitely Mal's job to try and make amends.

Mal drew a long breath then quickly tapped out the number Rob had given him. The phone began to ring and simultaneously he heard a tinny ring tone from a car a few yards down the road.

The car door opened and Rob got out and waved his phone at Mal. "Might as well speak to me in person," he said, so Mal turned his phone off and slipped it into his pocket.

"Let me guess," Mal said. "Betty?"

Rob shrugged. "Yeah. She doesn't mean to interfere, she just does."

"She means well," they both said together as Mal went across to the car and faced Rob across the roof.

"I'm glad she did," Mal added. "I wanted to apologise, both for our disagreement and for earlier today. I honestly had no idea you were there."

Rob nodded. "I could see that. You have this face when you're really concentrating on something. 'Course, the only time I've ever seen it was when you were blowing me, but once I'd calmed down I realised that was it. And, I dunno, I s'pose I shouldn't, but I sort of found that a bit flattering when I thought about it. I know how important that burial is to you."

"And to you," Mal said. He tapped his fingers on the roof of the car. "Are you going to let me apologise by buying you a pint?"

Rob tilted his head then grinned. "Get in the car," he said. "Go on. I dare you."

"What? What's the dare?" Mal asked, even as he opened the car door.

"You'll see," Rob said. "Buckle up. This is going to get a bit bumpy."

Their route was complicated and Mal's sense of direction had let him down completely by the time the car drew to a halt.

"We're here," Rob said. "Come on. Quiet as a mouse."

Mal got out, shivering a little in the cold October air. Raindrops ticked against the car roof and he grimaced, then the clouds shifted and he saw the blocky shapes of Portakabins.

"Rob?" Mal whispered. "What are we doing here?"

Rob had been delving around in the back of the car but straightened up with a grin. Then the moon was gone and Rob was just a dark shape that grabbed Mal's hand and towed him down the hedge line to a gap, through the gap and along the edge of the Heras fencing.

Even though their only contact was their hands, Mal could feel that Rob was laughing and the whole situation was so ludicrous that Mal couldn't help but join in.

"Where are we going?" he whispered between stifled chuckles.

"Here." Rob drew him into the darkness beside a huge piece of machinery. Mal glanced up at it and saw the cab of the JCB as a bulk of black against the stormy sky. Rob put something down with a rustle of plastic then put both arms around Mal's waist.

"I accept your apology," he said. "And I'm sorry for getting so stroppy. I – I dunno. I was on edge and –"

"I understand. A bit, I think. But, Rob, I'm sorry, the bones can't stay where they are. Gaskell's got approved plans and there's a local precedent for removing archaeological remains if they'll be destroyed by staying where they are. If it was something massive like another Chedworth, or something, then there might be some changes made to accommodate it, but this …"

"No, I understand," Rob said. "But right now, this minute, I don't want to think about rules and regs, unless it's to maybe break a few."

"And how would we do that?"

Rob smiled against Mal's ear, bit the lobe. "Have you ever done it in the bucket of a digger?"

"You're joking."

"Nope."

The bulldozer end of the digger was, indeed at quite a convenient height, had a tarp over it, and seemed to be half-filled with sand. "It's not big enough," Mal protested.

"Course it is," Rob said. "I measured it." He picked up the rustling thing and shoved it under the tarp, followed it and after a moment offered Mal his hand. "Come on, quick, before the night-watchman sees you. Trespass, breaking and entering. And it's Rother on tonight so …"

Mal wasted no time in scrambling into the bucket with Rob and found himself cushioned by what felt like the silk nylon of an old-fashioned zip-sided sleeping bag. "Did you plan this?" he asked, gasping at the chill as Rob, wasting no time, shoved a hand up his sweater.

"Nah, brilliant spur of the moment idea. I always have a sleeping bag in the back of the car just in case."

"In case you get lucky?" Mal asked.

There was a hesitation so brief as to almost be imaginary but Mal was pretty certain that what followed would be a lie. "Of course. Gotta be prepared, haven't you?"

There was a pillow too and a bag that Mal pushed out of the way but that felt as though it might have toiletries in it.

But then Rob's lips moved across his cheek, feeling for his mouth and he forgot about the bag, the digger and everything but Rob.

It was November and a chilly one, but the little space under the tarpaulin was sheltered and the sand yielded under their sides as they moved together. Kisses became hot, dirty and increasingly frantic and clothes were opened, pushed down, shoved aside with scrambling haste. It didn't take long before they were both laughing again as first one then the other discovered just how cold the massive metal of the bucket was when touched with a bare buttock.

"Couldn't we have done this in summer?" Mal asked.

"Could you have waited that long?" Rob asked, and closed the gap between them until they were chest to chest, cock to cock and moving slowly and deliciously, creating their own heat. Mal slid his hand down Rob's back to get a firm grip on one buttock and allowed himself the indulgence of sucking Rob's lower lip. Rob groaned and thrust against him a bit harder. Mal gasped, eyes closing as the tension mounted. Rob's phone trilled.

"Fuck," Rob scrabbled around for it, lost in the darkness. It stopped. A moment later Mal's phone broke into the opening bars of AC/DCs *Hell's Bells*.

The death knell tolling had seemed a more ironically amusing choice for a ring tone to represent Betty when he had picked it than it did right now. Rob let out a helpless hoot of laughter as Mal thrashed around trying to reach his jeans pocket which was down by his ankles. The ring tone cut off but Mal grabbed the phone anyway and almost broke his thumb on the off button. Then he put his head on Rob's hip and sobbed with laughter.

Rob jiggled as he laughed silently but he shifted and gave Mal's head a gentle push. "While you're down there ..."

That set Mal off again.

"Who's there?"

They both froze.

"Where are you, you little fuckers?"

"Rother," Rob whispered and pulled Mal up to face him again. "I think we ought to be very quiet."

"So do I." Mal rested his forehead against Rob's and tried not to breathe too loudly, a difficult thing to do when Rob shifted against him and he felt the strong grasp of Rob's hand, the wicked sweep of his thumb across the head of his cock. "What are you doing?"

"I said we should be quiet. I didn't say we should stop."

It was very difficult to be quiet while laughing one's socks off and simultaneously having the world's most bizarre hand job. Mal crammed his fist into his mouth and bit his knuckles, but it seemed rude not to reciprocate so he took a firm hold of Rob and began to get into a comfortable rhythm.

Rother shouted a few more times but wasn't much of a distraction once pleasure took over from mirth. Soon Mal was gasping into Rob's mouth as they heaved against each other. Rob came first, his normal triumphant whoop reduced to a stifled squeak and Mal lost it, muffling his howls of laughter against Rob's shoulder even as he spurted over their hands.

They were both still laughing quietly and cleaning themselves up as best they could in the darkness, when they heard Rother coming back, first as a snarled list of threats, then as the thump of boots.

"We should be all right," Rob said. "He doesn't normally look too hard. Might actually find someone."

"Fucking kids." Rother's voice was startling, seeming to be at arm's length. Mal shrank down against Rob, ears straining to pick up any clue of where the man might be and what he might be doing. Just as Mal's imagination supplied a headline for the local paper – 'Bulldozer Sex Romp Ends In Tragedy' – the tarp crunched and caved in a little as someone leaned against the bucket. They both tensed, then Mal heard the tiny beeps of a phone number being entered.

Rother grunted. "Pick up, you daft bint … Well hello darling."

Rob's chest quivered as he began to laugh again and Mal screwed his eyes tight closed trying not to make a sound.

Rother was making a date it seemed, and if Mal had to make a guess the lady in question had a husband.

"Yeah, Friday night. You can slip away, can't you? It's not like he'll notice." Rother snorted a laugh. "Well, obviously the silly old sod doesn't appreciate you the way I do."

Mal grimaced at the snide way Rother referred to the husband and it seemed Rob was offended too because he had stopped laughing. The call ended with some hideous baby talk then Rother thumped away down the hill again and they vacated the dozer bucket to get off the site before his patrol brought him back in their direction.

It was much warmer in the car, and Mal grinned at Rob. He had looked messy and debauched in the brief glimpse Mal had caught of him by the overhead light. Mal expected he looked the same. It was brilliant.

Rob started the car and reversed back to the tarmac then took the most direct route back into town. As they passed the entrance to the site they saw Rother, propped against the bonnet of his truck staring at his phone screen, thumb busy.

"He's such an arsewipe," Rob growled.

"You find rotten apples everywhere," Mal pointed out.

"Yeah, but on the whole us locals are pretty fucking spectacular."

"We are," Mal said. "I found out tonight that my great granny was one of the Derrys."

"No." Rob beamed at him. "I thought you'd got a bit of the look about you. Ah hell, this means we can't fuck again."

"What? Why?"

"Because it's probably incest."

Mal felt his jaw drop, then Rob curled up with another manic gibber of laughter, and Mal punched him in the leg.

On the whole, one of the best nights ever. Especially since Rob cashed his rain check.

Chapter 12

On Thursday Mal had a very full schedule but made time to visit Harvey, who was still in his sick bed at the Red Lion Hotel. Mal found him surrounded by paperwork, piles of used tissues and plentifully stocked with Lucozade and Lemsip.

"Well, someone's being looked after," Mal said, remembering his last illness, alone in a flat in Bristol, feeling like shit and with nobody to call to get him milk or bread.

"Benefits of minor celebrity, dear boy," Harvey said. He looked awful – moist eyed, pink nosed and with his white hair flattened on one side and sticking up in spikes on the other in one of the worst cases of bedhead Mal had ever seen. "But to be honest most of my creature comforts have come from you, or so I supposed. Have I been wasting my gratitude on the employer when I should be extending my thanks to the employee?"

"Betty's been here?"

"No, Sharon, that delightfully bubbly creature, has visited twice, each time improving my lot immeasurably."

Mal made an impressed face. "I think you've made another conquest," he said, "but – um – go steady. She's had a rough few years. Husband swapped home comforts for a short skirt and empty head and she's been managing as best she can on her museum wages and what little his accountant says he can spare. She's got a kid too. Girl of sixteen."

"Bastard," Harvey scowled. "Idiot bastard. Oh look out …" He grabbed for a tissue and sneezed lavishly into it. "Oh God, I feel horrible. Did you bring grapes?"

Mal laid out his offerings on the other half of the bed, Harvey letting out a hoarse yelp of approval when he saw the net of lemons, the honey and the half bottle of Famous Grouse.

"Toddy, immediately. You'd better have one too because we're breathing the same air. You're probably infected already."

"It's nine thirty in the morning," Mal pointed out. "I can't drink at nine thirty."

"Yes, you can, if it's for medicinal reasons. Whisky kills germs. Field

Archaeology 101. You know that."

"Well, okay, but I'm not in the field today. I have to be at County Hall for noon and can hardly go in and breathe booze fumes all over them, even if I have been celebrating."

"I thought you looked more chipper. May I assume that your relationship problems have sorted themselves out?"

"You may, indeed. To everyone's complete satisfaction, too." Mal grinned and added, "I have to catch the bus shortly. Is there anything I can do for you before I go?"

"Make my toddy," Harvey ordered, "and while you do that tell me how the excavation is proceeding without me."

"Slowly," Mal said as he got up to fill the kettle. "Gaskell and his crew are still nagging for speed. I don't think he has realised how delicate the work is. I've told him that, just as he has a way of going about things, so have we and protocols have to be observed, but he keeps saying 'but I've seen it on the telly' as though that's the answer to everything."

"*Time Team*'s fault," Harvey said cheerfully. "Popularising archaeology was great but turning it into a tense race against time is just bollocks. Ah well, I think I can see a way around that." He paused to instruct Mal in the preferred way to construct his toddy then settled back into his nest of pillows with a comfortable sigh. "Lovely, thank you. Where was I? Yes, Gaskell. If he's being awkward about the TV I think it might be as well to get in someone he can Google and whose credentials are a little more high-brow than mine. I'll make some calls." Harvey sipped his drink and shivered, pulling the blankets more closely around him. "In other news, I see you've had a haircut. You look remarkably sleek for an archaeologist."

"I know." Mal ran a hand over his hair, which was behaving impeccably. "I must admit to being a little surprised at how good it is."

"You were expecting a short back and sides with a dab of sheep dip?" Harvey sniffed. "One does find excellence in the sticks, you know."

"I found the best curry I've ever had in a little pub just down the road, washed down by some of the best beer too."

"When I'm back on my feet I insist we partake," Harvey grinned. "Hopefully in the company of your bulldozer driver? Oh Mal, do I detect a blush?"

"No," Mal said. "It's a bit hot in here. But, yes, we came to a compromise this morning over breakfast. First priority is to get the burial and finds made safe and into secure storage. I think he's very keen that the exhibition reflects the local community in some way. Also, that the bones are those of two men has made a huge impression. Validation, you know."

Harvey nodded. "I'm glad. I'd like to meet him. Maybe when we go for that curry. Or did I just say that?" He put his empty mug down and yawned. "Now I feel the need of a nap. Can you drop by later?"

"Of course." Mal got up. "Is there anything else you need?"

"Wi-Fi?" Harvey rolled his eyes. "The hotel says it has it but the signal is so rubbish up here that as far as communication goes I might as well be waving out of the window."

"I'll see what I can do," Mal promised.

"So will I." Harvey yawned again. "But a nap first so bugger off, there's a good boy."

As Mal crossed the little lobby of the hotel the receptionist hailed him. "One moment, please, Mr Bright. I – um – have a message for you from the manager."

Expecting some comment about the history of the building, Mal was completely blind-sided when the girl went a deep embarrassed red and added, "He wants to know how long Mr Biddulph will be staying. He feels it's inappropriate for him to be here because we don't have the facilities for looking after invalids."

"Oh." Mal stared into space for a moment, working out how to make his spare room more comfortable, where to get a new mattress and how to transport it on his bike. "Can Harvey at least stay for today? I'm on my way to Hereford now, but I can try to make alternative arrangements."

"I'm sure that will be fine, sir." The receptionist glanced over her shoulder at the closed door of the office then whispered. "To be honest, we're short staffed. I pop up when I can but …" She gestured to the desk.

"No. No, I understand. I'll get back to you after lunch. Sorry, got to go."

Harvey's state of health was on Mal's mind all through the morning. He called Betty while he was on the bus and she was outraged that the Red Lion wasn't keen on Harvey staying.

"Understaffed, my arse. It's his own fault for laying everyone off when the tourist season ended. What do you need us to do?"

"A more welcoming alternative, for preference," Mal said. "Failing that a decent standard four foot mattress that can be delivered to my flat today. Oh God, I won't be there, will I? Delivery to the museum? What do you think? Would Argos do that?"

"Why not go local? Jones's down the back of the bus station would be your best bet. I'll give you the number. Have you got a pen?"

"Have you met me, Betty? Of course I've got a pen."

"Duh." Betty rattled off the number. "You pay for it. Sharon and I will make the rest of the arrangements. See – things would be so much easier if you had a car, wouldn't they?"

Mal admitted they would and worried about Harvey all through an incredibly boring and irrelevant meeting where museums were mentioned once, in an 'acknowledging that they existed and were a good thing' context. As soon as the meeting wound up he turned his phone on again, intending to call the museum to check on how the mattress hunt was progressing, and startled the remaining meeting attendees when it blared the opening of La Grange.

Mal hastened to answer it. "Rob?"

"That's me." Rob's voice was blurred by engine noise and birdsong.

"Oh God, you haven't found more archaeology have you?"

"I wish. Get yourself down to the car park, sunshine. We've got a crisis. Harvey's been taken to hospital."

On the way, Rob told Mal what he knew – that the Red Lion receptionist had found Harvey passed out on the floor and had let Betty know. Betty had called Glyn and since Rob was between jobs Glyn had sent him to get Mal.

"We figured it would be quicker," Rob said, easing the car to a halt at traffic lights. "I'll drop you at A&E, 'cause that's where he was taken, and come and find you. It'll take me a while to find somewhere to park and besides, I'm not really dressed for a hospital visit."

"I think you're fine to come in with me. A&E must see blokes in working gear all the time. Thank you, Rob." Mal put his hand on Rob's overall clad knee and squeezed. "Remind me to show you my appreciation properly at the next opportunity."

"I like the sound of that. You need to thank Glyn, too, but I'd suggest a few bottles of Speckled Hen instead. Oh, here we go. The traffic round here is the worst."

A combination of being in the right place at the right time and Rob's lightning reflexes won them a parking place close to the entrance to the hospital car park. They jogged across to A&E, the jog turning into a run as the heavens opened, and they arrived at the reception desk dripping and laughing.

The woman there greeted them with a disapproving glare when they told her who they wanted. "Are you family?" she demanded. "Because if you aren't, I can't give out any details."

"Harvey's family live abroad," Mal said. "I have contact details if he's seriously ill but he'd be a bit peeved if I summoned his son back from California or his daughter from Melbourne for a nasty cold."

"That's as may be." She scowled at Rob. "Since you aren't on his ICE list, I can't give you any information. Next, please."

Outside listening to the rain drum against the roof of A&E's porch, Rob blew out his cheeks and said, "Sorry about that. She'd probably have told you if I hadn't been there. She's Phil Rother's mum."

"Oh, bugger," Mal said.

"Might as well." Rob grinned. "We're not doing any good here. Oh, hang on, though." He headed for a man in a green uniform having a smoke break further along the building and Mal followed him. "'Lo, Frank, how's it hanging?"

Frank grinned and blew smoke out before saying, "Same as usual, bigger'n yours. What you doing here, Rob? Nobody hurt up at the site, I hope."

"No, thank God." Rob introduced Mal and explained their predicament. "We just need to know if we should hang around to take Harvey back or if he'll be kept in."

Frank rolled his eyes. "Harvey Biddulph. Administration went into spasms when a TV star was brought in. Word has it he'd got out of bed to go to the loo, lost his balance and he clobbered his nut on the bed frame as he fell. Once he was down there he decided he might as well stay there. The hotel receptionist who found him panicked and was going to ring the doctor's surgery but the manager called an ambulance instead. Our lads would have told him to fuck off, only the old boy's temperature was too high for comfort and they didn't think he'd be properly looked after there, if you know what I mean. Doctor diagnosed a chest infection so he's staying in tonight. We'll know more tomorrow."

"That gives me time to get my spare room sorted out before he's discharged," Mal said. "Thanks – um – Frank."

"No problem, just don't tell anyone I told you, okay? See you next darts night, Rob."

They rang the museum from the car and reassured Betty and Sharon then headed for Pemberland.

"I'll drop you off," Rob said, "but I'd best get back to work."

"I'll give Glyn a call to thank him," Mal said. "Um, are you free later?"

"Thursday night at the Coach," Rob said. "Sacrosanct that is. Come along and then maybe we can see exactly how grateful you are after a game or two of pool."

"I did promise, didn't I?" Mal said.

But when Mal got back to the museum he found a message from Lillian to say that Jones's driver had dropped off the mattress in the middle of her hair salon. "The thing is, Mal," she said. "Terry's not here at the moment and the girls and I can't shift the damn thing. And it really is very much in the way."

Mal offered abject apologies to Lillian and more apologies to Sharon who was manning the museum desk alone.

"You go," Sharon said, laughing. "Honestly, could this week get any worse?"

Thursday night, Rob couldn't make their date. "I know I said it was sacrosanct," Rob said over the phone, "but there's been a landslip up in Longtown and it's covered the road to the village. And I really owe Glyn for this afternoon."

"And you're the best man on the digger. Friday, then. I'll cook – something. Not sure what. Something with plenty of meat."

"Hurr hurr hurr, only one sort of meat I'm interested in," Rob said. "Carry on being grateful!"

After the alarms and excursions of Thursday, Friday was blissfully calm. Mal answered his mail first thing, called the hospital at 10 a.m. to discover that Harvey had spent a quiet night and was mad as fire at being, as he put it, 'institutionalised'.

"They went through my wallet and called my agent," Harvey said. "She has expressed the intention of coming to rescue me but I nipped that in the bud. I have a number of delightful nurses at my beck and call, and I know if I need anything you are just a phone call away."

"And a bus ride," Mal pointed out.

"Well, no, because I rang my insurers this morning and you can drive my car. That young girl at the hotel has promised to pack my things and will have them and the car keys ready for you."

"That's very generous, Harvey. Thank you."

"Not at all. I plan to exploit you shamelessly, if I need anything, or I get bored or – where was I? Yes, I settled my bill with the Red Lion and do *not* let them try to tell you I owe for another day."

"I won't. But how are you feeling? Honestly, Harvey. This is me, not your agent. You're not providing a sound bite for an audience."

Harvey was silent for a moment then sighed. "Honestly, Mal, I feel a little frail. It's not a feeling I'm accustomed to and not one that I'm enjoying. This is the first hospital stay where I feel they may have a point. Apparently I'm staying in for another night so they can be sure that the infection clears up and … I don't mind. I expect they'll chuck me out fast enough if a proper emergency comes in –"

"And when they do, you call me and I'll come and fetch you. I can drive you home to Bristol if you like, or you can stay at mine. I've bought a new mattress for the bed."

"My goodness, how domesticated of you. I wish I'd been there to watch you try to carry it up the stairs."

Mal gave Harvey the full account of how he and Adrian, Lillian's gothy boy apprentice, had been twanged all over the place by the mattress and Harvey laughed until he began to wheeze.

"I really can't, dear boy," he said. "I'll be delighted to stay with you, but probably not until I can breathe again."

"Have a nap, old man," Mal advised. "I'll call you later."

In the afternoon, Mal visited the development site and repeated his thanks to Glyn for his loan of Rob.

"No problem," Glyn said. "He was getting bored stooging round here, anyway. We left him up in Longtown last night to carry on with clearing the road and making the bank safe. The one good thing about all the council cuts is that private contractors like me reap the benefit."

Berkley, Gaskell's manager, was less cheerful and gave Mal a very aggressive grilling about when they could expect the burial to be cleared away, so they could continue with widening the lane. Mal gave polite answers and came away feeling he'd defended his position quite well.

Then he went to Tesco and bought steaks.

"Steak and beer!" Rob whooped when he saw their supper. "My favourite. How did you know?"

"Because it's my favourite too," Mal said.

They tenderised the steaks with the back of a carving knife – Rob made a lot of jokes about beating the meat, but Mal had been expecting that – then they fried them while the oven chips, onion rings and battered mushrooms cooked.

Steak and the trimmings, beer and an *Iron Man* movie later, Rob said, "Shall we watch the next film or what?"

"What," Mal said with a grin, and easy as that they went to bed.

This time there was no urgency. Rob had Saturday off and so did Mal. They were comfortable enough together to use the bathroom and put phones on to charge, plump the pillows and throw back the covers. Mal really enjoyed watching Rob undress, knowing that the strong, slightly olive-skinned body was going to be his playground for the next few hours and he was positive Rob was looking forward to it as well, from the hot jut of his erection against Mal's belly. They kissed for a long time, gently exploring each other's mouths, then Rob muttered, "Just how grateful are you, Mal?"

"Enormously." Mal's voice was a little muffled against Rob's chest but he knew Rob had heard him by the way he chuckled.

"Well, I was just thinking," Rob said. "The first time I ever had a cup of tea with you there was that mug."

Mal rested his chin on Rob's chest. Rob had an arm behind his head and was grinning at him, eyes crinkled at the corners with affectionate amusement. Mal smiled back, guessing his own expression was equally sappy. "The one that says 'Museum Curators do it Meticulously'? That one?"

"Yeah, that one," Rob said.

"And you were wondering if it's true?"

"Can't deny that the thought crossed my mind a time or two."

"Well, then," Mal said and drew up the sheet to cover himself and most of Rob from the chin down.

This was a labour of love. Mal used his hands as carefully as he would when lifting the most delicate and precious relics from the earth, but let Rob feel the edge of his teeth at unexpected moments. Rob's sighs and moans grew more frequent and louder and, when Mal took his cock deep into his throat, Rob abandoned those for a broken little whimper.

"Too much?" Mal asked.

"No." Rob lifted the edge of the sheet and peered down at him. "You're doing fine. Don't let me interrupt."

"Good," Mal said and went, slowly and meticulously, back to work. It didn't take him long to get Rob arching up off the bed, clinging to the headboard and making that delicious little whimpering sound again. Deep under the covers, his head cradled by Rob's thighs, Mal spun it out until his jaw really ached before going in for the kill.

"Oh, Mal," Rob gasped. "I'm …"

And he did, bucking and moaning, holding Mal's head until he collapsed with another deep groan. "Damn!" Rob breathed. "Just give me a moment, then it's your turn. I'm gonna see if I can make you squeal."

Mal chuckled and began to pull the covers back, so had a perfect view of Rob's face as the door crashed open.

"Surprise! Oh Jesus Christ!" The door slammed again.

"Who the fuck was that?" Rob demanded.

Mal clambered off the bed and grabbed for his bathrobe. "My bloody sister," he yelled. "I'm so sorry, Rob. She didn't see anything, did she?"

"Only my head and shoulders. Your sister?"

"Yes, and I bet she's pissing herself laughing the other side of the door. Aren't you, Zoë?"

"I didn't mean it," Zoë shrieked. "You should have locked the bedroom door."

"I didn't think I needed to because the street door was locked," Mal bellowed.

"My brother has his short-comings," Rob said, "but I can honestly say he's never walked in on me shagging." Then he curled up with a howl of laughter.

By the time they were dressed, Zoë had made tea and was at her ease in the kitchen. She apologised profusely to Rob, much less sincerely to Mal and they admitted the tea, and the tin containing a home-made sponge she took from her bag, made up a bit for the intrusion.

"How the hell did you get in anyway?" Mal asked once they were all settled.

"I could see the light on so I rang the doorbell loads. I guess you were a bit … preoccupied. Then this big guy came out of the barbers." Zoë grinned. "He's a sweetheart. Said right away he knew who I was related to."

"Well, he would," Rob said. "Terry knows that kind of thing. Also, you and Mal are like as two peas apart from the you being a girl thing. Same hair, same eyes."

"Thank you kindly." Zoë grinned. "This where I can admit that my brother is very good-looking and share the credit."

"You can if you like," Mal said. "So what happened then?"

"Anyhow, the big bloke said that he knew you were in so he was sure it would be okay if he opened the door for me."

"It would have been, under other circumstances. As it is, I'm going to thump Terry."

"Oh, come on, we're all grown-ups." Rob, with tea in one hand and cake in the other, looked as happy as could be. "And you can't hit Terry because he might hit you back and, ya know, I kind of prefer you conscious."

"See," Zoë gestured to Rob with her mug. "A man of very good sense. And he's pretty too. Well done, bro'. I want to know *all* about him."

"Mal." Rob reached for his hand and gripped it tightly. "She's just like Betty, Mal. We can never let them meet."

"Betty?" Zoë's eyes lit up. "Meeting her will be my project for tomorrow."

"Tomorrow? Just how long are you planning to stay?" Mal asked. "Not that you aren't welcome, sis, but …"

"I have an afternoon shift on Sunday," Zoë said. "If Harvey had been staying here I'd have slept on the couch but, well, I really wanted to see you."

It didn't take long to get Zoë settled in the spare room and Mal rejoined Rob in a thoughtful frame of mind.

"This isn't like Zoë," he said as he settled back into the warm embrace of his bed, then shifted across into the even warmer embrace of Rob. His libido gave a lazy twitch to remind him that it had unfinished business, but it was late and he was tired so he told it to take a hike.

"No, she's got something on her mind," Rob murmured, his eyes already closed. "She'd have said if I hadn't been here. I'll get off first thing."

"I was planning on getting us both off first thing," Mal said, and smiled into the dark as Rob chuckled. "And Zoë will have to be patient. It won't hurt her."

"There's a big brother talking." Rob chuckled and gave him a squeeze.

Zoë slept in on Saturday morning so Mal and Rob had a leisurely and mutually satisfying fuck, then showered and made breakfast.

"She must be tired to be ignoring bacon," Mal said, turning the rashers under the grill.

"Only thing that wakes my Dad up," Rob admitted. "Hey, she's a nurse. Don't they run mostly on coffee? Like long distance lorry drivers and merchant bankers?"

"That's a point. I've got a coffee maker … somewhere."

They found the glossy piece of kitchen sculpture on a top shelf in a cupboard Mal rarely opened. Rob had fun twiddling the knobs, claiming he was trying to pick up signals from Mars. "This doesn't look like something you'd buy, Mal," he said. It beeped. "Shit, I think I just ordered a nuclear strike on Welshpool. Just isn't your style at all."

"No, it's not. It was a birthday present from an ex."

"But you only drink tea?"

"That's why he's an ex." Mal grinned. "When I left I took it with me out of spite."

There was an unopened pack of coffee grounds in the same cupboard. It was labelled 'Best Before December 2016' but Mal doubted that mattered much. It certainly smelled all right and it did the trick where Zoë was concerned.

"Mmm coffee," she muttered as she zombied into the kitchen and made grabby hands at Mal until he put a mug in them. She was wearing

Spiderman pyjamas, and Mal found himself overwhelmed with affection, both for Zoë who was sipping, barely awake, and for Rob who seemed to be appreciating the vision as much as Mal was.

Two coffees and a bacon sandwich later, Zoë had woken up enough to talk. She curled up at one end of the sofa, Rob took the other, and Mal took the lopsided little armchair.

"That hit the spot," Zoë said. "Do you always live this well, Mal? Or are you trying to impress Rob."

"He doesn't need bacon banjos to impress me," Rob said. "You feeling better now?"

"Yes, why the sudden visitation?" Mal cradled his tea mug in both hands. "What's happened that needs to be told face to face rather than your usual text or phone call? Honestly, Rob, this is a girl who once texted me 'in car crash, car totalled, please pick cat up from vets'. I was frantic."

"Oh Mal, it gave you the information you needed. If I'd been bleeding out at the roadside I'd hardly have been likely to be texting you."

"She's got a point," Rob said.

"And that vet closed at seven and I couldn't afford an overnight stay for the stupid cat."

"All right, if you two are going to gang up on me …" Mal said, and grinned when Rob leaned over to punch his leg.

"If it's super secret family stuff I'll be on my way," Rob said. "Got to see a man about a digger sometime today, anyway."

"Oh no," Zoë put her hand on Rob's shoulder, pressing him back to his seat. "No secrets. It was just one of those impulses that made a lot of sense at the time. You know? I'd done a week of nights which is always tough, and was trying to stay awake to get back onto the other shift's sleep cycle so in the evening I thought I'd give Mum a ring – since I'd tried you and you were out –"

"Oh, so it's my fault?" Mal asked.

"Usually is," Zoë said, "but I don't really begrudge you a social life seeing how you're spending your time with a man with a sense of humour. No, I rang her to ask what Dad wanted for Christmas."

"Bit early, isn't it?" Rob and Mal spoke almost together.

"Men!" Zoë rolled her eyes. "Christmas Eve is two months today, guys. There's been stuff in the shops for weeks. Wake up and smell the – what's

Christmassy? Pine, peppermint, cinnamon? Whatever. So I rang Mum and we were chatting and she reminded me that any present I wanted to send would have to be there by the fifteenth so he could take it with him on holiday."

"Holiday?" Mal stared at her. "They are going on holiday. For Christmas? What? This is the first I've heard of it."

"I'm not surprised. You know what Mum's like. Oh darling, I'm sure I told you all about it." Her voice rose into an affected RP lilt and her cheeks flushed. "And I rather lost it for a moment, because she honestly hadn't *and* had made that big fuss about us all getting together for the holiday so I had to trade an arm, leg and kidney to get those days off. But no, no family Christmas for us. Dad's decided he fancies a cruise. I hope it's choppy."

"And so you decided that you needed a bit of big brotherly sympathy?" Mal asked.

"Well, yes." Zoë shrugged. "And maybe a little reassurance that I'm not a totally evil person for being upset about having to spend Christmas on my own."

"But you don't have to, surely." Rob's puzzlement was obvious. "Come here. Mal has a spare room. We can move the books."

Mal and Zoë contemplated that for a moment, then both snorted.

"Why not?" Rob insisted. "This place is nice and warm. There's a telly. You don't have to do turkey and stuff. The fridge isn't very big but Tesco's will be open again on Boxing Day and how many bottles of wine do you think you'll need to chill? You could have a brilliant time. Eat exactly what you want, watch what you want. Buy paper plates so there's no washing up."

Mal caught Zoë's eye and suspected that she too was thinking of the parental home and its massive fridge, the glorious food, the comfort and ease of returning to the nest. "Well," he said, "since Zoë doesn't seem to be inviting me to the nurses' home …"

"Dear lord no." Zoë reached a foot across Rob's lap to poke Mal's knee with her toe. "Go on, Mal. It'll be fun. And if Rob gets fed up with turkey he can come and join us. I mean it's not as though Mum actually cooks, is it, apart from the bird."

Mal shrugged. "We can go to Marks and Spencer and microwave a pudding just as well as she can."

Rob patted Zoë's shin, settling her calf comfortably against his knees. "I'm a dab hand at a Sunday roast. Turkey is just a big chicken, if you think about it. Pigs in blankets, chestnut stuffing, all the rest of it." He grinned at Mal's goggle-eyed stare. "Yeah, I know that I look far too manly but it's just a bit of chemistry and a load of organisation. If you wanted the full Monte you could have it."

"Jeez, Mal," Zoë clutched Rob's arm. "Come on, say yes. We can buy a *Radio Times* and a tree! Say yes."

Christmas in Pemberland would include Rob, and it occurred to Mal that there were other things to do on Christmas Eve than attend a carol concert. "Yes," he said. "And the 'what to get Dad' problem is solved too. We can buy him a life jacket and a packet of Kwells."

Chapter 13

Saturday was one of the most relaxed days Mal had enjoyed since moving to Pemberland. Zoë and Rob got on really well, and Mal was pretty certain they weren't just putting it on for his sake. Rob tried a joke and Zoë topped it, then they both ganged up on Mal, poking gentle fun until he retaliated. After a trip to Tesco where they bought food for the evening, Zoë drove them all to Hereford to see how Harvey was doing. He was looking a little better and greeted Zoë with delight. Apparently the nurses were making a huge fuss of him but Mal felt he seemed more pleased that Sharon and her daughter had visited.

Best of all, Mal persuaded Rob to stay Saturday night as well.

"You really like him, don't you?" Zoë asked on Sunday morning after Mal returned, pink and a bit dishevelled, from seeing Rob out of the door at the foot of the stairs.

"I do." Mal shrugged, pretending a nonchalance he didn't truly feel. "He's genuine, you know? Right from the moment I first met him I felt that what I saw was what I'd get and he made no bones at all about what he wanted. I can relax with Rob."

"He's a little bit in awe of you." Zoë made a face. "And that's not a good thing."

"He's not." Mal laughed. "He thinks I'm funny, and impractical. And he's bright, Zoë. He's always surprising me with the things he knows. He was talking about entasis last week."

"En *what* now?"

"Greek columns aren't straight sided, they have a tiny bit of a convex curved taper to them that makes them look straighter. Apparently some modern buildings have it too."

"Who knew?"

"Rob did." Mal grinned. "Said he'd read it somewhere. I don't think he did much in school but, boy, has he made up for it since. He's always poking around in my book boxes."

"And you? Are you finding out about what he does? Oh, Mal! It goes both ways, you know."

Zoë had a point. After waving her off for her drive back to Bristol, Mal set about his neglected housework while making a mental list of the things he should ask Rob about his work. Unfortunately he didn't get a chance to bring any up because the building site had gone on to a new phase of construction and Rob's expertise was needed on a brown field site up in the Welsh valleys.

"Glyn's scheduled us four days of work," Rob explained in a phone call on Monday morning, "and the only way we'll get it done is if we B and B it. But I'll be in touch."

"You will?"

"You betcha. I'll give you a ring – um – Tuesday night? Eight-ish. Make sure you're on your own and wearing loose clothing."

"And will you be on your own wearing loose clothing too?"

"Either that or shocking people on the checkout in Sainsburys."

Mal chuckled. "That's a date then."

Mal paid a fleeting visit to the development site to pass on his regrets to Berkley. "An excavation of this nature isn't really a one man job," he said. "But Harvey Biddulph is on the mend and should be back with us by the end of the week."

"Really?" Berkley scowled. "I thought we had impressed upon you how vital it is that we widen this lane."

Mal cast a pointed glance to the lane. The broken surface bore tracks of broad wheels. "What are you planning on bringing along it?" he asked. "Glyn Havard has assured me that the area can be worked around for the time being – at least another month – and I'd have thought that the advantages of having a nationally acknowledged expert on hand to verify all the findings would be a bit of a coup for Gaskell Developments. It shows a real commitment to 'sensitive development that isn't detrimental to the heritage of our beautiful country'."

Berkley snorted; as well he might because that last phrase had been taken directly from Gaskell Developments' website. "Well, do your best to hurry it up."

They left it at that but Mal took care to spend an hour on Tuesday afternoon making busy with a surveying table, camera and ranging rods 'locating the burial in the landscape'. Gaskell, who was on a site visit, was most impressed when Mal explained the theory behind ley-lines but got restless when Mal began to delve into semiotics.

"I'll let you get on, then." Gaskell rubbed his hands. "I can't wait to see my exhibition."

Mal told Rob all about it on Tuesday evening, but not until they had taken care of other business. "Before you ask," Mal said, as he answered the phone, "I had my hand in my pants as soon as I heard your ring tone."

Half an hour later, damp, sweaty, mildly satisfied and fairly happy, Mal listened to Rob's news and shared his own.

"With Sharon?" Rob hooted with laughter.

"Yes! I rang to make arrangements to pick him up on Monday evening but Harvey was already packing. He's moving into Sharon's spare room as a paying guest for the duration of the project. Part of the deal is that he helps her daughter with her history homework."

"Aww that's nice. Good for both of them, I reckon, and Katie might appreciate another adult about the place too."

"I've never met Katie," Mal admitted.

"Yes, you have," Rob scoffed. "She served our meal that night at the White Horse. Pemberland's not that big a place, you know."

"Oh Rob, what would I do without you?" Mal said, then realised that he actually meant it and that should be acknowledged. "I miss you."

"Yeah." Rob's sigh sounded more satisfied than sad. "But I'll be back Friday to remind you why."

Friday morning, Mal was ready early, and went to fetch Harvey from Sharon's house. He looked a little pale and had lost weight but was otherwise really cheerful.

"Sharon is a gem," Harvey said as he put his work boots in the car. "An absolute gem, and her daughter wants to do something with history. Maybe archaeology, maybe something more academic. I told her she has time to make up her mind. Oh, here she is now."

Katie looked very different in school uniform but beamed at Mal when he greeted her by name. "Mam says you forgot your lunch." She offered Harvey a large Tupperware container. "She said she put enough in for two, Mr Bright, because a Mars Bar is not enough."

"Your mother is a very wise woman," Mal said. "Please tell her I said thank you."

Betty was already at the museum when they went to collect their kit. She greeted Harvey politely then nabbed Mal while Harvey was putting the ranging rods in the car. "Please tell me he's a decent bloke," she said, "because Sharon goes pink and giggly every time his name is mentioned. I don't want her upset again."

"Harvey is a perfect gentleman, far too sensible to raise hopes and far too nice to dash them unnecessarily. He's staying with Sharon because he says my place is too nasty." Mal grinned. "After I bought him a new mattress and everything."

"I heard about that." Betty grinned. "Also that you had a visitor. So when do I get to meet your sister?"

"Never, if I have my way," Mal said and left hurriedly.

It was a perfect day for resuming the excavation. The ground was dry and the sky clear. The breeze was a bit chilly but both Mal and Harvey had dressed for the weather. Glyn came to meet them when they arrived and loaned them a couple of men to help carry their gear and open up the site.

"Rob's over on the far side but I'm sure he'll be over when he has his break." Glyn grinned. "He normally enjoys his trips away but this time he couldn't wait to get back. They did four days' work in three and a half. I wonder why." Then he left them to it.

"That was nice," Harvey murmured as they hoofed it up the hill. Mal didn't reply but couldn't deny feeling a warm glow.

They made short work of checking that the site hadn't deteriorated over the past week, then they began work. Photographs, drawings, soil samples, everything meticulously plotted and described in Harvey's smooth tones into Mal's phone. Everything was going beautifully, when a stir down the hill drew Mal's attention and he spotted Gaskell getting out of his Jeep.

"Look sharp," he said. "Mr Gaskell is here to see how his excavation is getting on."

"His?" Harvey sat up. "*His* excavation?"

"He says he's looking forward to his exhibition, too," Mal said and grinned at Harvey, but Harvey's face had fallen into a disbelieving gape.

Gaskell, dressed to the nines, was picking his way towards them accompanied by a tough looking man in combat trousers and a padded gilet who raised a hand in a cheery wave when he saw them.

"God's teeth," Harvey muttered. "Lock and load, Mal. It's Culmstock from the British Museum. The man's a bloody pirate."

Gaskell hurried up, pleased as punch. "Mr Culmstock, I believe you know Harvey Biddulph, and this is our local museum curator. Mr Culmstock was trying to get in touch with you, Harvey, but came through to my office instead. He's come to offer his expertise."

Harvey nodded. "Yes, we have met. I – um – was in talks with Ormistead in the Bronze Age department and he promised to get back to me."

"I'm doing it for him," Culmstock said. At no point had he so much as glanced at Mal, so Mal watched Harvey instead, picking up the subtle signs of his absolute boiling fury. "Ormistead is very busy but he made time to tell me about some of the more interesting aspects of the find, so I said that I'd fit it into my schedule. Mr Gaskell has been very helpful. Now, if you can let me see what you have here I'll have a better idea of the equipment we need and the size of team."

"For what?" Harvey said.

"To undermine the cist and lift it intact. It will be a spectacular piece of archaeology and really put the site on the map. The cist will make a brilliant addition to our exhibition on Early Peoples, especially with the 'special interest' of the posing of the cadavers."

"And where do you anticipate this exhibition to take place?" Harvey demanded.

"At the BM of course." Culmstock smiled. "In 2025. But, of course, Mr Gaskell's generosity will be acknowledged long before that. With the publicity package I can put together we should make the main news on most of the channels."

"Isn't that wonderful news?" Gaskell beamed. "A really big exhibition – no disrespect to you, Mal, but a few rooms in a building shared with a library isn't a patch on the British Museum."

"No, it wouldn't be," Mal said, feeling gutted. He wanted to punch Culmstock's smirk right off his mouth. Then he suddenly remembered that that might actually be Rob's reaction and angry disappointment turned to fear. But he smiled as best he could and said. "It will be an education to work with you, Mr Culmstock."

"Oh no, I'll bring in my own team. But you can observe if you feel you can spare the time." Culmstock's smile was an insult. "Mr Gaskell has told me how little time you've been able to devote to this important find and I wouldn't want to take you away from your own duties any longer than necessary."

Which told Mal. He caught Harvey's eye and Harvey turned what he had been about to say into a coughing fit. When he was finished, he broke into Gaskell's excited speculation about how many newspapers they could get to cover the story and maybe even some TV crews as well.

"Gaskell, you do realise that, as a local find, this is of considerable interest to the local population? Don't you think they should be given a say in how the finds are displayed?"

"Why?" Gaskell shrugged. "It's my land. It was found on my land so this is mine too. It's not as though there are precious metals or anything. Just stones and bones. If it goes to the British Museum, at least our little town will be represented in the most famous museum in the world."

"Indeed," Culmstock grinned. "And you'd get an invitation to the preview. Always worth doing – champagne, canapés, a chance to meet the movers and shakers."

He spared one sly glance at Mal who forced a smile. "Movers and shakers are something we're short of round here."

"I wouldn't have said that," Culmstock said with a respectful nod to his host, who glowed with pride.

Conversation petered out then into a lecture, delivered by Culmstock with plenty of hand-waving and pantomime to ensure Gaskell followed, on how he intended to get the heavy stones of the cist, the earth it was set in and the precious cargo of bones out of the soil in one piece. Then he and Gaskell went off to set the wheels in motion.

Once they were out of earshot Harvey put both hands in his hair and said, "Fuck."

"I'll see your 'fuck' and raise you a 'how could Gaskell be so bloody venal'. Doesn't he realise that the cist will probably go straight into stores? They must have a couple of hundred."

"Stupid." Harvey blew out a long breath of total exasperation. "Me too. I knew Ormistead was busy but he promised to ask around for advice. I'd hoped we might be able to get some interest in exactly this – a one piece lift is incredibly good publicity, but pricey so I didn't want to get your hopes up. Then Ormistead implied that that you might be offered a trade-off. There is going to be a big Early Peoples special but your boys could be on display here until 2025, then have a little holiday at the British Museum for six months, then they could come home again. I never thought the BM'd sent a bloody shark like Culmstock."

"I only know him from his papers," Mal admitted. "Has he got a track record for doing things like this?"

"He'd make Elgin look like *Médecins sans Frontières*." Harvey rolled his eyes. "He's ostensibly part of the Early Peoples organisation, which is the new overall body that oversees all the prehistoric bits, but actually his department monitors local news and swoops in and picks up anything interesting. He has an arrangement with the other big national museums too. If this was a few miles further west he'd be negotiating on behalf of *Amgueddfa Cymru*."

"Oh God," Mal let his legs go and flopped down onto the tarps around the pit. "We have no choice, do we? How am I going to tell Rob and the others?"

"You probably won't have to," Harvey was peering down the hill to the growing knot of men around Gaskell's Jeep. "It looks like Gaskell's doing it for you. Right, I'm going to call a meeting. Your place?"

"I've only got five chairs!" Mal knew he was wailing but felt the situation called for it.

"Then I'll sort something out and let you know where to go."

The whole of the rest of the day turned into damage limitation for Mal. Within minutes of Gaskell's departure, Rob, Sion, Glyn and half a dozen of the other local lads were standing around the site howling for Gaskell's blood.

Rob had come straight to Mal's side and made no bones about putting an arm around him. "It's not true, is it? They're not going to take them off to London?"

"I'm as upset about this as you are," Mal said. "The thing is, landowners have a lot of say in what happens to finds on their land. If he decides he'd sooner donate to a bigger institution, then there's not a lot we can do to prevent him. But I promise that we're going to do our best to stop it happening."

"We're not blaming you, Mal." Glyn looked angry but a bit more contained than some of the others. "It's the way people like Gaskell operate. Always got to grab for the next shiny thing. He could be one of the biggest benefactors in the area, could do an awful lot of good *and* be a very successful business man but no, he wants to be the biggest developer in the county, in the West, in the South."

"Prat," Sion added. "Sometimes what's right in front of you is the best possible thing you could hope for. Still, we've all agreed Gaskell's a dick, so what next?"

Everyone seemed to be looking at Mal, including Harvey for once, so Mal took a deep breath then said, "Glyn, you've got everyone's phone numbers. Harvey and I are going to close the site up and make safe for today, then we'll make some calls, and set up a meeting when we've got more of an idea of our options. I'll ring you, Glyn, and maybe you can let the others know when and where?"

"Or you could call Rob," one of the other men said with a cheery grin. "He's got us all on speed dial for the darts."

"Erm, yes," Mal said. "Or I could do that."

The impromptu meeting broke up then as Glyn urged his men to get back to work, but Rob ignored him and stayed at Mal's side. "Don't worry," he said and gestured to the burial pit. "It'll all work out. They'll see to it. That's what they are here for, to guard the track and the way into the valley. Pretty poor show if they can't guard themselves."

"Back in their day, in their own way, no doubt," Mal said. "But money talks and so do people like Culmstock. You know what they'll say. This is an important find with all kinds of important messages about strength and love and loyalty and as many people need to see it as possible. We can't argue with that, but Culmstock will add that having it on display in a place like this where it will be seen by about twenty thousand people a year isn't nearly as good as it being in the British Museum where it might only go on display once *ever* but in those six months will be seen by millions. It's simple arithmetic, Rob."

Rob punched Mal in the shoulder, one of his gentle love cuffs that hurt but in a good way. "Never was much good at sums," he said. "See you tonight?"

"Please and I'd be very pleased if you'd come home with me. I don't care if you wake me up at 5 a.m. I'd like to have you there."

"Ah man," Rob smiled, eyelids drooping in a way that made Mal's breath catch. "You could have me pretty much anywhere. I best get on, no rest for the wicked."

Mal snorted and watched him go with wistful appreciation for the swagger.

Chapter 14

Back at the museum, Mal tried to work while Harvey used the museum phone to bend ears in London.

"Dammit," he said, when he put the handset down. "Ormistead is at a trustees' meeting and is unavailable for the rest of the day. I've left urgent messages but I'd really like a chance to speak to him before our meeting. Do you think we can put it off until tomorrow?"

"I don't see why not," Mal said. "Culmstock's planning to come back with his team on Tuesday. Let's go and see if we can arrange a meeting space in the museum."

"I'm not sure that would be appropriate," Harvey said. "Give me a moment, I'll see what I can do."

Harvey hurried off and when Mal carried coffee down to the desk he found Harvey watching Betty and Sharon making a list.

"If you can bring half a dozen of the fold-up chairs in the stores, I can seat about twenty people." Sharon added another item in her sprawling loopy hand. "When I get home tonight I'll take some cookie dough out of the freezer."

"Brilliant. I'll bring pizza," Betty said, "because I can't cook and I don't think you'd want me to bring beer. And I'll run off a load of plans of the site and the sketches we did of the possible layout in the new exhibition hall. Damn their eyes, they'll take those skeletons over a whole load of dead bodies."

Harvey beamed and gave Mal a nudge. "The meeting is all set up. Sharon's house at 8 p.m. tomorrow. We'd best make those phone calls."

On Saturday evening Mal arrived at Sharon's neat little semi-detached house at twenty to eight and was welcomed in by Katie.

"Mum has been hate-baking all afternoon," she said. "And Harvey has been shouting at people in the British Museum. It's the most exciting thing ever."

Betty arrived at quarter to with additional supplies, and the two ladies set Harvey and Mal to getting the room ready for the other visitors. They all fetched and carried chairs, then made tea and coffee, filled Thermoses with hot water to save time and went to the door to let other attendees in. Rob was one of the first to arrive whooping "Hello, Peaches" as Betty let him in then boldly coming across to Mal to demand a kiss.

"Since I didn't get one this morning," he said. "Damn, Mal, you're a sound sleeper."

Sharon noticed Mal's flush and snorted. "Did you think it was a secret? I've known Rob since he was in nappies so nothing he does would surprise me."

"For God's sake, don't try to prove her wrong," Mal muttered and Rob snickered all through helping him to shift the sofa.

Soon they had what Harvey described as a quorum. Some of the men from the site, all the museum custodians, and Marcia Stenhouse with two of her minions arrived at ten to, followed by Veronica Garth – Chair of the Ladies Circle – gently conveyed into the house by Terry the barber. Cadaverously thin with a wonderful meringue of white hair swirled up on top of her head, she offered her diamond-ringed hand to Mal very much in the grand manner and husked, "Call me Ronnie, dahling, everyone else does. I've heard so much about you. And who is this wonderful man?"

Mal introduced her to Harvey who seated her in the room's most comfortable chair and fetched her a small gin.

Terry nudged Mal and said, "Isn't she like Joanna Lumley?" then went to help Sharon make tea.

Glyn Havard arrived next with Gary and Morris, though when Gary saw how crowded the room was he turned about to put Morris back in the car. He returned with Sion and a smallish, stocky, grey-haired man of immense dignity who Sion introduced as 'my father, Sergeant-Major Rai'. Mal shook his hand, complimented him on his cooking and was surprised by Rai's impish smile.

Councillor Pugh was last to arrive and Mal felt a twinge of disquiet. Surely Pugh would be as keen on the new development as Gaskell but, no, he made his outrage obvious. The only downside to Pugh's presence at the meeting was that he felt he was the best person to take charge of it.

"Has everyone got their drinks?" Pugh asked on the dot of eight. "Because I think we ought to call the meeting to order and get on. I propose that firstly someone fills us in on what has actually happened. I've been hearing all kinds of rumours since yesterday. Then I propose that we have a discussion about the best way to stop it."

"Harvey?" Mal said. "I think you'd tell it best."

Harvey rose to his feet with the confidence of a man used to speaking in front of an audience for a living. He didn't waffle but described how he had come to be involved in the discovery, the legal requirements associated with archaeological material when discovered as part of a development and the responsibilities of the landowner. Then he described the find, making the story a good one. That caused the first interruption.

"But surely," Melilot said, "if they are arranged as a couple it would *have* to be a man and a woman?"

"Why, pray?" Ronnie Garth raised pencilled eyebrows. "'Couple' can mean anything, all shapes and sizes and sexes, always has, and a bloody good thing too."

"Also, it has been confirmed by the skeletal evidence, dear lady," Harvey said with a smile.

"But surely there's room for doubt?" Pugh was frowning. "It seems odd given the context."

"Nothing odd about it at all from where I'm sitting." Rob leaned forward, his expression belligerent. "If you got to die and be buried, wouldn't you want it to be with someone you loved?"

Pugh, wisely, shut his mouth and Harvey jumped in to settle the matter.

"The bones of our fathers cannot lie. The two people who were placed so carefully in that grave, to sleep through the centuries in each other's arms, were two strongly-built men in their thirties, both of whom died by violence."

"I knew it," Rob slapped his knee. "I told you to look at the map. It's all there."

"What is?" Harvey asked.

Mal winced at the sharp pang of guilt as he recalled what Rob had said the night of their quarrel and how he had never followed it up.

"How do you mean, Rob?" he asked.

"Some of us went to school in Brynglas which is just over the border into Wales and so we had to do Welsh. All around here you've got a muddle of English and Welsh place names, like Escley which is Welsh esk for water and Saxon ley for a field or meadow."

"Aye," Terry nodded. "That's right. It all gets mangled up over the years because the English can't roll their r's or pronounce Ll."

"So it gets called High Rifles Lane," Rob added, "which seems to make sense because the local militia used to have a shooting range up there, but the track is much, much older than rifles or guns and we should be calling it Heol Rhyfelwr which means the warriors' road."

"Warriors' road." Harvey's voice rose with excitement. "Are you sure?"

There were several nods.

"I don't remember that," Betty admitted.

"That's cuz you're a girl and were busy braiding Lizzie Pritchard's hair and said soldiers were boring," Rob pointed out, "but I bet you remember about the name of the hill."

"What? Carew Hill?" Betty frowned for a moment. "Well, yeah, that was Bryn Carwr, wasn't it?"

"Which means Lovers' Hill." Sharon pinked up and shot an apologetic glance at Mal and Harvey. "I'm sorry, I thought you knew those. I was so pleased when you told me about the burial because it seemed so fitting."

Marcia Stenhouse cleared her throat. "In the reference section of the library we have a book by Augustus Farriner, an antiquarian, published in eighteen twenty. It contains a beautifully illustrated map of the town with all the road names in Welsh. Like Ross Road. It doesn't go to Ross, but it does go onto the common. Heol Rhos means Moor Road. If you come to me on Monday morning, Mr Bright, I'll have one of my girls check the book out for you."

"Thank you so much, Marcia," Mal said. "That's very helpful."

Marcia gave him a tight little smile and added, "Even Pemberland has got Welsh in it, hasn't it, Terry?"

"I reckon so," Terry said. "Pen is top or head or chief, something high up anyway, and a perllan is an orchard. You can see how over the years that might corrupt into Pemberland."

"I'm sure we've got a copy of that map in the collection," Betty said.

"I need to get those maps out," Mal said. "First thing tomorrow. Thank you, all of you."

"But what do we do?" Rob seemed to be simmering with fury. "It was bad enough those two men being taken out of the ground where they belong but at least they'd still be here. We can't let them go off to

London."

"I agree with you." Harvey scowled. "Culmstock thinks he's bloody Indiana Jones, swooping in to scoop up artefacts. He can bring up all kinds of persuasive arguments – better storage facilities, access to expert conservators, a far greater reach in terms of accessibility to an audience –"

"A chance for Gaskell Developments to be mentioned in big letters in a big place." Sion's dad spoke with a fine edge of contempt. "He was talking about it at the Chamber of Commerce meeting last Tuesday night. A big chance to put the town on the map, he said, but I'm sure he was thinking more of the free publicity. I think that it would be better to keep your soldiers here. Let them continue to guard the valley as they have in time past."

That suggestion got a quiet cheer from some of the people present and a reminder from Harvey that, as yet, they had no real evidence but healthy supposition never hurt anyone.

"An argument could certainly be made that that is the case," Pugh said, "but we still have no clear course of action."

"It's early days yet," Harvey said. "First of all, someone needs to approach Gaskell to try and get him to see sense. I'm sure he hasn't thought it through. He's assuming that his name will be up in lights immediately but museums don't work like that and, frankly, although the find is of immense importance, I don't think that many people will understand its significance. If there had been a slew of gold jewellery buried with them or something to suggest that they had been murdered and hastily concealed the press would have been all over it like flies – but a burial with honour? Where's the scandal in that?"

"Some of us appreciate the significance," Terry murmured, "and I think that if it was displayed locally and with the right sort of publicity it would bring a lot of outside visitors to the town."

"Which would be good for everyone," Pugh agreed. "Well, I'll talk to Gaskell. Mr Biddulph, could you sound out your contacts at the British Museum. Presumably Culmstock has *someone* to whom he is responsible who could rein him in. Mal, can you come up with a – what? – a three year plan for the refurbishment of that Early Peoples gallery you mentioned in your last email?"

Mal nodded. "I'll keep it to a tight budget."

"Don't you dare." Harvey shook his head. "You've got something the BM is desperate to get its paws on, which means it's really worth splashing out on. I'll look into available grants and sponsors."

"You can count on Havard Plant Hire," Glyn said. "Not perhaps for much financially speaking but I'll do what I can, and you can count on us all the way in other respects. I'll sound out some of the other local businesses as well."

"That's brilliant." Mal made another note on his tablet. "Guys, we'll all do all we can to keep – er – the bones of our fathers etc. here in Pemberland."

"Bloody good name for an exhibition," Harvey said and gave him a thumbs up. "I thought so the moment I said it."

Pugh clapped his hands together and nodded approvingly. "Then I suggest we wind this up, unless anyone else has anything to say?"

The meeting broke up soon after that. Pugh hurried off in his Jaguar, saying he had another meeting to attend but offered to detour to drop off Ronnie Garth on the way. She shook Mal's hand again before she left and leaned in to brush an air kiss beside his ear and whisper, "Harvey's not the only one with contacts at the British Museum. All of us old fossils keep in touch. I'll do what I can."

Terry and some of the other lads expressed an intention to go to the pub, Betty went with them, and Harvey shooed Mal and Rob out of the door.

"Sharon, Katie and I can manage," he assured them. "I'll bring the folding chairs back on Monday morning. Goodnight."

"Well, I reckon he's got his feet under the table there." Rob opened his car door and leaned on the roof. "Might be nice for them both. Do you want to go to the pub? I can drop you off there if you like?"

"You're not interested?"

"Daren't. I'm on edge. All it would take is for bloody Rother to come in and shoot his mouth off and I'd take a swing at him." Rob scowled. "But, as I said, I'll drop you off."

"Or we could swing by the Spar, buy some cans and go back to mine?" Mal suggested. "I've got a lot on my mind too and some company would be nice."

"You don't mind?" Rob asked, his smile more wistful than Mal had ever seen it. "I mean – we always end up at yours."

"No, I don't mind at all, and we can just sit and watch TV if you like."

Rob grinned. "We could see what's on Movies for Men, have a beer or two, and a shag?"

"Sounds like a plan." Mal opened the car door and got inside.

Chapter 15

Day by day they fought a losing battle against Culmstock's smooth promises and Gaskell's utter refusal to accept that the name of Gaskell Developments being blazoned across the front of the BM in illuminated letters was beyond the bounds of possibility. Harvey was tearing his hair out at Ormistead's apparent reluctance to call Culmstock to heel. Meanwhile, Mal was sick at heart from fielding phone calls from interested locals. Opinions were quite sharply divided. Some were outraged that he, as an incomer, would allow such a thing to happen, others that he, as an incomer, couldn't appreciate what a brilliant opportunity it was for the name of Pemberland to be heard far and wide.

"We might be on the telly, even," one said. "That lovely Dan Snow might do a programme."

Rob's mood deteriorated as Friday, the day Culmstock had approved as the day for the lifting of the cist, approached.

"It's ridiculous," he said on Wednesday evening. "Why take it all that way just to put it on a shelf?"

"That's the way museums work." Mal flapped a hand towards the stack of DVDs he had just unpacked. "Remember that bit at the end of the first Indiana Jones movie, where they put the ark in a crate on a trolley and wheel it away into that huge warehouse? Well, that's what the storage facilities of some of the big museums look like. Even ours has got *far* more stuff in stores than on show. We collect and conserve. Display and accessibility was always a lower priority."

"Maybe it shouldn't be?" Rob said. "What's the point of keeping it if nobody can ever see it?"

"Most people don't want to," Mal said. "Look, we've got stacks of bits of pottery, most of which look identical to someone who hasn't studied it. But that pottery can be used to date sites, and the only way to train people to be able to date sites is by handling stacks of bits of pottery and getting used to what they look and feel like."

"S'pose so." Rob leaned back in the seat, can in hand, and pointed Mal's remote at the TV. "Coming to the park tomorrow night?" he asked.

"Bonfire Night. Always a big bash. Pugh and his pals put on a good firework show and there's a beer tent and a burger van."

"I was planning to stay in and catch up on paperwork," Mal said.

"Hell no!" Rob grinned. "If you want to be a local you have to join in the nice things as well as doing all the boring paperworky stuff. Come on, Mal, it'll be fun. I'll buy you a burger. They are huge and greasy and covered in onions, and the best thing ever."

"Well …"

"And then we'll go to the Coach and I'll let you beat me at pool?"

"Promise? All right then." Mal grinned and stole the remote. "What'll it be? Sport, film?"

"Well, I came for Netflix and chill, but I guess we could watch something first."

Mal had been aware of the adverts for the annual fireworks celebration but it hadn't occurred to him that he might go. He was neither a fan of cold damp nights nor of the blare of piped music, but once he got to the field he found himself getting excited in a way he remembered from attending similar celebrations when he was about ten years old. Not that there hadn't been some much needed changes. Burning effigies of Guy Fawkes, for instance, was very much a thing of the past. But he still felt that excited flutter of anticipation.

The park wasn't a huge one but was nicely laid out with flower beds, paved walks and trees around the edges, and a broad expanse of grass in the middle that could be used for anything from cricket and rugby matches to shows and fêtes. In the middle of it a section of turf had been lifted and a bonfire made from off-cuts of timber and pallets. Upwind of that was a well shielded area where the fireworks would be set off. Plastic matting had been laid to protect the grass from the milling feet of the crowd. But when Mal arrived none of that could be seen for people.

It was a huge turnout. Kids rushed around waving glow sticks. Parents rushed around trying to find kids. The beer tent and burger van were doing a roaring trade. Mal paid his entrance fee and tried to remember where Rob had said he would meet him.

Eventually he found Gary. Morris was at home, Gary said, because he didn't like fireworks. Instead, Gary had Betty at his side and Mal was pretty sure that, until he had got close enough for them to recognise him, they had been holding hands.

"Yes, I saw Rob about ten minutes ago," Betty said. "He was with Sion and they were looking for you."

"Do you mind if I stay with you?" Mal asked. "I think we've got more chance of meeting up then."

"Good idea." Gary nodded. "Or you could, like, phone him and tell him where you are?"

"No, because his phone's at home, charging." Betty rolled her eyes. "He was complaining about it. Oh look, they are going to light the fire."

A whoop went up as the announcement was made and Mal joined in the count down, laughing a little at the bubble of joy expanding in his chest. As entertainment it wasn't sophisticated but he kept catching glimpses of faces he recognised, all of whom were smiling and many of whom gave him a nod or a wave. He felt at home, he realised, in a way he never really had in Cheltenham or Bristol, and that felt really good. He just wanted Rob, and all would be well.

The fire blazed and the crowd whooped along with a favourite track on the Tannoy. Mal bought a pack of sparklers from a vendor and shared them with Betty who drew hearts and stars in the air and shouted at Mal until he did the same. He caught the eye of Marcia Stenhouse and drew her a heart, laughing as she actually giggled and clutched the arm of the man next to her. A few moments later he saw her with a sparkler of her own.

"It's sad I couldn't bring Morris," Gary said. "He'd have loved the burger van."

Reminded of the burgers, Mal left them to go and get something to eat. He recalled that Rob had promised to buy him one and wondered if it was worth asking the man who was frying the onions if he had seen him, but the smell was so savoury that by the time it was Mal's turn to be served he was salivating too much to do more than pay. He wandered then, savouring the soft bun, the succulent meat and the tangy onions. He had lost track of Gary and Betty so looked for them as well as Rob. Instead he found Councillor Pugh, who was preparing to announce the commencement of the firework display.

"Well, what do you think?" Pugh asked. "I'm sure the bigger cities have larger events but I doubt they have such good natured ones."

"You're probably right," Mal said. "And I do enjoy a good burger. Where's the best place to watch the fireworks?"

"Oh, over by the beer tent." Pugh grinned. "Always a good view from there, and even better through the bottom of a glass."

"Great idea," Mal said, and ate the rest of his burger as he circumnavigated the fire and joined the throng buying bottled beer at exorbitant prices. But Guinness was good whether on tap, canned or bottled, and Mal took his can and stood to one side, hoping for a glimpse of one of his friends. Leo Farriner passed, neat in a long overcoat and sporting a magnificent furry hat. He nodded to Mal and paused to ask him if he was enjoying the event. A few minutes later Mal was joined by Brian Farriner, the police constable, off duty this evening and looking relaxed in a business-like cagoule and huge walking boots.

"You ready for this?" he said and grinned as the Tannoy crackled again and the music cut out.

Pugh's voice boomed over the chilly field in a half heard admonition to be careful and stay back behind the guide ropes. Then he passed the mic over to their special guest Harvey Biddulph.

"I didn't know Harvey was going to start it," Mal said, laughing at Harvey's excited shouts.

"I guess he's the closest thing we've got to a celebrity in town today," Brian grinned. "Though I guess I'd best not let him hear me say that. Gaskell must be pissed, though. He usually does it."

Mal shrugged, not much caring one way or another how Gaskell felt. He was concerned that he hadn't found Rob.

With a whoosh and a shower of sparks the first fireworks traced a glittering path across the cloudy sky – and Mal started as a hand patted on his hip.

"There you are!" Rob said. "I've been all around the place looking for you. Gawd, what a turn out. Hi, Brian."

"Hi, Rob." Brian stared up at the sky where pink and gold sparks were spreading like chrysanthemums. "Was Sion with you?"

"No, I lost him when I went to the lav," Rob said. "He's here somewhere. Hard to spot someone that short in this crowd."

"Cheeky," Brian said. "You wouldn't get away with saying that if he were in earshot."

"If he were in earshot it'd be an unkind thing to say, even if it is the truth." Rob stole the Guinness can from Mal's hand and took a swig. "God, I needed that. Can I get a round in? Or would you prefer mulled cider?"

"I never had that," Mal admitted. "Is it good?"

"Oh, heck, yes. Brian?"

Brian gave him a thumbs up and offered him his empty glass.

Even the crush of the beer tent was more fun when Mal could squeeze in beside Rob.

"I kept missing you," Rob said as they edged forward in the queue. "Every so often I'd spot you but by the time I got there you were gone again."

"I was looking for you." Mal laughed. "Next time we have to have a plan."

"Beer tent," Rob said. "There will always be a beer tent so next year that's where we'll meet."

Oh I hope so, Mal thought. *Or better yet we could go together*. Planning ahead for festivals and fun, year after year, was something he had never done with Oliver, whose work schedules had been erratic – this week Paris, next week San Diego – and Mal found the idea quite enchanting.

They had left the beer tent and were enjoying their cider a little closer to the fire when they spotted Harvey and Culmstock head to head in a widening circle in the crowd. Alarmed they headed for them.

"Completely unethical," Harvey was shouting when they reached them. "And I protest in the strongest possible terms."

"Harvey!" Mal darted to his side and grabbed his arm, relieved to see Rob grabbing on the other side. "I don't think this is the time and place."

"Nor do I," Culmstock said, his trademark smirk still in place. "Go home and sleep it off."

Harvey looked around at the interested onlookers and sighed. "All right. Mal, is there anywhere we can get coffee?"

Mal who had expected more of a battle, acquiesced and led him over to the beer tent where there was at least a chance of soft drinks. But Rob disappeared for a moment and came back with a paper cup, fragrant with beans.

"There's a coffee machine in the burger van," he said. "Bottoms up."

Disaster averted, Mal grinned at him and thought about the rest of the evening. "Harvey, what are you doing after the show finishes?"

"Back to Sharon's. Neither she nor Katie like bangs so they elected to stay at home and watch at a distance through the double glazing," Harvey said. "Why, what did you have in mind?"

"We can give you a lift to the pub," Rob suggested, and slung his arm around Mal's shoulders.

"You know, all things considered," Harvey sighed, "I think I may as well get back. But you two have a good time."

The last of the fireworks faded from the sky leaving a chill wind and a scent of cordite. The fire began to burn down too and the crowds began to disperse. Mal didn't envy the parents wrangling over-excited kids back to their cars. He imagined it would be even worse getting them up for school in the morning.

He checked his watch. "Nine o'clock? It feels much later. What usually happens now?"

"Usually we'd go to the Coach. Thursday night, pool night," Rob said. "But I don't really fancy the pub tonight."

"We could go back to mine?" Mal squeezed Rob's arm. "I found a box of DVDs I haven't looked through. Could be something in there worth watching."

"I got to get up early," Rob said, "but – yeah, why not?"

It wasn't a long walk. They strolled, shoulder occasionally knocking shoulder, unable to move any faster because of the press of people. Mal found he was enjoying the silent companionship. It wasn't until they had entered the flat and he was rummaging in the kitchen cupboard for snacks that he realised that the silence had continued. He and Rob often enjoyed some peace but Rob wasn't usually this quiet. He popped his head round the edge of the kitchen door and said, "Beer, or shall I make tea?"

Rob started, his phone in his hand. "Er – what? Sorry, I didn't hear."

"Beer or tea?" Mal repeated. "Are you okay, Rob?"

"Yeah, sorry, just tired. It's been a really long week. Tea would be great, if you don't mind?"

In the end, with Rob yawning before the opening credits of the film had finished running, they took their tea to bed. Mal was tired too but that didn't stop him feeling a little surprised when Rob just huddled close, nudging his way into Mal's arms. His skin was hot and Mal rubbed his cheek against the top of Rob's head and said, "I hope you haven't got Harvey's cold."

"Naaah, I never get sick." Rob shifted enough to kiss Mal's neck. "I'm just knackered. Got to be up at five again. Sorry, love."

The endearment was an unexpected surprise and Mal smiled. "Let's sleep, then," he said.

Chapter 16

Mal was a little late into work the following morning. He had woken up when Rob did and had made him tea while he showered, but then had made the mistake of going back to bed and falling so soundly asleep that he hadn't heard his alarm.

Now he had a buzzing head and was desperate for coffee. But he was even more desperate for someone, preferably one of the big guns at the British Museum, to step in and solve the problem of Culmstock. The man was behaving appallingly and it wouldn't be long until the press reminded Gaskell that his will wasn't the only thing in play here. Public opinion counted for a lot with Gaskell's type, and being sneered at up at the golf club would carry more weight than anything Mal could say.

Betty had already opened up the museum and gave him a cheerful wave. "Well, what happened to you last night?" She produced a cup of coffee for him and led him to a chair. "It's not like you and Rob to miss pool night. Are you okay?"

"I am. Not too sure about Rob, though." Mal shook his head, winced and reached for the paracetamol. "No, he's probably okay. He was up with the lark and made himself bacon and egg to, as he put it, get off to a good start. The only comfort is that he'll be a bit late too and Glyn will shout at him."

"Naah, Glyn was at the bonfire too. He was lit up like Christmas. He'd told all the lads they could have a nine o'clock start. Not much point getting there earlier when it's so dark in the mornings. And it rained around midnight, the ground'll be a bog at the bottom of the slope."

"Oh that's good." Mal relaxed into his chair and took a sip of coffee. "Until we hear from the BM whether they can rein in Culmstock, I guess we'll have to hope it's too wet to lift the cist this afternoon. Keep on raining, I say. Look, Betty, how about you make a start on clearing that back room. For now I think we just need a list of everything that's in it and some kind of notation system so we can keep track of where it all is. If we make it over as a display area we'll have to figure out where to put the stuff stored there."

"Okie doke," Betty said, and grinned. "Have fun with your inbox."

Mal didn't but he did get it cleared within an hour. There was remarkably little of interest, but an email from an old friend working at a museum in Newark expressed sympathy and repeated a rumour that Culmstock had been responsible for the removal of another large impressive find which had since disappeared into the stores and never been seen again.

"Don't let the bastard have it," she said. "Because what he does with them nobody knows. I think he just gets off on it."

So a proven track record of tomb raiding, Mal mused. *I think I could use that.*

He was just imagining a scenario where he used facts, wit, skill and unnatural eloquence to not only persuade Gaskell to give up his daft scheme but also to bear the expense of the entire new gallery when his phone rang.

"Dammit." Mal abandoned the day dream with regret. "Hello?"

"Mal," Betty's voice was tight, "can you come down? You might want to bring your coat?"

"What? Why?"

"There's something wrong up at the site. Brian – I mean, PC Farriner is here to fetch you."

Mal grabbed his coat, his bag and, as an afterthought, a pair of wellies. He clattered down the stairs to find Brian waiting at the desk, his face a study in suppressed grimness.

"Morning, Mal," he said. "Sorry to say the site seems to have been vandalised."

"Is there much damage?" Mal asked, his heart in his boots.

"I – er – I think you'll need to see for yourself. Could we get Mr Biddulph to meet us there, or would it be better for us to pick him up?"

"He'll meet us there. Betty can you give him a call? I want to get up there asap."

It was a short car ride. Any other time, Mal would probably have enjoyed seeing cars wave Brian's police car on but today he was too on edge. At the site he got out of the car and looked around. The place was a sea of mud; pallets had been overturned, scattering building materials, and further up the hill he could see Rob's digger, leaning at a most peculiar angle.

"This way," Brian suggested and took a slightly less muddy route around the quagmire and up onto the side of the hill.

"Oh, God in Heaven," Mal groaned as he saw the rags of the gazebo flapping in the wind. "What the heck did they do? Didn't the night-watchman see anything?"

"Ah well, he had been taken care of," Brian said gravely. "When the first guys arrived this morning they found Phil Rother was trapped in one of the Portaloos. He'd been there for most of the night. Says he went in to – er – you know – at about the time they were setting off the fireworks and someone shoved a screwdriver through the bit where the padlock goes." Brian's calm expression didn't waver but his tone lightened. "He lost his temper and threw himself against the door and managed to tip the whole unit over. Good job it had just been emptied."

"Oh, very good," Mal agreed. "Though a night spent sitting in your own piss can't have been pleasant."

"Most unpleasant, I should think."

Mal put that thought to one side for later. He was sure at some point that the idea of Phil Rother trapped in a plastic toilet would be hysterically funny but right now he was too worried to savour it. All his attention was on the site further up the hill where the neck of the digger towered like a drunken giraffe surrounded by men in hi-vis jackets.

When he reached the clot of men he couldn't at first make sense of what he was seeing. The gazebo had collapsed onto the cist, and the tracks of the digger ran across the fabric.

"Mal." Glyn came to his side and put his hand on his shoulder. "We think they hot-wired the digger, took it for a joy ride and lost control of it. Rob's gutted. It's his pride and joy."

"I know," Mal said, his eyes on the swathe of water-logged canvas. "Is it much damaged?"

"We waited to look until you got here."

"I meant the digger?" Mal looked at Glyn. "Is it much damaged?"

"Nothing we can't fix," Glyn said. "But it went into the ditch and it'll take a bit of work to get it out. This ..." He nodded to the burial site. "This is a bit different."

"All right." Mal took a deep breath and stepped forward. "Can some of you give me a hand?"

They each grabbed a bit of the sodden canvas and crab-walked it towards the old hedge line to get it off the cist. Water cascaded, slipped icily up Mal's sleeves and filled his boot as the canvas dipped on his side. "That's got it," Glyn called. "Let it go. Ah … Mal?"

"I'm scared to look," Mal said – but he went to the edge of the hole to join Glyn and Brian.

And that was all it was – a hole filled with water and scraps of the plaster the Culmstock had used to stabilise the base of the burial.

"It's gone." Mal shook his head. "It's bloody gone. Who'd do a thing like that?"

Brian made a face signifying complete bafflement. "This is just weird. Mal, up to now I thought maybe some of the kids might have got on the cider and been messing about but this – this is theft. I think I need to call in a higher rank."

Higher ranks all round. Harvey arrived about ten minutes later, hair flattened by the rain which was beginning to come down really hard now. On Brian's advice they had used the canvas to shield the pit again though, as he said, any evidence was surely waterlogged.

Harvey joined Mal, and Rob hurried across to greet them. He gave Mal a sympathetic fist bump.

"I'm so sorry," he said. "I can't believe this. Look, I got to get the digger out of the ditch before the water backs up enough to affect the engine. I'll be back in a bit, okay?"

Mal nodded and watched the activity, too dispirited to talk. In fact the whole site was unusually quiet.

Culmstock and his team more than made up for it when they arrived. Culmstock was incandescent, demanded a greater police presence than the calm eyed detective who had just arrived from Hereford, and then had a good rave at Mal and Harvey. "What are you just standing there for?" he demanded.

"What do you suggest we do?" Harvey said. "Until a scene of crime team get here we can't work on the site. But I do have one suggestion for you. How about you get in touch with the press? I believe you'd invited a bunch of them to come and witness you lifting the cist out this afternoon. They might find the change in the story interesting?"

"Oh Jesus, there's a film crew too." Culmstock grabbed for his phone and stalked off down the hill.

"There goes a really unhappy man." Brian Farriner approached, collar of his uniform waterproof turned up against the rain.

"Yes, he looks upset." Harvey frowned. "You know, constable, while of no real intrinsic worth – there are no extensive grave goods, no precious metals – this burial is actually of great potential value to the right buyer."

"Really?" Brian tilted his head. "I know about people stealing art and antiques to order, even garden statuary, and shipping it abroad, but archaeological material? Is there much of a market for that?"

"Have you been on eBay lately?" Mal asked. "There's a lot of interest in archaeological material, a load of collectors, and if word had gone out about this burial and its more unique features, I'm sure there would be people interested in owning it."

Brian grimaced. "I'll go and tell the DI," he said. "Because we wasted two hours this morning thinking it was kids messing about, but if that was just camouflage …" He hurried away, and Mal and Harvey sighed and found a quiet place to stand.

They spent half an hour or so watching Rob use the digger's own backhoe to ease the huge machine out of the ditch and onto flatter ground. Mal joined in the round of applause as the digger straightened up but he truly felt numb. That was probably just as well because otherwise he feared he might punch someone or burst into tears.

"I can't stand around here," he muttered. "Let's go and make everyone coffee?"

"Great idea." Harvey took his arm as they slipped and slid across the muddy ground to the Portakabins. "Everything's better with coffee."

They were washing up mugs when they were found by the ladies and gentlemen of the press. Lisa Parrish, a rounded lady of boundless curiosity who wrote for the Pemberland Free Press, fluttered into the Portakabin and for one moment Mal thought she was going to give him a sympathetic cuddle.

"Mal, I'm so sorry this has happened. Oh, er – Mr Biddulph, isn't it?" She offered her hand to Harvey and went very pink when he stooped over it. "Pleased to meet you, Mr Biddulph. I'm Lisa and this is Mike."

Her photographer, a morose beanpole of a man, had entered so quietly that Mal hadn't even noticed him. He nodded a greeting, then stood by the wall and apparently went into stand-by mode until needed.

"So, what can you tell me?" Lisa produced a notebook and pen from her enormous handbag. "Inside job or shadowy international organisation?"

"I'm sorry?" Mal stared at her. "I think maybe you're mistaking this for a James Bond plot?"

"Well, you never know your luck." She grinned at him. "So, how did you find out?"

Mal gave her a bare account of his morning but since she was clearly dying to interview Harvey he brought him into the narrative and let him take over. As usual, Harvey made a good tale of it, describing the utter desolation of the site and their shock at the discovery that the burial cist had been stolen. Lisa scribbled frantically, making encouraging sounds. Once, when Harvey came out with a particularly mellifluous phrase, she let out an excited yip and said, "Can I quote that?"

"Full attribution will be required," Harvey said with a smile, then went into a full blown rant about night hawks, their lack of morals, antecedents and personal hygiene.

"And do you agree with that?" Lisa asked Mal, who scowled a moment before answering.

"The person – or persons, rather because this can't have been a one man job – who did this are the scum of the earth. I know that it has to figure well down the list from crimes of violence or selling narcotics to teenagers but this stole knowledge from us. This burial could have told us things we didn't know about ourselves. It could have been an example of tolerance and respect, something often lacking in modern society. Those things have been taken from us and now we'll never know. I have nothing but contempt for the thieves."

"Nice one." Lisa scratched an underline across her page. "I need to get this to press a.s.a.p., but can I follow up in a day or two? I'd like to do a more complete interview with you. I understand you've got big plans for the museum."

"I had big plans," Mal said. "I have no idea what to do now. But I'll think of something."

Mike whirred into life and Lisa directed them back out into the rain for a photo. Mike took off the lens cap and nodded to the hole. "Point at it," he barked and they all obeyed, Mal eyeing Harvey with puzzlement.

Around them the other observers had paused to huddle close and the hole was indicated by a dozen mud and oil stained digits.

"Nice," Mike said, peering at the little screen on the back of his camera, then headed back down the hill to the car. Lisa twirled her stripey umbrella and thanked them, then followed.

"What was that about?" Mal asked

"Tradition," Glyn said. His pointing had been particularly bold. "Mike does two sorts of photos – a line of people so we can see all their faces and it's easy to put their names underneath, or if the photo is of a thing he likes to get people to point at it. Human interest, he says, when he can get a word in edgewise. That Lisa can talk."

"Well, as far as I'm concerned, we've given her an exclusive," Mal said. "Any other press types who turn up can be redirected to the Free Press office."

"Good idea," Harvey said. "Look, I've got water running down my back. Shall we get back to the museum and see what our options are?"

"I think so. Glyn, is there anything we can do?"

"No." Glyn looked around at the mud. "I'll get this lot cleared away. At least we can get working on this part of the site now. We'd about finished at the bottom of the hill."

"Small mercies, eh?" Harvey said. "Come on then, Mal. I'll give you a lift."

Once back at the museum, Mal filled Betty and Sharon in on what had happened, made them and Harvey tea, and left Harvey to chat to them. He hurried up to his office and began to do what he could to prevent the burial from leaving the country. There were official channels, of course, and the police would go through those, but Mal knew a few channels they probably wouldn't examine and spent an annoying half hour calling people in the trade who might conceivably be offered something of that nature.

"Good grief, Mal," said one man in Bath. "If something like that did come on the market I would definitely hear about it – my special interests are well known in the trade. But you know I wouldn't touch it, don't you?"

Mal did know, but he also knew that it would only be after much agonised soul searching that possession of such an evocative object would be rejected. "And you'll let me know?" he asked.

"Of course, I'll be in touch as soon as I hear anything."

They left it there, Mal uneasy at using an old acquaintance like that, and presumably the old acquaintance cursing his promise.

Later he joined the rest of the staff in the reception to field a sudden influx of reporters. Denied the opportunity to witness and photograph the raising of the cist from its bed, they wanted to get photos and sound-bites from the bereft museum staff.

"Speak to Lisa at the Free Press," Mal advised. "We gave her an interview this morning. Failing that I have a press release that I can give you." He passed out copies of the terse half dozen lines and refused to pose in what might have been the new gallery, though he didn't object to one cheeky photographer who admitted to having grabbed a candid shot as he and Harvey exchanged resigned smiles.

"That's a good one," Harvey said, peering at the camera's display. "Mal, you have both eyes open. I think that's a first."

Mal laughed then, but that was the only time for the rest of the day. He made phone calls, answered phone calls, and listened to Harvey having a shouting match with Ormistead at the BM and another with his agent who appeared to be worrying about ratings. Throughout it all, Mal fixed his mind on the evening. He would be seeing Rob. That the thought calmed his thumping heart said a lot, he realised, about his feelings.

They had arranged to meet at the Coach and Horses, and chatted over a pint and a game of pool.

"We've been working like pit ponies," Rob said. "But it looked a lot worse than it was, actually. Mostly building materials scattered about. The digger was okay, just a bit of a ding on the track cover from hitting a bush and a load of mud. I've been stripping it down. They'd hot-wired it, bastards."

"I'm glad it wasn't damaged," Mal said. "And that the site was easily sorted."

"Well, we'd written most of today off anyway, what with expecting that tit Culmstock and his circus to be there fannying about with his press people and film crew. Film people don't like machinery droning along in the background. Oh, and Rother came back after lunch. He wasn't hurt, just a bit cold. Lucky the loo had been emptied that morning or he could'a drowned."

There was a light in Rob's eye that meant he was trying to be grown up and responsible and not think about Rother spending the night laying in his own urine, so Mal decided to encourage the responsible bit of him.

"I should imagine that he's relieved," Mal said. "Relieved. Ha, get it?"

"Oh very clever. Yeah, nobody can blame Rother for not tackling the thieves if he was locked in."

"That whole scene – Rother locked in the loo, the silly but almost damageless vandalism – made it look obviously like some kids had had a spree after too much cider."

Rob nodded. "That's what the bloke who came on at midnight thought. He said he saw the mess, rang it in and didn't think any more of it. That plus a bladder like a bucket took him through 'til daylight and bought the thieves a good ten hours before it occurred to anyone to check the burial."

"Clever," Mal said. "So basically that cist and its contents could be out of the country by now. Straight into a container then on a lorry to Harwich."

"Awww, Mal." Rob leaned across the corner of the pool table to grab him by the back of the neck and pull him into a cuddle. "Never fear, Brian and his boys in blue could find it yet."

Mal had the impression that the boys in blue acted more as general peace keepers than steely-eyed investigators but was happy to agree, then changed the subject to football and they spent the rest of the night happily, firstly at the Coach then back at Mal's.

"I feel bad about always coming here," Rob said in the sleepy comfortable aftermath of loving, "but you don't want to be at mine. Christ, I don't want to be at mine. So thanks for letting me come here."

He nestled, there was no other word for it, into Mal's side and, amused and touched, Mal tightened his grip on Rob's shoulders and nuzzled the top of his head. "You're welcome," he said. "Always."

"Even at Christmas?"

"Especially at Christmas. Oh God, it's gone twelve. I need my beauty sleep."

"Yep, you do," Rob agreed with a chuckle, and they slept.

Next morning Mal woke up to tea and toast and Rob already dressed. "Saturday," he said, "but I'm going up to the site. Glyn agreed to give us an extra day to make up for yesterday. See you later? I'll be off four-ish."

"Could go see that film," Mal said.

"Cool," Rob grinned at him, then stooped and gave him a goodbye kiss. "Jeez, Mal," he said when he straightened up. "Morning mouth much? See ya later, hot pertater."

"I'll clean my teeth," Mal promised and picked up his mug. Eight weeks, he realised. He had known Rob for less than two months and was more relaxed with him than with Oliver who had shared his flat in Bristol for two years. Too soon to be thinking long term, of course, but he couldn't deny that a future with plenty of Rob in it had a definite appeal.

Chapter 17

Mal's good mood saw him through his Saturday morning routine of laundry and vacuuming, his trip to Tesco to stock up on necessities and a phone call to his parents. Or rather to his mother. Dad, as usual, was out in the garden somewhere. But Mum exclaimed in outrage over his problems with the burial, made a couple of completely impractical suggestions that at least showed an interest, then filled him in about their plans for their winter cruise and reminded him to check his father's Amazon wish list.

"And what would you like, Mum?" he asked.

"The usual," she said. "Yes, I know I'm boring."

Mal grinned and scribbled himself a note to order a box of Turkish Delight.

At ten to four Mal was trying to decide whether to have tea now or wait until Rob arrived when the doorbell gave its wheezy chirrup. Mal flicked the switch on the kettle and hurried to the door.

"I'm really going to have to give you a key," he began as he opened the door.

"I don't think that will be necessary, sir." The big calm detective who was in charge of the theft case gave him an affable nod. "May we come in?"

"Of course." Mal put the door on the latch so Rob could get in, then stood aside to let the detective and PC Farriner pass. "Up the stairs and to the right."

The DI – Cowper – wasted no time in getting down to business, refusing a coffee and taking a seat at Mal's tiny kitchen table with grave authority. Brian removed his hat and stood back against the kitchen wall, giving Mal a small but encouraging smile.

"We have been looking at this theft," Cowper said, "from all possible angles. One suggested by Mr Biddulph is that word of the more unusual aspects of the burial got out and someone somewhere ordered the theft. It's less common than people think but it does happen. We are monitoring the sites where such items are usually advertised but so far no luck."

"I wouldn't imagine you'd see anything this soon," Mal said. "They usually let the furore die down a bit first before putting it on eBay or wherever."

"These sites aren't as easily accessible as eBay," Cowper said with a small smile. "You have to know how to get there, if you know what I mean. But there's another line of investigation that may actually be more promising. I don't know if you'd heard but the site has been trespassed several times over the past couple of weeks. On one occasion the night-watchman heard someone's ring tone and claims to have heard it again recently."

"Good grief. No, I hadn't heard that." Mal made a mental note to change his ring tone. "Did you discover anything?"

"We've only just heard about it. Sites of this nature always have a trespassing problem. It's not usually serious. But now the head of Rother Security is claiming that the theft is part of a campaign carried out by people in the local community to try to discredit his business."

"Why would anyone want to do that?" Mal asked. "Reliable security staff must be quite desirable and Morris alone must be worth his weight in gold."

"Morris?" Cowper had turned to Brian, and Brian nodded.

"Gary Havard's dog," he said.

"Ah yes, and Gary is Glyn Havard's son, I understand?"

"Well, yes," Mal said and smiled. "He seems like a nice lad."

"At odds with his father," Cowper said. "They have had several loud fallings-out about Gary working elsewhere when he could be working for the family. It's possible that he might have organised this."

"But why?" Mal frowned. "What would Glyn have to gain from vandalising his own building site? Or did you mean Gary? What would Gary have to gain from discrediting Rother Security? What would either have to gain from stealing the burial? Surely just the vandalism would be enough?"

"So one would think, but the possibility has to be examined. Speaking of which, there is another possibility, one which was suggested to us by Mr Gaskell."

"And that is?"

"Professional rivalry," Cowper said. "It's well known that Harvey Biddulph and Culmstock can't stand each other, also that plans were afoot to make the burial the centrepiece of an exhibition at the local museum.

Gaskell and Culmstock claim that Biddulph backs the local display and organised a local task force to prevent the burial being taken to London for conservation and display, with the added advantage that Culmstock would be publicly humiliated. Gaskell claims that you are involved since you have ingratiated yourself with some of the local ne'er-do-wells, his term not mine, who are the type of people who could easily carry out the robbery."

Mal listened with growing fury. "He does, does he? So, what do I have to do to prove him wrong?"

"He suggested that I search the museum," Cowper said.

"Well, that's fine," Mal said, bouncing to his feet. "I'll get my coat and we can go round there right now."

"No need," Cowper said. "We got a warrant and did that before we came here. The custodian let us in. She also claims that there was some kind of conspiracy involving men from the building site and you and Mr Biddulph."

"Conspiracy? We called a meeting about Culmstock sweeping in to pirate the damned burial if that's what you mean? A local councillor was present and so was the Chair of the – I dunno – Women's Institute or something. You can't get much more official than that."

"One man's official meeting is another man's, or woman's, conspiracy," Cowper said. "We asked, and one of the custodians present at the meeting confirmed that means were discussed by which Culmstock could be prevented from taking the burial off the local patch. Something about maps and old place names."

Melilot. Mal sighed. "Yes, I think I know who you mean. At the time she seemed more appalled that the two skeletons might both be male than that they were being taken out of the county. But a conspiracy is a bit rich. It was more – letting off steam in an environment where we thought we could trust everyone."

Cowper shrugged and made a 'well more fool you' expression. "Anyhow, I thought we'd let you know that, while of course we will examine every possible angle, for the moment you aren't under serious investigation. Some of what I've heard in the past twenty four hours seems fanciful, some ridiculous and some, frankly, just bigotry. That we searched the museum without first getting in touch with you was a matter of expedience, but we acknowledge that it was discourteous and you have my apology. The advantage was that some people spoke more freely than they might have done had you been present."

"Apparently so." Mal shook his head. "I know that I have no proof of this, but I can assure you that I would never have been a party to this theft. Large museums pirating good quality items from smaller ones is fairly routine in this business. That's why national collections are always so much more exciting. They get the whole pots, we get the broken pieces. They get the fantastic glittering hoards, we get the single chance finds."

"I see." Cowper pursed his lips. "Wouldn't this class as a single chance find?"

"Normally, yes. Bronze Age cist burials are ten a penny. I'm sure that the British Museum has dozens packed away in store. The only reason this one is special is because of the two skeletons and the attitude in which they had been placed. Burials that look as though they are couples or families are quite rare and they are popular with the general public. It's the difference between a pile of old bones and evidence of a human connection." Mal caught his breath, aware that he had slipped into lecturing mode, but Cowper smiled a small, tight smile and gestured for him to continue. "This display would have been something that you could look at and think 'I recognise this. I know this. This is the same kind of love I feel for my wife, or husband, or partner', and that makes the history come alive. We can feel it more. And this burial – this may be evidence of a same sex relationship that has endured for four thousand years. It's enormously exciting and should be examined, properly, and exhibited in such a way that the bigots can't deny that LGBT relationships have *always* been part of human life and that, at this time, they were afforded great respect. Those two men weren't just dumped into the ground – shoved out of sight in one grave to get them out of the way. They were buried in a way that reflected their relationship. Laid to rest with honour and with respect."

Behind Cowper, Brian Farriner was staring at Mal, those lovely grey eyes blazing in a carefully blank face. It struck Mal that even in today's modern police force, being a gay copper probably wasn't at all easy. Then Cowper cleared his throat and nodded.

"I see," he said. "And that they are local lads and should remain local is another part of it. Thank you, Mr Bright. We may need to speak to you again but we have your contact details. I will follow this up as far as we can with the resources available but you do realise that if, as Mr Biddulph suggested, the item was stolen to order, it has probably already left the country?"

"I do, and I'm gutted." Mal stood up as Cowper rose to leave. "At least we have the grave goods safely in store, unless Culmstock intends to take those?"

Cowper shook his head. "He said it wasn't worth bothering unless he had the whole thing. He's on his way back to London."

"Thank God for small mercies," Mal said.

"Not that small, Mal!" Rob whooped as he opened the door from the stairs. "I ... what the fuck's going on?"

"Ah, Rob." DI Cowper's bland and careful expression was back again. "I wondered if I might see you here. We were just leaving. Thank you, Mr Bright. We'll be in touch."

Mal closed the street door behind DI Cowper and Brian and clicked the lock. The experience of being suspected of a fairly major crime was a novel one, and one that he hated, so he guessed that he looked pretty grim when he turned to go back upstairs. Rob was halfway down the stairs, scowling furiously until he caught Mal's eye.

"Oh Mal," he whispered. "What on earth's going on? Why were they here?"

"I'm so glad to see you," Mal said. "I'll tell you upstairs. God, I'm so angry I could punch someone."

"What's happened?"

Mal just gestured to the stairs and followed Rob up them. Clean jeans, he noted, showing off that perfect muscular arse and powerful legs. *So there is something to be grateful for*, he reminded himself.

"Do you want some tea?" he asked, heading for the kitchen. He was scared that if Rob showed too much sympathy he'd lose it. He'd learned to cope – both he and Zoë had to, with parents who provided for them lavishly by maintaining two careers – and he hadn't been able to rely on Oliver for emotional support. In that relationship he had been the one to listen to Oliver's frustrations and provide comfort, and had been used to keeping his own problems to himself. He was absolutely prepared to do that now, but Rob gripped his arm firmly and pulled him back.

"Yes, I do want tea," Rob said, "but not until you tell me why you look like your puppy just died. Jesus God, Mal, they don't think you had anything to do with the burial going missing?"

Mal took a deep breath. "It has been suggested to them," he said. "Gaskell, maybe prompted by Culmstock. They've already searched the museum. They probably would have searched here except how would I get the fucking cist up the stairs." He began to laugh and was shocked to hear his voice break.

"Oh Mal," Rob said again, and his arms closed around him. So tight, so comforting. Mal knotted his fists in Rob's clean, fabric softener-smelling shirt, pressed his forehead into Rob's neck and allowed himself to lose it for a little while.

Chapter 18

The rest of Saturday was difficult. Mal couldn't believe that he had, frankly, snivelled into Rob's collar and Rob seemed to bear no ill-will about it, but Mal couldn't help but feel he'd let the side down. Okay, it had been enormously comforting while it had been happening but as the day went on they both got further and further on edge.

On Friday, Brian had warned Mal that if the thieves weren't found quite rapidly they probably never would be. Anticipating the worst, Mal settled down during the afternoon with his files of notes and sketches to see what kind of exhibition he could mount without the big spectacular focus of the cist. Rob watched a rugby match on TV and brought him tea from time to time. Mal thanked him but couldn't help but notice how unhappy he looked and how much time he was spending staring at his phone screen and sending texts.

Changing your mind, I bet, Mal thought. *Deciding that I'm too high maintenance? Or just bored?*

The fifth time the phone pinged to warn of an incoming message, Rob caught Mal looking. "Darts match Tuesday. We're playing the Dog at King's Norton and that's always edgy." He rolled his eyes. "Dead posh they are over there."

"Oh, right," Mal said, and Rob frowned.

"What did you think I was doing? Oh fuck, Mal, this isn't about earlier?" Rob reached across to give Mal's hair a friendly ruffle. "You rant away if you need to, you've every right to be upset. I don't mind."

"Oh God, I'm sorry, Rob." Mal's throat was tightening again but he closed his laptop with a decisive click. "Tell you what, why don't we go for a pint this evening?"

They went to the Coach and shared a basket of chips. Later they watched a little TV before going to bed to rock against each other in the darkness until satisfied. Not an exciting evening by any means but Mal felt it was what they both needed – comfort and normality even under difficult circumstances. But neither of them slept well and both were up early on Sunday.

"I best go see Mum," Rob said. "Dad's being … difficult."

"I'm sorry. I hope you can sort things out," Mal said. He hesitated for a moment, because Rob also had responsibilities and Mal felt a bit guilty for taking up so much of his time, then asked, "Will you be back? I mean, no problem if you've got things to do –"

"I'll be back," Rob said. He smiled down at the car keys in his hand. "I love being here with you, Mal. Never think otherwise."

"And I love having you here," Mal said. "I'll leave the door on the latch for you."

That little exchange cleared the air. Mal felt much happier and cracked on with his work, re-jigging the design of the gallery and wondering what to do with the extra money that would be left over. "I'm counting my chickens here," he said to his laptop. "Who knows if any sponsors will be interested now? Still, we'll do the best with what we have."

After lunch he rang Zoë. She was outraged about the theft, but also looking forward to Christmas and told him a story about the squeamishness of a new father that had him both snorting with laughter and curling up with embarrassment on the man's behalf.

"That's better," she said once he'd got his breath back. "I don't like it when you sound sad. Give Rob my love."

"I will," Mal promised. Then he changed the sheets and put them in to the wash and took the time to run the vacuum around the flat. By six he was checking his watch, wondering whether to put dinner on now or wait until Rob came in. Not worried exactly, but very aware that neither of them had specified any times. Also Mal was beginning to get hungry. He was very relieved to hear the street door open and feet on the stairs – not Rob's usual two steps at a time rush but a slow plod.

"Hey," Mal said by way of greeting as Rob entered the room. "Oh Christ, Rob, what happened to you?"

"Hmm?" Rob glanced down at the blood on his shirt. "This is Dad's. Silly old bastard broke a glass then trod on it. I've been at A&E with him all day." He rubbed absently at the rusty marks.

"Get that shirt off," Mal ordered.

"Jeez, Mal," Rob said, "give me time to get the door closed."

"No," Mal laughed. "Well, yes, obviously, but I meant that we'll put it into soak with some salt. Take the stain out. There's clean laundry on the end of the bed. Should be some of your shirts in there."

Rob let out a long breath and smiled. "Thanks Mal," he said, and headed for the bedroom.

When he came out he didn't seem much happier. Mal pulled him into a hug as they sat on the couch and Rob rested his head against Mal's shoulder. Mal would have been happy to stay like that, except that he could hear Rob's stomach rumbling as loudly as his own.

"I think we need to eat," Mal said.

"Yeah, s'pose so."

"We could cook or go out, maybe somewhere different? We could go to Hereford, have a pint in the Spread Eagle? Or over to King's Norton to the Dog. I've never been there. My treat," he added.

"You could give me a treat right here."

Mal glanced down to see the expected leer but didn't feel Rob's heart was in it. "Later," he promised, "but for now shall we eat in or out?"

"Out." Rob sat up and stretched. "We need to blow the cobwebs away. But we're not going to the building site for *al fresco* nookie because it's freezing cold and blowing a gale and I like my nuts right where they are, thank you very much."

"God, no," Mal said. "It's not the night for it."

"Come on then," Rob offered a hand to pull him up. "I'll show you the sights on the road to King's Norton."

Mal only knew the countryside around Pemberland from a couple of excursions with Rob and from looking at maps in the museum files but he recognised the White Horse, knew that King's Norton was straight ahead and was surprised when Rob turned into Escley village.

"We're going the pretty way," Rob replied when he commented, and Mal had to admit that the village seemed very sweet. Neatly presented black and white houses lined the roadside leading to the solid bulk of a Norman church whose tower shouldered up against a sky bright with moonlight.

"Is this the family seat?" Mal asked, and was surprised by the wry twist to Rob's mouth.

"Not as such, no." Rob halted the car by a construction at the entrance to the church yard that was just a little too small to be called a lych gate.

"But there's a load of my family buried here. Loads. Grandmas and grandpas and one of my uncles, then others, back, way back and some with just stones because their bodies stayed out in Flanders and France. It's a nice place. The church door has got a – whaddaya call it – tin pan, with angels?"

"Tympanum?" Mal craned his neck. "Shall we go for a look?"

"No, save it for daylight," Rob suggested. "We could come on a nice day. There's an honest-to-God Olde Tea Shoppe." He pronounced all the Es with relish. "And they do a mean scone. With jam. But none of that clotted cream stuff because Cornwall has it copyrighted or something. Mrs Bray calls it virgin butter."

Mal snorted. "We just have to have some of that."

"You do. It's good. The Derrys make it." Rob started the engine again. "Just another mile or so." Out of the village, Rob turned off the B road onto a lane that snaked between high banks topped with hedges and stopped the car when they reached a wide gateway. Mal peered at the huge stone pillars and wrought iron gates of the type that normally graced stately homes. The modern black and white sign fastened to them looked out of place, and that it said 'Havard Plant Hire. No admittance without appointment' was a shock.

"Good grief. What's Glyn got in there? Chatsworth?" Mal asked.

"No, he rents the yard and buildings. Can you get the gate?" Rob asked, offering him a keyring. "It's the big brass one."

"You really are showing me the sights." Mal grinned as he got out of the car.

"You never know your luck," Rob said. "Just sneck the lock on the chain and push the gates to. Nobody'll come in while we're here."

The key turned easily in the outsized padlock and Mal swung the gates open enough for Rob's car to pass through. The wind was bitterly cold so he hurried back into the warmth of the car and looked around with interest as Rob drove into the site. There were enormous dumper trucks, two more JCBs, a low loader and no end of smaller vehicles. "This is a heck of a set up." Mal pointed at a truck with tires like a tractor. "Those can't come cheap."

"They don't. A full set's the best part of three months' wages for me." Rob parked beside the massive machine and got out of the car. "I got a surprise for you," he said.

"Oh yeah?" Mal grinned. "Does it involve virgin butter?"

"Jeez, Mal, have you got a one track mind or what?" Rob didn't look too disturbed about that. He slung an arm around Mal's neck and began to manhandle him across the rutted yard towards some buildings. "Sooner we get inside, in the warm, sooner you'll see."

The area was bounded on two sides by tall wire fences inside leggy hawthorn hedging and on another by a massive stone wall with a couple of lit windows, but Mal couldn't see how big it was due to the pack of machinery and the scatter of solidly constructed buildings. Some were little more than open fronted shelters designed to keep the rain off machines or materials, but the one to which Rob led Mal was substantially built from rendered breeze block painted white and had large wooden doors suspended from rails fixed to the side of the building. Rob unlocked another enormous padlock and slid the door open a foot, so they could get in then closed it again. Inside it was profoundly dark and Mal started as Rob touched his face.

"Hold still," Rob said and put his hand over Mal's eyes.

"Didn't know you were into this kind of thing," Mal muttered, and grinned as he heard a snort. There was a sharp click and Mal was aware that light leaked around Rob's fingers but all he could see, by squinting down, was his own nose.

"You'd be surprised what I'd do for the right man," Rob said. "Okay, forward a bit. Don't worry, I won't let you walk into anything."

"I'll trust you. Dozens wouldn't."

"I know. That's why we're here."

Mal felt his way forward, smelling cool dry air, a sharp not unpleasant smell that a moment's thought identified as raw cement and Rob's familiar combination of aftershave, sweat, and engine oil. It was a scent that he relished. Waking to a lungful of it on a cold morning was pretty damn good even if it was only on the pillow from the night before, because he knew that soon he'd have the real thing again.

"Okay," Rob said. "Er – not sure how you're going to feel about this."

He took his hand away just as a sudden awful sensation swept over Mal. He had a feeling he knew what he would see and kept his eyes closed, not wanting to open them because if he didn't he wouldn't have to deal with what would be a horrible situation.

"Mal?" Rob said. "Aww, Mal, please."

There was nothing for it. He couldn't just stand there.

"Oh, dear God."

There was a specially constructed pallet, well padded. There was the blocky squarish shape of the cist, the four slabs that had formed the lid rolled in protective foam, and the cist itself packed and braced to prevent collapse. There was the evidence that he had been deceived and lied to and taken for a fool. Abruptly, fear turned to anger.

"Why did you do this?" Mal asked. He tried to keep his tone even but even so his voice shook.

Rob looked as though he was going to be sick. "I couldn't let them be taken off to London, could I?"

"Yes," Mal snapped. "Yes, you could. Because there's a good chance we'd have been able to demand it back again. And to hide it here? In a fucking concrete store."

"S'not concrete, it's –"

"Have you any idea what the chemicals ... Jesus Christ, this is a priceless discovery. Just because it's not – not *treasure*, doesn't mean it's not precious. It needs handling with care. It needs controlled humidity. Bloody hell." Mal's voice rose to a yell. "You could have destroyed it."

"Well, I didn't." Rob put his arms around Mal's waist. "They are safe. The humidity in here is controlled – low but –"

"But you don't know what you're doing." Mal tried to shrug Rob off. "Too low is as bad as too high. I have to call the police, tell them – shit, I don't know. Tell them there's been a misunderstanding, or something. Christ, what a stupid thing to do."

"It was for you." Rob's voice had risen too, and he was still trying to keep his hold on Mal even as Mal struggled to get free. They lurched against one of the stacks of cement bags as Rob continued in a rapid babble. "Because I want you to have that great exhibition and put the museum back on its feet because that means you'll stay and maybe you'll stay with me. I care about you, see, and lying to you about this is just about killing me. That's no way to treat someone you love."

"No, it fucking isn't!" Mal bellowed and slammed both hands into Rob's chest, shoving him so hard he stumbled over the heap of bags and slithered to the ground in a billow of grey dust. "I've lived with that before. Not doing it again. I'm giving you twenty-four hours to get this sorted out or I go to the police."

"There's no need for that —" Rob's voice swooped high, panicky, but Mal spoke over him.

"You lied to me," he said. "I trusted you and you lied to me. No, just — no."

He turned and ran to the door, heaving it open, squeaking along the track then darted out into the shivering darkness. Behind him he heard Rob's shout, but he kept running.

Chapter 19

Mal woke slowly, blinking at the light in his eyes, then curled up with a groan as pain blossomed in his head.

"Oh God in Heaven," he groaned and turned away from the window. He ached all over, with sharper pains here and there, but the thump of a king-sized hangover was by far the worst thing. He did not want to move – but now he was awake, his bladder informed him, he better bloody well had.

Mal levered himself into a sitting position, letting his feet down to the carpet. There under his toes, were the pants and shirt he had worn last night. He was still wearing his socks and on one shin there was the lavender-stained egg of a sizeable bruise.

"How the heck did I do that?" he wondered, and got up to go to the bathroom.

Washing his face and cleaning his teeth made him feel fresher even if they did nothing to ease his throbbing head. He found clothing and went to the kitchen to make tea. There on the little table that he had shared with DI Cowper stood his bottle of Scotch, empty but for a scant inch. No wonder he felt so wretched. But then he did have reason. Just thinking about it turned his stomach.

He made toast and took it and the tea to the sofa and sat down to try and make sense of his life.

He supposed that he should have realised that Rob would have been involved in the robbery. Initially he had been misled by the damage to Rob's prized digger. But of course a really good driver could make it look a lot worse than it was. The damage on the site had been cosmetic too. Hardly anything had been destroyed and even Phil Rother had been inconvenienced in such a way that he would remain safe, if somewhat humiliated, rather than do something stupid like try to attack. Because Rob would have fought back, Mal knew, and what could have happened then didn't bear thinking about.

Rob was so passionate about everything. That was one of the things that had attracted Mal most – his zest and commitment and enjoyment, his insistence that whatever he was doing right at that moment was the most important thing in the world, whether it was taking a pool shot, arguing over the offside rule or making love to Mal. And – Mal took a moment to reflect – had Rob actually said something about loving him? He dredged back through the throbbing haze of his hangover to that horrible scene in the cement store. Yes, he thought he had. Mal put his elbows on his knees and rested his aching head in his hands. Rob had as good as admitted he loved him and all Mal had done was threaten to have him arrested. That was – actually, that was a really shit thing to have done.

Could Mal consider turning his boyfriend in to the police? What Rob had done was completely illegal. For Mal to keep the location of the cist a secret was unethical, and as a responsible museum curator and archaeologist committed to preserving the history of the land he had no choice but to get on the phone to the police and let them know what he had found out.

"And then ring the museum and hand in my notice," he muttered, "because I couldn't stay here. Not after that. I couldn't walk down the street and look Sion and Gary in the eye if I'd put Rob in jail."

The ringing of his phone made him jump, and he got up with a groan and hobbled to the table where it was charging. "Hallo," he muttered and winced as Harvey yelped a greeting. "Hold it down, there's a love," he said. "I've got a hell of a head this morning."

"That's unlike you, Mal, especially on a week day." Harvey sounded annoyingly cheerful. "But I have some good news that should bring a smile to your face."

"Okay," Mal tried to put a smile in his voice. "What's that then?"

"I've spoken to Collins. Culmstock's ultimate superior at the British Museum? He assures me that Culmstock's been given a reprimand and told not to interfere when small museums ask for help. That is, just because a small museum requests advice it doesn't give him the right to run up the Jolly Roger and sail in to help himself. As far as they are concerned, the find is ours and they are pleased to have been able to offer his expertise – free of charge, I might add. I suspect that word got out about his activities and they are scared that the little local institutions won't 'fess up to any future finds, and the dear old BM does like to have its finger on the pulse. Also, he said that if the cist turns up could they maybe borrow it at some time if they are doing a suitable special? I said they'd need to consult you. So – er – your plans can go ahead … Mal? Are you still there?"

"Yes. That's grand news, Harvey. I'm so glad we won't be getting an invoice." Mal took a deep breath and made what he hoped wouldn't be the worst decision of his career. "As for the exhibition, I have no idea whether I'll be able to stage it. The expense – well, it would have been justified with the whole burial. As it is we have nothing particularly special and it doesn't seem worth it."

"Not worth it?" Harvey's voice had dropped. "Oh dear, you really are off colour, aren't you. So – er – there's been no news then?"

"No," Mal said. "It's probably out of the country by now."

"But you've got the rest of the finds. The swords and axe. Those amazing flints. The beakers. The jet and bone and amber beads?"

Mal scowled at the blank, black screen of his TV. "Yes, I suppose so. Look, I have to get ready for work. Have fun on set."

"All right, though filming on a site in Northumbria with this weather forecast is unlikely to be fun for anyone. Take care, Mal, and I hope you feel better soon. Ask Rob to fetch you some aspirin or something."

"I don't need Rob to fetch me anything," Mal snapped. "I've got to go now. Take care."

He cut Harvey off, tossed the phone onto the table and stared at the bruise on his shin. "How the fuck did I get into this situation?" he asked, then got up and limped off for a shower.

Work was horrible. All day long Mal twitched every time the phone rang, anticipating a call from the police to say that the cist had been turned in, or that arrests were being made. The hangover of the morning had developed into a full body ache with a churning stomach and a tightness in his chest that made him wonder if the virus that had laid Harvey low was paying him a visit. As each call proved to be just sales pitches for double glazing or racking, or demands for news from the press, Mal's tension rose.

At three o'clock he finally snapped. Marcia Stenhouse had come up to his office to complain about bad parking in the car park. After suggesting that perhaps he should do something to ensure it never happened again, she said, "After all, now all that business with the building site is over, it's not as though you're busy."

Mal sighed and got up from his chair. He reached for his coat and said, "Mrs Stenhouse, if you want your many patrons to park more sensibly why don't you get one of your many members of staff to go out there and tell them? Better still, do it yourself. If you have time to come up here and nag me for twenty minutes, you have time to go be a parking attendant. But I am going home."

"Well, really," Marcia said and swept regally back to her own domain.

He dropped into Tesco on his way home and bought a basket full of perishables plus some aspirin, then hurried back through the gathering darkness and let himself into his flat.

Work would take his mind off his troubles. He turned off his mobile phone, turned on his laptop and began to go through those emails he hadn't yet addressed.

He worked until six, then knocked off for half an hour to warm some soup and rolls for supper. He still felt fragile, not being a heavy drinker normally, and a large meal was out of the question, but chicken noodle soup was the mainstay of sick days of his childhood and soft white rolls with real butter would fill the crevices. Not quite as well as one of the Sergeant Major's kormas, perhaps, but that Rob had poured out his heart to his friends at the Coach seemed very likely and Mal just didn't want to have to deal with them.

Mal's self-pity soared to new heights as he contemplated the loss of that treat. It was healthier, he felt, to concentrate on the shallow material things. There were other losses – love and trust for instance – that were too great to bear.

He had just finished his soup and was contemplating the choice of an early night – a good idea because he had started to type rubbish – or to stop work and watch something loud and violent with a lot of guns and explosions when the door buzzer sounded its broken wheezy hiccup. Mal looked at his watch; 7 p.m. which meant that the twenty-four hours he had given Rob were just about up. The buzzer sounded again. Mal hurried down the stairs hoping to see PC Farriner. DI Cowper's calm regard made Mal feel far too guilty.

"Sorry to keep you waiting," he said as he opened the door, then stopped, confused to see the very last people he might have expected.

"Mr Bright." Leo Farriner looked as though he had just come out of court, his hair swept back neatly from his high forehead, his white shirt collar as pristine and crisp as Mal expected it had been first thing that morning. His suit, under a heavy cashmere overcoat, was perfectly pressed. "Good evening, I hope you will forgive us for intruding but when we saw your light on … I believe you have met Mrs Gaskell."

"I – er – only once," Mal said. "I – um – please come in. I'm afraid I'm not really geared up for visitors but you're most welcome. Upstairs and through the door to the right."

Mrs Gaskell gave him a small smile and slipped past in a waft of Opium. Leo followed in his own cloud of cool yet spicy scent. Mal suspected they both smelled a hundred times better than he did.

In the flat he took their coats, hanging them on the hooks nailed to the back of the door, hastily moved his laptop from the couch to the table, and suggested they took a seat. He turned one of the hard chairs from the little kitchen table and sat down, resting his elbows on his knees.

Vanessa Gaskell was looking about with more interest than the condescension he had expected. "I always wondered what was up here," she said. Mal had expected the rounded vowels of elocution lessons but her quiet voice lilted and hummed with the local accent. "I knew there was a flat. I used to try to imagine what it would be like to have a little place all of my own. I love your fireplace."

"Thank you," Mal said. "It's not particularly grand but I'll improve it, given some time."

She nodded and bit her lip, apparently at a loss for words. Mal took in the flawless skin, glossy blonde mane and perfect symmetrical features and wondered suddenly if, despite appearances – those boots had to have cost more than his sofa – maybe she was just a small town girl blessed with extraordinary beauty and used to being judged on that and not on anything else. She seemed shy and maybe a little apprehensive.

She looked sidelong at Leo Farriner and he gave a small, reassuring smile and said, "It's getting late and we don't want to keep Mr Bright from his – um – work. Shall I fill him in on the details?"

"Oh, please do," she said, and leaned back against the scruffy IKEA upholstery.

"Well." Leo squared his glasses on the bridge of his nose and sat a little straighter. He levelled his calm intelligent gaze on Mal in a way that made

Mal sit up straight too. "We are all aware of the situation regarding the High Rifles Lane development and the archaeological find up at the top of the site close to the road. However, while it is generally believed that the land is the property of Gaskell Developments, such is not the case, and therefore Mr Gaskell had no right to agree to the removal of items from the site or to allow them to be taken to London. In short, the land belongs –"

"To me." Vanessa nodded. "He put it in my name for – I don't know, some kind of tax reasons I think. But anyhow, it's my land, so anything found on it belongs to me and I did not agree that anything from the site could be moved out of town."

"I see." Mal didn't really but his heart had begun to thump a little harder. Could it really be as easy as this? Was Vanessa Gaskell the least likely *Deus ex machina* ever? "So what would you want me to do? The cist has disappeared –"

"No, it hasn't," Vanessa said. "As of two o'clock this afternoon it was still safe as houses in Glyn Havard's concrete store, where I told him to put it."

"What?" Mal stared at her. "You … what? You knew where it was all the time? And have you informed the police of this?"

"We have." Leo took an envelope from his inside pocket and presented it to Mal. "Here are copies of a letter sent to the British Museum in which Mrs Gaskell has expressed her extreme displeasure in the way Mr Culmstock swept in and attempted to appropriate the finds illegally, and her desire that everything discovered on her land should remain at the Town Museum for the benefit of the people of Pemberland. This includes the cist and the bones, and all other finds, also the archival material assembled during the excavation. There's also a copy of a letter to the police laying out the situation and how it arose, apologising for the confusion, and offering to pay any fines accrued should charges be made for wasting police time."

Mal took the envelope but didn't open it. He was lost for words.

Vanessa Gaskell eyed him, her pretty face concerned, as though she suspected he might shout at her, or burst into tears. Mal himself wasn't sure which was more likely. When he neither spoke nor opened the envelope, she glanced at Leo and took up the tale. "I was so shocked. I was away, see, on a spa break with some friends, when Terry rang me to tell me what was going on. So I called Leo to check what my rights were, then called my PA and told her what to write in the letters to Culmstock and the museum. The silly girl was supposed to sign 'em *per pro* and send 'em straight off, but she hung onto them for me to sign when I got back. I gave her a right bollocking when I saw them in my in-tray this morning. I'm really terribly sorry, Mr Bright."

"I … I understand." Mal ran his finger under the unsealed flap and took out the papers. "I can see how that would happen. I don't really understand why they staged a theft, though."

"I think I can help there." Leo smiled, wryly. "The nature of the burial has been a topic of conversation, as I'm sure you can imagine. I believe that on a Friday a couple of weeks ago at the White Horse there was a purely theoretical discussion of the best way to steal something that large using the resources available. When it seemed as though the removal to London was going ahead I understand that Terry organised the – er – rescue of the cist almost at the last minute."

"I don't know what to say," Mal shook his head. "So all this is because some letters weren't posted."

"They should have been sent first thing Tuesday last week." Vanessa leaned across and touched her French manicured fingers to Mal's knee. "The museum might not have been able to do anything to stop Mr Culmstock, but the police would and then Terry and the boys wouldn't have had to do what they did. I'm really so sorry.

"There's a letter in there for you too," Vanessa added. "About your exhibition. And I expect you to treat them kindly. Because those two poor men belong here and nowhere else."

Chapter 20

The visit of Vanessa Gaskell and Leo Farriner gave Mal another bad night. That the situation had been at least partially resolved – assuming the police didn't press charges – was a relief, but that didn't take away the hurt and anger at how he had been made to look foolish. If Rob, Vanessa, Leo, and Terry had known, then surely others must have too. Mal could just imagine their derision at his distress then their annoyance at what they surely must see as lack of gratitude. But how could he feel grateful when what they had done had been without the careful control provided by experts and had put his professional reputation in jeopardy? Then there was Rob, so sure that what he had done was right and that Mal could be conveniently side-lined until he needed to know. That had been Oliver's standard MO. Mal cringed at the memory of a time when he had caught a reference to Oliver making some kind of exciting trip, obviously long in the planning, and Oliver had smiled and said 'I'm sure I told you, babe, but you probably had your nose in a book'. But Rob had been so upfront about everything else. Frank and straightforward, he'd told it like it was. Mal couldn't believe that Rob had taken him in like that.

The thoughts chased themselves around in his mind until the church clock struck midnight. Mal must have dozed off because he awoke with a start at around 3 a.m. He was shivering, cold to the bone, with a pounding head, but when he got up to fetch extra blankets and caught a glimpse of himself in the bathroom mirror he realised his face was flushed and his eyes glassy. He took aspirin and curled up to try to sleep it off.

No such luck. He tossed and turned until seven then got up and went to take another aspirin. Mal had always hated being ill. It always brought out his inner four-year-old and he wanted nothing more than for his mum to come into the room, clucking and maternal, and take control of his life. It had happened, he was sure, maybe when he'd had chicken pox when he was six. He wanted what he'd had then – cool wet flannels for his forehead, orange juice in a sippy cup, a cartoon on TV and warm blankets tucked tenderly around him. Instead he had a Tetrapak of cranberry juice, undrunk because he didn't much like it, and a quarterly budget report to write. But first he had to call in to work.

"Oh Mal, I'm so sorry." Sharon's quiet voice was so soothing. "You take care of yourself. Don't worry about anything apart from getting better."

"Thank you, both of you. Tell Betty I said 'hi'." He grinned as he heard a muffled 'Hi' in response. "And if someone really needs to get hold of me, give them my mobile number."

"Only in emergencies," Sharon said, then chuckled. "At least you don't have to worry about the local press bothering you. This horrible bug has gone through the Free Press offices and they are all laid up, too. Do you need anything?" Mal heard a rustle and could imagine Sharon with her pen in hand poised to make a shopping list. "I can pick up some stuff at lunchtime."

"I'm fine," Mal said. "But thanks for the offer. That's very kind."

By eleven he was halfway through both the report and the cranberry juice. He squinted at the screen, head thumping. Typos, bad grammar and unnecessary repetition. Okay he wasn't writing War and Peace but he should at least look as though he'd tried. He saved the document and went to the Museums Association website to see what was going on in his small academic world, but that soon palled and he found his cursor hovering over the Jobs tab. It would be a pity to move on. He was sure that he could do some great things with the museum, and the history of the area was fascinating, but he wasn't sure it would be fun staying. Not any more.

On the other hand that could just be the illness talking. Mal put his laptop aside and scowled at the ceiling. He really didn't want to think about Rob right now, but he kept coming to mind. The desolate look on his face when Mal had pushed him away. His earnest belief that he had done exactly the right thing and that if only Mal gave it some thought Mal would realise he had as well.

Had he?

No, obviously not. Theft, vandalism, and shutting Phil Rother in the Portaloo could not be condoned no matter how irritating the man was. No matter how good the intention had been, what Rob had done was wrong and Mal had been right to let him know. Perhaps pushing him so hard had been a mistake, but he definitely couldn't give in to the kind of loving coercion Rob had been about to apply. No, it was for the best. The carefully-wrapped cist would be discovered, and perhaps the whole sorry business could be swept under the carpet of short memory?

And that exhibition could be such a good one. He had it all in his mind's eye, with the cist set into a ramped plinth so visitors could look down into it and all around the interpretation of the rich lives of the Early Peoples, from the first tiny Mesolithic flints to the layouts of the massive hill forts of the Iron Age. The text, of course, would be informative but not too wordy and he'd have to source some really good illustrations. In fact the whole museum could do with a facelift, from the stores to the museum gardens. Just a few quid out of petty cash for bedding plants would make a world of difference to first impressions.

He must have drifted off then into a happy dream where he was discussing whether to plant petunias or lobelia with someone who he desired very much who smelled of soap and engine oil and beer and …

"Rob?" Mal blinked blearily and sat up. The door buzzer hiccupped again. Mal groaned, got out of bed and pulled on a dressing gown to go and let his visitor in.

"Oh bloody hell, don't you look a wreck." Betty pushed past him with no further greeting and scampered upstairs to his flat. "Come on, you. Back to bed. Sharon and I talked it over and I drew the short straw. I've been shopping and I'll leave the receipt by your kettle. You can settle up with me when you're back on your feet. Jeez, the things I do for my job. Mal, didn't you hear? Go back to bed, you twat."

"Hello, Betty," Mal said, and did as he was told.

Twenty minutes later he was regretting ever moaning about wanting his Mum. Betty was no substitute for the soft-handed angel of his daydreams. Brusquely, she reorganised his room, opening the window to let an excruciating blast of cold air waft through the place because, she said, "It smells like something died in here." Her pillow plumping was achieved with sharp angry punches and she banged a bottle of Lucozade down on his bedside table with enough force to make it impossible to open unless he wanted his ceiling to be dripping.

It took Mal a while to work up the courage to speak to her. "Um, Betty, it's not that I don't appreciate you coming but you don't seem to be very happy."

"Of course I'm not happy." Betty put her hands on her hips and glared at him. "First off, you went to Sharon to whine about being ill. Just because she's all cuddly and mumsy and shit doesn't mean that I'm not perfectly capable of giving you comfort, *capisce*? Secondly, I've had to rush over here in my lunch hour in the rain and Marcia was giving us both a hard time and Sharon doesn't really want to be left on her own in the museum with her. Fuck sake, she's a grown up, she could just tell Marcia to piss off like I do, but no, she's scared of losing her job and doesn't seem to think that you've got our backs even when lolling there on your bed of pain – which I think you have, really, in your own wussy way, and – and – where was I? Yeah, thirdly, or was it fourthly, what have you done to Rob, you wanker?"

"What do you mean, what have I done to Rob?" Mal had been expecting Rob to be mentioned but had assumed something a bit more specific. "I haven't done anything to Rob. I haven't seen him."

"You haven't?" Betty's eyebrows rose. "After several weeks of being joined at the hip, you haven't seen him. That could explain why he had a face like a bulldog licking piss off a thistle in the pub last night, while I understand you've been wandering around in a daze being unprofessionally forthright about parking problems? And now, boo hoo, you've taken to your bed."

"I'm fucking ill." Mal hadn't meant for his voice to rise but it did and his voice caught and he dissolved in a bout of painful coughing. Betty reached for the still too lively Lucozade, swore and made him a Lemsip instead.

"There you go, though I don't know why I bother. You were the best thing that's ever happened to Rob, you know. Jeez, he's had some rough years but … well, I guess it might be for the best."

"Shall we agree not to interfere in each other's love lives?" Mal suggested once he could speak again. "Otherwise I could make some comments about how friendly you seem to be getting with Gary."

"Hey, lay off Gary," Betty raised a warning finger. "Gary might not be the sharpest knife in the drawer, though I reckon he might surprise us all yet, but he is good at one particular thing and that's making me happy. Who do you make happy, Mal? Give that some thought, all right. Oh, who's that now?"

"Thank God." Mal's phone was vibrating on top of the dresser, where he had left it charging. At that moment anyone would have been preferable to talk to, so he threw back the covers to lunge for it. But Betty glared at him, grabbed it, and answered.

"Malcolm Bright's phone? Who's this? I asked first! Ohhhh!" She turned interested eyes to Mal. "Zoë, Mal's sister. My name's Betty. Yes, that Betty. How lovely to speak to you. Yes, I'm looking at him now. He's poorly bad, poor dab, and I popped round in my lunch hour to make sure he was still alive. Yes, he looks awful and his temper's worse. Well, if you're sure? I have to be getting – oh shit, is that the time?"

Betty tossed the phone into Mal's hands, hurried out of his bedroom shouting a promise to visit again.

"Bye, Betty," Mal croaked, before putting the phone to his ear. "Zoë?"

"Oh dear Lord, you sound awful! You poor thing. Now that's enough sympathy. What on earth have you been doing to upset your staff?"

"Me upsetting the staff? What about my staff upsetting me? And that wasn't nearly enough sympathy. Zo – I feel dreadful. And I've done something really stupid."

"Again?"

In the background of Zoë's voice Mal could make out the sound of voices and cutlery echoing in a large room so he guessed she was in the hospital canteen. "Yes, again. Look, have you got time to chat?"

"Always for you, bro'. Though I have to be back on the ward at two fifteen. What have you done?"

Mal took a deep breath and said, "I broke up with Rob," then jerked his phone away from his ear as she shrieked, "You did what?"

"I had reason, at the time. I thought. Now I'm not so sure."

"Well, tell Zoë all about it," she said. "You've got ten minutes!"

Talking to Zoë took up the last of Mal's energy so for the rest of the day he alternated between napping and browsing the net. He took one look at his email inbox and decided that since he was ill he'd let himself off going through it, and felt better for allowing himself that indulgence. It was probably for the best, he thought, remembering horror stories about people not at their best accidentally sending the wrong messages to the wrong people. The way he was feeling that moment, he could imagine himself sending a hopeful dick pic to the county council hub or something equally unfortunate. Not that he had any dick pics. He considered that a great misfortune and had actually uncovered and begun to angle the web cam of his laptop before it occurred to him that his high temperature might be clouding his judgement.

"Sorry, pal," he told his dick, "now is not the time for a close-up. And anyhow, who would I send it to?"

That was such a miserable thought he closed the laptop and curled up with a whimper. He'd had weeks and weeks when he could have sent Rob a dick pic and been pretty sure it would have been well received. But now, for the first time since coming to Pemberland, he felt truly lonely.

Zoë had been a bit more sympathetic than Betty but not much. "You were sickeningly sweet together," she had said. "And I really think you should try to make it up with him."

Mal agreed, but right at that moment his thoughts were too fuzzy to figure out how. And he wanted Rob so much, just to see him and make sure he was all right, and to apologise, abjectly if necessarily. Twice he picked up his phone and began to pick out a message but the words wouldn't come. So he set it aside and concentrated on trying to get better.

At half past six, Sharon let herself into his flat bringing with her a large bowl of chicken casserole and all the sympathy he could wish for.

"It's cut up small so shouldn't hurt your poor throat too much." She smiled at him. "Betty was going to bring you a pizza."

Mal shuddered. "No, thank you, Sharon, this is much better." It looked grand and Mal was fairly certain it would smell good too, if he had been able to smell anything at all. "Thanks for going to all this trouble."

"No trouble. I have a freezer full of the stuff. Batch cooking is such a comfort when you don't have much else to do. Betty asked me to make her apologies. Gary rang and offered to take her to the cinema, her choice, even those chick flicks, she said. I think it must be love."

Mal snorted. "Yeah, first time I saw him he couldn't keep his eyes off her."

"I don't see the appeal of him myself, though I've heard he's a kind lad," Sharon said, "and I'm convinced that at least part of the allure is Morris, but it's good to see her with someone who has the same amount of energy."

"They are amazing, aren't they? People like that, I mean. Harvey's like that once he's interested in a project. He'll move heaven and earth to bring it round to what he wants to happen."

Sharon nodded, looking a little wistful. "He's a kind man too. Very good with Katie. It really was a pleasure having him to stay those few days.

Now, eat your casserole. If you can't manage all of it, I'll fridge it and you can have more later."

"It's brilliant, honestly." Mal ate a few mouthfuls, taking his time and Sharon leaned back against the foot of the bed, leafing through one of his text books. Once Mal had eaten as much as he could manage he put the bowl and spoon on the side table and gave her a tired smile.

"Sharon, Betty said something that bothered me a bit, earlier. About Mrs Stenhouse giving you both a hard time? You know, if she does something you don't like you can come straight to me?"

Sharon picked at the fringe of the coverlet. "I know that, but – well, it's just Marcia's way. She'd only just come to terms with the move into the museum building when the previous curator retired and she was left to mind the whole building. So, part of it is habit, from being our boss, even if it was only nominally, and part is not wanting to give up too much control to you. When the library moved in, it was chaos for months while they sorted everything out. Now they aren't as busy, she still comes to us with the practical jobs we used to do just to help out. It's just her manner that's difficult and that's very hard to pin down as being actually offensive. It's in tone and body language and the look in her eye."

"A sort of 'you had to be there' situation?"

"Yes, exactly. She's so tall and slim and beautifully dressed and her hair is always perfect, so when she steams up to the desk to demand that I stop doing what I'm doing to run an errand for her it can't help but come over as condescending, especially when she really shouldn't be asking me anyway."

"Certainly not, if it means you leaving the desk while the museum is open." Mal frowned for a moment, then said, "Next time she does it ask her to hang on a moment and ring for me. I'll come straight down and deal with her myself. As you said – when was it? I feel as though I've been stuck in here forever – she's probably going to need a couple of reminders to pack it in before she does. And if I'm not there," he added quickly, "call for Betty. Between the two of you, you can pour on the pathos and tell her that your horrible boss won't allow it. Get some female solidarity going there. I don't mind being the villain in a good cause."

"You a villain?" Sharon giggled. "Mal, you really don't look the type."

"There's lots of different types of villain. They aren't all muscles and attitude. How about I get a white cat, one of those really hairy ones, and a Nehru jacket and cultivate an aloof expression?" He picked up a pillow and caressed it while fixing her with a heavy-lidded eye. "Minions, prepare the piranha tank!"

"Absolutely chilling," Sharon said, and picked up his bowl. "Ice cream for pudding, if you feel up to it."

Mal did and, after she had gone, watched a few episodes of a crime drama on Netflix, then had another Lemsip and went to sleep.

On Wednesday he felt so much better. His temperature had broken during the night, leaving him soaked with sweat but without that awful fuzzy shivery feeling. He got up, had a much needed shower, dressed properly, and relocated to the kitchen table for breakfast.

The museum would be opening soon and Mal imagined his quiet but chaotic office and the mail that was surely piling up. "Shall I go to work today?" he asked himself because while he still felt dire, he supposed he really should.

The answer came almost immediately in the form of a phone call.

"Mr Bright?"

Marcia Stenhouse's voice had been the last he had been expecting. "Oh hello, Marcia, what can I do for you?"

"Nothing at all," she said. "I am standing here with your custodial staff and they are making bets that you will try to return to work today. Now I haven't seen you myself but I am assured that you look like – what was it, Betty? – death warmed up. If that is the case, I would prefer you to stay away. None of us want to catch what you've got *and* we have vulnerable customers to consider."

"Er – no, quite." Mal couldn't help grinning as he felt a lightening of spirits. 'Should' go to work didn't mean that one was fit to go.

"Do you need anything?" Marcia added. "Are you registered with a doctor yet?"

"I – no – I'm not, but honestly, Marcia, I am feeling much better today."

"Well, see that you take care of yourself, and if you do need anything feel free to call. Someone can bring round a box and leave it at the foot of your stairs."

In the background Mal heard Betty snort and say "He's got man-flu, not the plague," and he chuckled and said, "That's a very kind offer. Much appreciated. I'll work from home today."

"If you feel well enough." Marcia cleared her throat. "And don't overdo it. We – umm – have got used to you being about the place but there's no need to hurry back on our account."

"Of course not." Mal said, and made a request to talk to Betty or Sharon.

"But they both have work to be getting on with, Mr Bright," Marcia said. "Good morning."

By lunchtime his private inbox was clear and the work one down to a few links to professional journals, so he spent a satisfying half hour going through what he could remember of the Early Peoples collection. The goal was to design an exhibition that would please all ages and levels of knowledge. Impossible, but with hard work and a bit of luck he could come close.

At half past one he made himself tea, using the last of the milk, and ate the rest of Sharon's casserole. While he let his lunch go down, he picked up his phone to address the problem that had been lurking in the back of his mind all morning. The Rob Problem. He looked at the texts he had started the day before and had abandoned, thanking God that he'd been sensible enough to do so. One sounded whining, the other both whining and needy. Rob was a grown up and so was Mal. Surely it would be better if they communicated like adults?

He turned over various wordings in his mind then settled for, "I'm sorry. I over-reacted. Please can we talk?" and sent it before he could change his mind.

Ten minutes passed. Fifteen. At two o'clock Mal sighed and stopped checking his phone. Rob was probably on site, unable to hear over the roaring of engines. He'd pick up his messages later. Mal would put off worrying until – he checked his watch – eight o'clock. Meantime he had a more minor crisis to deal with in that he had run out of Lucozade and his Lemsip supply was critical too.

Having the kind of morality that dictated that, while off sick, he shouldn't really leave the house or do anything that might be construed as enjoyable, Mal felt very guilty as he pulled on his coat and hat. He squinted at himself in the mirror. Yes, he still looked sick, pasty faced, red nosed, a bit glassy eyed, just horrible really. That would do. If anyone criticised he'd just breathe on them.

Chapter 21

Mal wrapped up well, found his wallet and phone – because Rob might conceivably pick up his messages if he had a tea break – and picked up a tote bag for his shopping. Then he let himself out of the flat and shuffled along to Tesco.

In the past few days it was clear that autumn had given way to winter. There was a vicious bite in the air and a hint of sleet on the wind that ruffled the tinsel on the decorations strung across the road. Christmas was just around the corner as far as Pemberland's retail establishments were concerned. He guessed he ought to think about presents, especially with regard to mailing them early to his parents. Zoë was easy – she had an extensive Amazon wish list – but he should try to think of something special for Harvey and there was Sharon and Betty and the weekend girls. He remembered how, a few weeks ago, he had sounded Rob out gently about what he might like for Christmas. The holiday had seemed a much more attractive prospect when he'd had Rob's company to look forward to.

In Tesco everything was red and white and unbearably jolly. Mal wandered round in a bit of a daze, quite enjoying the purposeful bustle of the other shoppers and adding items to his basket more on the principle of what he fancied than how useful they would be. That was the only upside of being ill. Normal healthy dietary considerations could go out of the window in favour of eating things that made him cheerful. He was in the frozen food department considering whether to buy a chicken korma or a beef lasagne for supper, when he was startled at the pressure of a hand landing on his shoulder.

"'Lo there, Mal. You feelin' better?" Gary, up in his personal space, seemed even bigger than usual.

"Hello, Gary. Back on my feet, but still not too good. Er, don't mean to be alarmist but hadn't you better step back. I wouldn't want you to catch this."

"Naaah, I don't get colds," Gary said. "Else I'd'a had it. Half the security guys have got it and so have most of my dad's boys."

"Really? Is it holding up your work?"

"Not mine so much. We're doing extra shifts to cover." Gary grinned. "I'll be able to afford a fortnight somewhere warm in January at this rate. But Dad's lost a few days. It's not safe to run a big site with too few men. Especially with some of the team leaders off. Silly buggers try to do too much too fast and that's when accidents happen. Rob's –"

"Rob's had an accident?" Mal was aware that his already husky voice had broken.

"No." Gary raised his eyebrows. "Not that I heard of, anyhow. He's been really sick. Probably got what you've got."

Mal grimaced, remembering the heat of Rob's kiss and the fevered look in his eyes. "Ah, sorry to hear that," he said. "Is he, um – on the mend?"

"Yeah, he's staying at mine. His dad's a useless fucker and his mam can't cope with 'em both so I went and got him. Mam's looking after him. Hey, but, what's happened between you two?"

"Happened?" Mal felt he was getting a little better at casual.

"Yeah, he's been miserable as fuck even without the flu." Gary frowned, glanced around and moved even closer. "Everything else is okay, but I noticed you haven't been about much and Betty's all tight lipped. You haven't stopped seeing each other or something, have you?"

Mal looked at Gary's collarbones, which were level with his eyes, and tried to get his head round the idea that this immense, intimidating, and very straight man was trying to facilitate his gay best friend's love life. It was one of the sweetest things he'd ever seen.

"We had a disagreement," Mal admitted. "Over something quite important too. I'm not happy about it either, Gary, but – well, it was a trust issue. I'm sorry."

"Trust?" Gary began to shake his head. "No, nuh-huh, Rob don't play around. Might flirt a bit, you know what he's like, but I'd never seen him as into someone as he was into you. And now he's absolutely miserable. I dunno what you said to him but that's not like Rob."

"I'm sorry," Mal said again. He hesitated, unsure how much to confide in Gary. "Let's just say it wasn't about our relationship. It was about something else. An ethical matter."

Gary stared at him. "Ethics. What the fuck have ethics got to do with who you love?"

"Could you love someone who didn't like Morris?" Mal asked.

"Oh? … Oh, yeah, right, I understand. Good job I got someone who thinks he's wonderful then. But hey, if you don't like dogs you wouldn't have to do anything with Flash. He doesn't bother with anyone apart from Rob's dad."

"Flash?"

Gary grinned at Mal. "The Escley family dog, duh? Hey, I got to go get ready to meet Betty from work. Bye, Mal."

Gary hurried to the checkout and Mal continued his shopping, part amused by Gary's misapprehension and part interested. So Rob had a dog that would only bother with Rob's dad. Mal had never had a pet. As a child it had been impossible because Dad was allergic, and ever since leaving home he had lived in rented accommodation with strict 'no animals' rules. He imagined himself living with a dog as big as Morris, then hastily downsized it to something more manageable. A Jack Russell maybe? Or a cat? Cats were easier, weren't they? Aloof and self-contained? Or maybe a goldfish?

Mal paid for his shopping, adding a little Christmas cactus to his basket as an impulse buy at the last moment. It had occurred to him that perhaps it would be a good idea to practice looking after something non-sentient before he committed to caring for an animal.

"You won't be much company," he told it as he stepped out of Tesco and headed for home, "but we'll see how we do. Who knows? This could be the beginning of a lovely friendship."

A stifled sound behind him drew his attention to two small girls in hats and mittens, one set pink and the other a strident purple, wearing matching navy blue anoraks. They were very small, carrying dinky little pink rucksacks, and scarlet in the face with trying to hold in their giggles. Mal blushed too, aware that he had been caught out talking to a small plant.

"Ladies," he said, and drew aside a little to let them pass.

"See, I told you," the one in purple muttered. "Ever so posh. Dad says he's giving Uncle Rob one."

"One what?" asked the other.

Mal stared at them, mortified, as a lorry rumbled past, drowning the reply. Rob's nieces – he couldn't recall their names – but surely they were no more than six? He looked over his shoulder, wondering where their mother might be, or Kevin. Surely someone should be with them?

He fell in behind them, trying not to walk so close that he scared them but close enough to be available should he be needed. Cactus in one hand and bag in the other, he followed them along the road and picked up that the purple one hated broccoli and would be sick if anyone offered it to her. The pink one said she felt the same. Then the purple one said she hated carrots and would be sick. She sounded as though she was looking forward to it. Mal wondered how far they intended to walk because the spit of sleet had steadied into a down pour. Almost immediately the answer came as the pink one sighed and said, "Are you sure we can walk to Brynglas? It's ever such a long way. Can't we go see Uncle Terry instead?"

"Uncle Terry makes us do our reading," the purple one said in tones of utter contempt.

Uncle Terry. The only Terry Mal knew was the benign mountain of a man in the barbers' shop. "Excuse me," he said.

The purple one glared at him. "We're not allowed to speak to strangers. Not even if you've got sweeties."

"Or puppies," added the other. "Especially puppies."

"I haven't got either," Mal said.

"Well bug'roff then," the purple one said.

"All right. It's a pity, though, because I've been sick too and I'm not sure I can cross the road to where your Uncle Terry works on my own." Mal coughed pathetically into the cactus. "That's a long way."

"No it isn't!" they chorused, and Mal walked the rest of the way home with a child each side, to show him how to use the pelican crossing and to make sure he didn't get lost. The child in the pink hat, who seemed a lot quieter than the other, had taken the cactus from him and was carrying it while the other held his hand. When they reached the hair dressers they insisted he come right in.

"Mal?" Lillian paused in blow-drying a lady who fixed Mal with a suspicious stare. "Paige, Kimberley, what are you doing with Mr Bright?"

"He was lost." Paige rolled her eyes. "So we brought him home. He di'nt know how to work the crossing either."

There were three ladies in the process of having their hair done and they all exchanged glances and said, "Awww, the little dear." Mal wasn't sure whether they were talking to him or the child. Terry had no doubt.

He came running in response to Lillian's yell and stooped to take the dripping hats, mittens and coats from the girls.

"What are you doing here? It's not Thursday," he said. "Mal, just give me five, 'kay?"

Mal waited on the doormat while the girls were settled in the waiting area with their homework and a biscuit each, then he followed Terry back into the barbers.

"What the fuck?" Terry asked. "Where did you find them this time?"

"This time? They were outside Tesco and said something that made me think they might be your nieces, and something about walking to Brynglas. I thought it would be better to bring them here."

"Jesus Christ –" Terry began then added, "Oh no, Mal, I'm not angry with you. Thanks so much for having the common sense to bring them here. No, but I'll swing for that Kevin Escley. He knows bloody well it's his turn to collect them from school on a Wednesday."

"Maybe he's been held up?" Mal asked.

"I'm going to find out now." Terry took a phone from his pocket and pressed a couple of buttons then put it to his ear. A moment later he said, "Yeah, of course it's me. Had you forgotten it's Wednesday, you clown?" The phone squawked and Terry's scowl grew darker. "Yes – yes, they are, no thanks to you. Where are you? You're where? Oh Jeez, don't bother. I'll call Julie. She can pick them up when she finishes work. Yes, of course I'm going to tell her. Yeah, you just do that." He finished the call with a stab of his forefinger. "Wanker's in Leominster. Says he forgot what day it was. The apple didn't fall far from the tree with that one. Um, sorry. I'm talking about Rob's brother."

"We've met." Mal grimaced. "A bit of a different approach to Rob."

"Yeah, not half." Terry was texting, big thumb moving without hesitation. "You sound like you've got what Rob's got."

"Yes, and I don't want to spread it around so I'd best get home," Mal said.

"Hazards of being in a relationship, I guess." Terry sounded a bit wistful. "Right, that's Julie informed. She'll go spare. That's the third time in the past two months. Thanks, Mal. You're a lifesaver. I'd give you a hug, but I'll let Rob do that."

"Er …" Mal felt his cheeks heat again. Terry had tilted his head and was leaning slightly towards him. For a moment Mal contemplated spilling out all his worries, his regret that he had ruined something that could have been so good, and just how much it hurt to know that he had hurt Rob – but Terry had problems of his own, sitting in reception complaining about having to do sums. "I'd best get home."

"Oh? Okay, then." Terry escorted him past the interested customers to the door. "You're looking a bit shaggy round the ears, boy."

"I'll make an appointment," Mal promised, "but not until I've stopped coughing."

"Yeah, that'd be good. You take care now." As the door closed behind Mal he heard Terry's voice rise. "Right, you two, what did I say about walking home on your own?"

By Friday Mal was back at work though still feeling distinctly fragile and prone to dozing off at the drop of a hat. The flu had left him with a hacking cough that tended to get worse at bedtime and no amount of cough syrup could calm it. Also the amount of spam in his inbox had reached epic proportions and he wasn't sure he'd ever reach the bottom of it. Consequently when he had a phone call on Friday morning he answered it with less than good cheer.

"You sound awful," Harvey said. "Oh God, you got my flu, didn't you? Haven't you recovered yet?"

"No," Mal said. "Though I'm not sure you should be taking credit for the flu. I think it's gone round the entire town."

"Nasty. Right, to make amends, I'll come and take you out for a curry. We'll go to that nice little pub, the Coach and Horses."

"No, we won't," Mal said. "I can't go in there. It's Rob's local."

"Of course you can." Harvey laughed. "I won't take no for an answer. Meet you there at seven? I'm driving back from Northumberland the pretty way."

"You can go if you like," Mal said. "I'll see you whenever."

"Oh dear. Then I'll get a takeaway and bring it round at about eight." Harvey said. "No arguing. I want to talk to you about the exhibition."

"Can't stop you." Mal was well aware that he was being less than gracious. "Always pleased to talk exhibitions with you, Harvey, but I'm not well enough to deal with exes and their disapproving and hostile pals."

"Don't be dramatic, Mal. It doesn't suit you. Eight o'clock. If you're still feeling rough, put the street door on the latch and I'll lock it behind me when I come in."

"Why does everyone feel the need to manage me?" Mal demanded.

"We'll stop when you show signs of managing yourself. Later. Now, put me through to the desk again. I want to talk to Sharon."

There was no point in arguing with Harvey in that kind of mood. Also, when Mal put Harvey back through to the reception, Sharon's tone was such that Mal wondered just who it was that Harvey was really coming to see, and that made him stop and think a bit.

Okay, he and Rob were over. He had texted Rob again and had also left a voice message that he hoped had sounded rational and not too needy, requesting a meeting to talk things over, but all his efforts had been ignored. He had to face up to the fact that their relationship was at an end because he had stupidly over-reacted. He had parted from lovers before and he had still been part of their social circle. The only one from whom he had parted without any sympathy had been bloody Oliver, but that was a completely different situation. He still missed Rob, a lot, and this hurt far worse than leaving Oliver, but he loved his job in this quiet and close knit little town and wasn't going to give it up for anything. All the same – the Coach and Horses tonight with a runny nose, red rimmed eyes and hardly any voice? No, he couldn't. He'd accept the curry though.

By half four he'd had enough of emails, the cool disapproval of Betty, and Sharon's anxious attempts to cheer him up. He said goodbye to them, fended off Marcia who felt that changing a printer cartridge might help his recovery, and headed for home.

His intentions were good. He changed the sheets on the spare bed and started to tidy the flat, but he sat down with a cup of tea at six and didn't wake up until quarter to eight. By then the best he could do was to put things in neat piles and push the vacuum cleaner around, wincing at the noise. There had been an occasion when he and Harvey had shared a disgusting 'hole in the ground' toilet filled with flies in a corner of a field in Wiltshire. If Harvey could survive that he could survive a bit of mess.

Vacuum back in its cupboard, he popped down the stairs to put the door on the latch and then settled down to read through his report on the development and the finds. At eight fifteen he heard a voice in the hallway and feet on the stairs and realised, with panicky horror, that Harvey had brought people home with him.

"If one of them's Rob, Harvey," Mal muttered as he went to open the flat door, "we're going to have words."

But to his surprise the first person in through the door was big Terry, the barber, his arms laden with bags belching fragrant steam. "There you are! He's awake," he shouted over his shoulder. "Hi, Mal, got the plates out?"

"Er, yes. Kitchen's that way." Mal stepped aside to let him in and smiled a greeting to Glyn Havard and Leo Farriner, each of whom were carrying bags of poppadums. Harvey brought up the rear brandishing two bottles of wine, one white, one red.

"Mal! We stopped at the off licence. I wasn't sure if you'd have any vino in."

"No, I haven't," Mal admitted. "Hello, guys. I wasn't expecting visitors. Please excuse the mess."

"Oh, don't apologise." Leo offered Mal one of his fleeting little smiles and a white envelope addressed in a beautiful cursive script. "I was going to put this in the post for you but Harvey suggested I come round and give it to you now. I – um – can't stop. Got to get home to the dog, you know how it is."

"Are you sure?" Mal was struck that every time he had seen Leo he had been alone or leaving in order to be alone. He had never actually seen him relaxed and looking comfortable. "You'd be very welcome. Please, stay and share. It looks like you brought masses."

"That's kind but Jolly will be expecting her walk," Leo said. Terry returned from the kitchen with a smaller package which he handed to Leo and after a brief round of goodbyes the solicitor was gone.

"That's a pity," Mal said as he chivvied people into chairs and helped to provide plates and eating utensils. "Am I the only one who thinks he maybe doesn't get out enough?"

"Still grieving," Glyn said.

"Oh, I'm so sorry to hear that. I knew he was divorced but I didn't know –"

"Oh no, she hasn't died." Glyn shook his head. "Sweethearts since college, set up in business together, but it turned out she was more ambitious than he was. Went off to London to get her Silk but Leo didn't like it there and it's hard to keep a marriage going at a distance."

"He misses her," Terry said. "We keep an eye on him and sometimes make him do stuff for his own good. But usually he plays the dog-walking card and it's a bit hard to argue with that."

"Maybe another time then?" Mal looked around. "Has everyone got what they need? Thanks for bringing me my supper."

"No problem," Harvey said. "And I hope you don't mind me bringing Glyn and Terry. Like Leo they had intended to call on you this weekend anyway. I've just accelerated things a bit."

"Oh yes." Mal eyed Terry, who was already digging into his lamb rogan josh like a champion. "And why's that? Or shall we eat first?"

"Let's take the edge off," Glyn suggested, grinning at Terry who waved his fork in agreement.

Mal picked at his food. He was hungry, he could actually smell the curry and it was fantastic, but there was an atmosphere in the room that made him nervous. Harvey had planned something. It had happened before. Once Harvey had tried to set him up with a gorgeous American student over here to study hill forts – blonde, sun kissed, leggy, with a killer smile, but unfortunately female. After some polite explanations, a few months later Harvey had set him up with an Italian linguist, right sex this time, which had been more fun. Then there was the time Harvey had decided the entire dig team needed massages to work the kinks out of their backs after a particularly gruelling series of fingertip excavations, and they had ended up in a place that may have had massage parlour on its advertising material but offered many other more startling services. Harvey always meant well.

To while away the time Mal put down his fork and picked up Leo's letter. It wasn't sealed, the flap just tucked neatly in. Mal opened the envelope, enjoying the feel of the heavy high quality cream stationery, and extracted the single sheet of paper. Actually, to call it paper was an insult. This was more like vellum, thick and crisply folded with a classy embossed letter head reading just 'Lockhart Farriner' with an address and a phone number. It screamed old fashioned reliability. It fitted the premises he remembered, with stone steps, a portico and the type of blue rinsed receptionist who would only allow you access to her charges if you had a bloody good reason. Then he read the typed words – actually typed, none of this new-fangled printing – and almost dropped the paper.

"Mal?" Harvey said. "What's wrong."

"Nothing," Mal said. "It's a letter, properly notarised, from Vanessa Gaskell's solicitor, that would be Leo, on his client's behalf, confirming that all finds from the High Rifles Lane development, large and small, are to be donated to the museum and inviting me to send them any necessary legal paperwork. Also, since she says she can trust the local museum staff to – er – here it is – 'do the right thing for the finds and for the community', she promises on behalf of Gaskell Developments to match any funding we raise elsewhere. That – that could be incredibly generous if the Heritage Lottery Fund comes through with some cash."

Terry gave an approving nod. "Good girl that 'Nessa. She deserved better than Gaskell."

Mal looked around at his companions. "None of you are surprised," he said. "What am I missing?"

"Community?" Glyn said. His tone was gentle rather than critical. "You've never lived anywhere like this. Like it never occurred to you to ask for help when you got ill. Here we don't leave people to suffer, we pitch in to help. It never occurred to you that poor Rob might be offering to take the blame for what had happened because he cared so much for you that he just couldn't keep lying to you. Stupid thing to do, because he's spent the past week wondering when to expect a visit from police accusing him of – I dunno, reckless endangerment of antiquities, or something. He's been sick with worry, and that's made the flu even worse. And that's not fair because we were all in it."

"All of you?" Mal's shock overrode his shame at how he had treated Rob, so the words came out a bit more loudly than he had intended.

"You betcha." Terry grinned at him. "We'd intended to draw Rother down to the other end of the site and put a sack over his head but seeing him go into the Portaloo was just too good a chance to pass up. I never thought the silly bastard would tip it up. That's something you gotta look out for, Glyn."

"Believe me, I am." Glyn grinned. "Everything's properly pegged down now. So, Mal, after that meeting at Sharon's we went to the pub and thrashed out a plan. Terry had remembered 'Nessa coming in to have her hair done and saying something about the High Rifles Lane land being in her name. We rang Leo and asked who would own what under those circumstances then Terry rang 'Nessa. Once she understood that she had the right to object, she was outraged that her property was being taken out of the town without her permission and got those letters made up. When it was clear that Culmstock was going ahead I offered to provide the equipment and a means of hiding the cist. Some of the other lads offered their muscles. We didn't want to involve Rob but in the end he did drive the digger. We needed the best to be sure of getting the cist onto the lorry without damaging it but that's all he did and he only offered because I said I'd do it and Rob said I'd fuck it up. And then he dashed off to join you at the bonfire and Sion put the digger in the ditch."

Mal tried to speak but Terry very calmly picked up the story. "I drove the lorry and Glyn moved the cist to the store with a forklift. Nice and cool and not too dry in there."

"What humidity level was it? How did you know it would be safe?" Mal demanded, but a gentle clearing of the throat from Mr Biddulph gave him his answer. "Harvey, you were a party to this?"

"I most certainly was," Harvey said. "I got wind of it by accident and there was no way I was going to let the burial be damaged, so you bet I checked the premises over. And I made sure that everything was packed to museum standards, too."

"Is there nobody in this bloody place I can trust?" Mal demanded. "What did you think you were doing?"

"Taking care of our own," Terry growled. "I told you we do that. You knew that. Rob told you that. You don't have any excuse. What was being done to that burial was shameful. That's no way to treat your ancestors, lugging them all over the country."

"But that burial is so special." Mal felt like crying. "Don't you understand how rare it is to be able to identify archaeological cadavers as a couple and even rarer for there to be an implication that they might be a same sex couple? This is one of the most important finds ever. It must be studied."

"Then study it," Glyn said. "Nobody ever said you couldn't do that. Vanessa has given you *carte blanche*. Study them, find out who they are. How about a DNA test? See if they match up with anyone round here. It could be a great project."

Harvey was nodding so hard his hair shook. "Yes, root the research in the local area. Find descendants. Build a display about longevity and community spirit, and about love too. Nobody who sees those bones could deny that they were buried with love and respect."

"And display them with respect," Terry added. "That's the least they deserve."

Mal stared at them. "I don't know what to say. You've put me in an impossible position professionally. Nobody will ever believe that I wasn't a party to this theft."

"Not a theft. If anyone checks we have a paper trail." Glyn grinned. "I wasn't going to do a thing without it. Okay, they were a bit late but I've got a copy of the letter Vanessa sent to Culmstock refusing him permission to remove the burial, a copy of his reply stating that he felt the permission granted by her husband was sufficient and that if she took matters further he'd have no choice but to bill her for his services, and her response saying he could keep his hands off and she'd expect his invoice. There's also a final document addressed to me requesting that in view of Culmstock's refusal to comply I should arrange for the burial to be removed to a place of safety. Not our fault if, due to an administrative error, it took a while to reach the police."

"Then they'll be charging us with wasting police time instead of theft." Mal shook his head. "It's still a criminal offence and the last I heard they took it pretty seriously."

"We took legal advice as soon as we realised what had happened." Glyn shook his head. "It's going to come down to whether they decide to prosecute for Wasting Police Time or reprimand us for a Failure to Act."

"You also might have noticed that we timed the – er – removal so you were in clear sight at a big public event the whole time?" Terry wasn't actually scowling but his grave expression was quite daunting. "Rob insisted on that. He didn't want anyone to assume that you might be involved. And you were so gobsmacked when you arrived at the site and thought the burial was damaged that the police were convinced. Nobody's that good an actor."

"Anthony Hopkins is," Harvey said. "Olivier. Ben Whishaw. But not Mal. He's completely transparent. Like now he's wondering if he could get away with killing us all so none of us can tell anyone just how much of a twit he feels."

"No, just you, Harvey." Mal snarled. "Glyn, Terry, I know that you meant well but you have no idea what a position you put me in. Harvey, on the other hand … Christ, Harvey, what do you expect me to do now? How do you expect me to react?"

Harvey had drawn breath to reply but Glyn cut in first. "I'll tell you what we expect you to do," he said, his tone sharp. "I expect you to get in touch with Rob – preferably in person but over the phone will do if you're too much of a coward to look him in the eye – and tell him that you're not going to press charges for – for criminal damage or whatever it was. I had to persuade him not to give himself up yesterday, he's so sick with worry. We could have forgiven you for letting the burial go off to London, there wouldn't have been much you could do to stop it, but I'm finding it hard to forgive you for what you've put Rob through this past week."

His words struck Mal like a bucket of ice water. "But I wouldn't have done that. I'd *never* have done that to him. If he didn't know that –"

"How would he know that?" Terry's brows had drawn down and Mal was reminded again of just how huge and intimidating the man could be if he wished. "Okay, you've been knocking boots but you've only known each other for a couple of months. Rob – idiot – tried to take the blame for all of us. And it didn't occur to you that he'd have had to have help? Or that Glyn would have had to be in on it because Rob would never have used his equipment without asking permission? Or that Rob wouldn't have been capable of coming up with a plan like that in the first place? He'd have been more likely to have chained himself to the cist – first hiding all the available bolt cutters – or to Culmstock's van. Or to have decked the fucker. You don't know Rob at all, and he sure as fuck didn't know you the way he thought he did."

"No, apparently not." Mal glared at them all, flushed with shame and anger and aching desperate sadness. "Which explains why, despite me doing my best to get in touch he hasn't responded. I've tried texting and calling. I've left messages. I'm sorry – more sorry than you can know – that he's been so upset but I've tried and he clearly doesn't want to know. And if I've messed up our relationship I'm not going to commit professional suicide as well."

"Oh, cut the bloody drama." Harvey rolled his eyes. "I've spent the past week dealing with TV divas in the Northumbrian fog. I was hoping for a bit more clarity and a lot less selfishness down here. Mal, you need to look hard at the situation here and realise that very little of it is about you. This is about the good people of Pemberland and what they see as being right and proper. You can either be a part of it and be helpful, or get out of the bloody way. An expert," he put his hand on his chest and gave a little bow, "will assure everyone that none of the finds are damaged, and in two to five years, depending upon availability of funds, a terrific exhibition will be unveiled at the Pemberland Centre for Heritage and Culture, and all the great and good will come to sip cheap champagne and nibble canapés. And they'll all agree that you've done a great job – unless you hand in your resignation to make a self-immolatory point, like a swishy little drama queen."

The words fell into a dead silence as both Terry and Glyn stared at Harvey. Mal stared too, not sure whether to be offended or impressed.

After a moment Terry cleared his throat. "Um …Harvey, while I don't entirely disagree with what you just said, can I just make the point that I'm the only person in the room qualified to be tossing homophobic slurs at Mal without sounding a bit –"

"Oh God, *mea culpa*, Terry, I'm so sorry."

"Apology accepted. So, Mal – what he said, right? And this is only going to be a big deal if you make it so," Terry said. "Culmstock should never have been involved."

"*Mea culpa* again," Harvey admitted.

Glyn nodded. "You only asked for advice, Harvey. You didn't expect him to steam in and take over. No, the job should have been handled locally and if that meant the cist was dismantled and moved bit by bit and the skeletons reassembled later that would have been fine. They looked like good strong lads to me and the local boys don't mind a bit of inconvenience in a good cause. What we need to know, Mal, is if you're going to play ball with us over this? Can you imagine we're in a position where, instead of Culmstock, some other boffin came here and helped us raise the burial without interference? No theft, no vandalism, no threat to your professional reputation, no countrywide interest from the media."

"No accusations of pulling a publicity stunt?" Mal flopped back into his chair. "What choice do I have?"

"There's always a choice, Mal." Harvey tilted his head. "But you need to really think through the consequences of making the wrong one. And I'm not talking about your professional position, either."

"Yeah, we think you could fit in well here, and be happy." Terry's grin was cheerful. "I reckon we'd best leave you to think it over, don't you, Glyn? And if I was you I wouldn't be phoning Rob. I'd get out there and find him."

Chapter 22

Much to Mal's surprise, as soon as Terry and Glyn had gone, Harvey disappeared into the bathroom expressing the intention of having a shower.

"And then I'm going to turn in," he said, sponge bag and PJ pants in hand, "and I suggest you do the same."

"I thought you'd be wanting to shout at me a bit more?"

"Lord love you, no." Harvey shrugged. "You're a big boy now and can make up your own mind."

With that he was gone and Mal had no choice but to take himself off to bed. He had hoped to catch up on his reading but his book couldn't hold his attention after the uncomfortable home truths he had heard, so he turned off the light and settled down to weigh the pros and cons.

So Rob had come to the plan late, and only then to prevent a possible accident to the burial. And he had felt so uncomfortable about lying to Mal he had confessed without implicating anyone else. And Mal had left him thinking that Mal was going to tell the police and Rob had been worrying himself sick about it.

That was … just awful. That was cruel. If the boot had been on the other foot – if Rob had been holding something like that over Mal's head – could Mal have ever forgiven him? How much would he have had to grovel? How much would he have had to beg? A hell of a lot, Mal suspected. On the other hand, maybe Rob was a kinder more forgiving person who was less up his own professional arsehole than Mal was?

"Basically," Mal murmured into the dark, "is my life going to be better with Rob than without?"

That was an easy question to answer but what to do about it was another matter.

On Saturday when Mal got up, the flat was empty of all traces of Harvey other than the lingering smell of curry and a bin full of takeaway containers. However there was a note propped against the kettle.

"Out.
"I hope you're feeling better.

"Your assignments today are:

- *To have a good hard think about how happy you are in Pemberland.*
- *To decide if you really want to be part of the community.*
- *Or would you sooner take a high moral stance and be miserable somewhere else?*
- *Finish filling in that grant application form. I looked it over and there are two spelling errors and a grammar cock up in the first paragraph.*
- *For God's sake get someone to proof-read it and correct it before you send it off!*

"Toodle pip
"Harvey
"P.S. I left you some milk but I used the last of the cornflakes."

"Well, thanks, Harvey. Only you could bullet-point a bollocking." Mal made tea and toast while pondering over the note. He had done his soul-searching the night before and had already made up his mind what he needed to do. As a result, yes, he did feel a lot better. So it looked like the first task was to finish filling in the form and get Harvey to check it when he got back. Once that was out of the way he would find Rob and do whatever he had to do to make things right again.

He had finished the form by 12.30 and put it aside where he knew Harvey would be able to find it. Then he put on coat, hat and gloves and went down to get his bike.

First call was the building site, where he could see some of the men were putting in some extra hours. He spotted Sion, who gave him a wave, but Rob's digger was standing idle with tarps over the buckets and well blocked in by other vehicles. Mal cycled away, feeling a little relieved. The building site probably wouldn't have been the best place for a confrontation.

Next on the list was the Coach and Horses. But Mal drew a blank there too.

"No, I haven't seen him," the barmaid said with a grin. "Not since last night. If the amount of beer he had is anything to go by he's probably at home sleeping it off."

"Ah right." Mal grimaced. "I should probably go there then. Um – any idea where it is?"

"No idea of the address," she replied, "but if you turn left opposite the church in Escley and go down that lane a bit you can't miss it. Just look for the Morris van."

Mal got back on his bike and pedalled hard into the chilly wind, trying to recall what a Morris van looked like. He hadn't gone far before a yellow-and-blue-chequered car overtook him and he saw a uniformed arm flagging him down.

"Hello, Mal." Brian Farriner gave him a cheerful grin as he pulled up alongside the car window. "I thought that was you. Where are you off to?"

"Escley," Mal admitted. "Um – was there anything you wanted?"

Brian chuckled. "I just thought you'd like to know that the pallet and contents are now safely stored in our evidence locker in Hereford. Mr Biddulph has promised to come and check the humidity and heat and so forth. We did call you first but your phone bounced straight to voice mail."

"Did it? It shouldn't have." Mal grimaced and fished it out of his pocket. "Oh, only one bar – nope, that's gone, too."

"There are so many dead spots round here," Brian said. "Anyhow, when I saw you I thought you should know. I'm so glad it was just a misunderstanding."

"So nobody's going to be getting it in the neck then?"

"Who would we prosecute? Mrs Gaskell, when she thought she'd sent the letters? Culmstock, when he thought he had permission from the owner? A group of people who knew he hadn't and took steps to prevent a theft, and have stated that they are absolutely prepared to pay any fines? That poor secretary who didn't put the letters in the post? Certainly not you – I don't think I've ever seen anyone look sicker when we pulled back the tarp and you saw the burial had gone." Brian smiled again, gorgeous grey eyes crinkling at the corners. "I've got to get on. Take care, Mal. Forecast's for rain later."

Mal thanked him and watched the police car pull away, not quite able to believe that DI Cowper would be as understanding about it all. But at least he'd have some good news to pass on to Rob along with his apologies.

Escley was further than Mal had remembered so he was very relieved to spot the cross roads by the White Horse. The car park had only a couple of cars in it and the doors were closed, so Mal refused to give in to his rather cowardly impulse to stop for a pint before tackling Rob. Instead he turned off and free wheeled down the slight slope into the village. At the church with its not-quite-a-lych-gate, Mal made his turn down a much rougher single track road with grass growing up the middle. He hoped he'd get there before he met a tractor or lorry because the road was steep walled and there was little room for manoeuvre. But, as the bar maid had promised, there was no mistaking the house. Amongst half a dozen elderly and partly reconstructed vehicles he saw the rusting carcass of an old postman's van. Mal knew they were worth a good bit to collectors. This one was wheelless, propped up on blocks and had a tarpaulin covering the windows so someone had taken care of it at some time. But it had obviously been there for a long time because ivy had grown up over the engine block and rank grass whispered against its side. The whole approach to the house was littered with car parts in various states of disrepair. Mal got off his bike, propped it against the van and picked his way through the debris, pricking his ears as a dog began to bark. Gary had mentioned that Rob's dog was called Flash, and Mal had imagined some kind of terrier, or maybe a whippet. This sounded like the type of dog that eats postmen, cold callers and Jehovah's Witnesses, so probably an asset in an out of the way place like this. Mal just hoped that it was sensibly restrained.

To a crescendo of barks the door opened and a rotund man in a grubby maroon rugby shirt stepped out. His face was almost as florid as his shirt and was further set off by a grog blossom nose.

"Who the fuck are you?" he demanded. "You from the Social?"

"No. I – um – was looking for Rob Escley."

"He ain't here," the man said. "I sent him off to town to fetch my beer but he's been ages. What you want him for, anyway? If it's money we haven't got any."

Mal frowned. "No, it's nothing like that."

"Well if you do see him, tell him to get his arse back here. And he better not forget my beer."

"Beer. Right."

Mr Escley cocked his head and gave him a hard stare. "Are you one of his nancy friends?"

"Well, actually," Mal said, feeling his temper beginning to rise, "as it happens, yes, I am."

"Fuck off then."

The door slammed, muffling more grumbling and Mal stared at the peeling planks for a moment.

He'd heard that Rob's dad could be difficult but hadn't expected such casual aggression. He returned to his bike, wondering whether to go back to town or to wait up by the church until Rob came back with the beer. He still hadn't decided when he heard the barking again and saw a small grey-haired woman come round the side of the house. She glanced back at the front door as she hurried towards him but gave him a nervous smile.

"You wanted to see Rob?" she asked. "Are you – Mal?"

"Yes." Mal let her lead him round the side of the old post van, out of sight of the house. "And you must be Mrs Escley. I'm pleased to meet you."

"It's my pleasure," she said. Her voice was cracked and her fingers were nicotine stained, but she was neatly dressed and, though her face was deeply lined, Mal could see Rob's likeness. She must have been a pretty girl once. "Rob told me about you and I hoped we might meet. I'm sorry, but I don't know whether to expect him. He and his dad – well, they don't really get on and it's been even worse since his brother moved back in. Rob and Kevin had a bit of a barney earlier, too."

"Mr Escley seems to think Rob's fetching his beer," Mal said with a lift of his eyebrows.

"Silly ol' fart." Mrs Escley shook her head. "He *asked* Rob and Rob said he would but then – Oh I don't know. Voices got raised and Rob slammed out of the house. It's not fair. He's been such a help to us but his dad can't see that." She smiled again, properly, revealing a chipped tooth. "He's been so much happier since he got to know you. Thank you for being there for him."

Mal's conscience twinged like stubbed toe. "But I haven't been," he admitted. "Not lately. We had a disagreement, and then we both got sick. I wanted to apologise and – well, to see if we could get back together. If he's still interested. It's a bit awkward."

"Oh, that's a pity. He never said." Mrs Escley glanced towards the house again. "If you want to find him, I expect he'll be at Glyn's place later.

Or the Coach and Horses. Sometimes he stays with Sion. Do you know Sion?"

"Yes, I do." Mal glanced at the house as the dog began to bark again. "Is there anything I can do?"

"Bless you, no. Not unless you've got a light?" Mrs Escley fiddled in her pocket and took out a pack of Embassy.

"Sorry, I don't smoke."

"Sensible boy. Good luck." She turned and hurried back towards the house.

Mal sighed as he cycled away. She'd looked totally dispirited, and Mal wondered how much of that was from the disagreements between father and sons and how much was from her own sadness. Her smile had been layered with so much tension it had been more like a grimace. But it did explain why Rob was so keen to spend time elsewhere. Mal biked back up the lane to the church and paused in the shelter of the big yews to catch his breath.

Mrs Escley had suggested that Rob might be at Glyn's place or the Coach and Horses. Somehow he doubted she meant the builders' yard, and since he had no idea where Glyn lived he decided to go back into town and check the pub again. Rob was bound to be there sometime.

Chapter 23

On the way back, just as Brian had warned, it began to spit with rain and an unpleasant chilly breeze got up. Mal felt that it reflected his current state quite well – cold and shivery with nerves. He rode past the museum and into the main street then looked up as he caught the sound of a familiar engine. Up until that moment he wouldn't have believed that he'd be able to pick Rob's car out of a bunch of others but there she was, mud-splashed and unlovely, idling at the zebra crossing as Rob waited for a couple pushing a buggy to cross the road. Mal pedalled hard and pulled up beside him.

Rob ignored the first tap on the window then glanced up and scowled as Mal repeated it.

"I need to talk to you," Mal said and pointed to the kerb. "Rob? Can you pull over?"

Rob's scowl deepened and as soon as the young family had cleared the front of his car he pulled away. Mal tried to follow then realised there might be a better way. He turned across the road and dived down the alley way between the bakery and Lillian's hairdresser's salon. Once Rob was in the one-way system, with the streets busy with Saturday morning shoppers, Mal would be able to keep up with him.

In the maze of small streets and alleys, Mal could move faster. He only had one really bad moment, when he found that the gate at the back of the Castle Inn was closed and he had to make a quick detour. But he still managed to get back onto the main drag ahead of Rob, catching him at the pelican crossing downhill from the clock. Rob's fingers drummed on the steering wheel as two elderly ladies with little tartan wheeled trolleys ambled across the road. One waved her thanks to Rob but they continued to chat.

"Rob?" Mal tapped on the window again. "Open the window. I want to apologise."

Rob's face flushed and he shook his head. "No," he said, his voice barely audible over the street noise. "Piss off."

"No!" Mal shook his head. "Not going to happen."

The light turned amber and Rob's car leaped forward. But there was a red light at the crossing opposite the castle. Panting, Mal tucked his bike in close to Rob's car door and tapped on the window again. "Open up," he begged. "Christ, Rob. I just want to say how sorry I am. And that I'm sorry you've been ill. And that I should never have left it like that between us."

"You tell him, boy." A total stranger halfway across the road swung her shopping bag and gave them both a grin. "Shall I stand here until he opens the window?"

The car behind Rob's blasted its horn and Mal, the helpful lady and Rob all looked at the driver and made gestures varying from Mal's apologetic wave to the lady's firmly raised middle finger. Snarling, Rob rolled down the window, but spoke to the woman not to Mal.

"I'll talk to him, Aggie. I promise. But not in the middle of the chuffing road."

She gave them both the thumbs up and began to get out of Rob's way. "When?" Mal asked. "Where shall I meet you?"

"When I feel like it," Rob snapped and accelerated away.

"Bugger." Mal gave chase, standing up on the pedals and swooping around the corner. He pulled alongside Rob's car again briefly, just long enough to shout, "I'm not going to stop following you, you know, and if you're on your way home I hope you haven't forgotten your dad's beer."

"Fuck Dad's beer," Rob yelled and the car pulled away again and turned into Ross Road.

"Shit." Mal put his head down and followed. Past the new houses, including the one with the garish yellow flints in the driveway, past the turn off to High Rifles Lane, along to where the houses thinned out and the countryside began proper. Up here, Mal knew, was a lane that would take Rob across to the Escley Road and there had been a Tesco bag bulging with the shape of beer cans on the back seat. Where the road began to climb across the side of Carew Hill, Mal had no choice but to slow and watch Rob's car dwindle into the distance, but he knew where they were going and was damned if he'd give up now. Rain spat on his shoulders, pattering audibly on the hard carapace of his cycle helmet. His fingers, even inside his gloves, felt frozen but his body was warm and his legs still strong.

"Nope," Mal mattered as a bend hid Rob's car. "Not giving up now I've come this far."

A few minutes later, he too rounded a bend and there, pulled up at the side of the road, was Rob. Mal could see his silhouette. His hand was raised to his head so he was probably on the phone.

Mal didn't pause, didn't slow down, but cycled hard right up to the car then put his hand on the roof. He leaned, taking a deep breath, hoping to get enough air into his lungs to talk, but all he could do was cough.

Rob wound the window down. "Yes, he is," he said into the phone. "He's soaking wet, looks like shit and is coughing up a lung. Yeah, I know. Well, it's all right for you isn't it? No – okay, if I must. Take care now." He ended the call, put the phone on the dashboard and gave Mal a measuring look. "That was Betty, telling me that a friend of Lillian's had told Lil, who told Betty, that you were chasing all over town trying to find me. Not that it was news, because I've had texts from Sion and from Lisa in the Coach, and I missed a call from Mum. Jesus, you look sick."

"I have been," Mal gasped between coughs. "Got your flu. Sorry you've been ill."

"Yeah, well, it would have been easier if I hadn't thought I was going to be arrested," Rob muttered. "Look, this isn't a good place to talk. You're still ill. I've felt better to be honest, and it looks like it's going to piss down. How about we meet up later?"

"You're in the car in the dry," Mal pointed out. "Just give me two minutes, okay?"

Rob's rather grudging nod was all the permission he needed.

"I've been a total shit," Mal said. "I realised almost immediately but I couldn't get past my own arsey attitude and being so intent on my job that I forgot that my job is all about people. Specifically the people of Pemberland and Escley, Brynglas and King's Norton, and all the countryside in between. About you, Rob. Of course you'd want to keep what's yours here and, if I'd been a better friend to you all, you wouldn't have felt the need to do what you did in secret. Secrets are for people like Gaskell, out for the advantage, for the quick quid. Not for us. But most of all I'm sorry I didn't get in touch in person to tell you I wouldn't be going to the police. That was unforgivable. I'm so sorry, Rob. I really shouldn't have done that."

"No, you shouldn't." Rob sighed then he shot Mal a glance and one corner of his mouth turned up. "You look like a drowned cat," he said. "You'll be getting your flu back."

Mal nodded, wiping drips of rain off the end of his nose with the back of his hand. "Wouldn't be surprised if it turned to pneumonia."

Rob nodded too, an expression of satisfaction on his face. "That'd teach you, wouldn't it? Aw, fuck, Mal, I was so scared. I didn't want to go to jail."

"Well, you won't because –" Mal lost the rest of his sentence to a sneeze.

"Bless you," Rob said. "And kindly don't sneeze on me. I don't want your germs."

"I don't mind yours. Look, Rob, can we start again? I've missed you so much."

"I missed you too." Rob drummed his fingers on the steering wheel. "Especially at night. Should have rung to thank you for looking after Kev's girls too."

"That was – I won't say a pleasure, I was too worried, but yeah. They were talking about walking back to Brynglas."

"Oh jeez, then thanks even more. I owe you one."

"Well," Mal wiped rain off his nose and tried a hopeful smile. "Could you – I dunno – come round to mine this evening so we can both settle our debts? You can bring your toothbrush, or a hazmat suit, if you want, but please come."

Rob hesitated but Mal could see the tension at the corners of his eyes that meant he was trying not to smile. "Eight-ish?" Rob asked. "I can't drink – still on antibiotics – but I could pick up some chips on my way?"

"That would be sensible." Mal fished a damp tissue out of his pocket and wiped his nose. "Because I'm not sure I've got enough brain cells left to cook anything edible. And I'll make sure we're not disturbed. Harvey's down."

"Ah, he won't disturb us." Rob grinned. "He's off out with Sharon tonight. Proper date. Didn't you know?"

"No!" Mal stared at him. "I'm behind with the gossip, evidently."

"Well, don't you worry about that," Rob said and there was that wonderful grin that Mal had missed so much, "because tonight I'll be sure to fill you in."

"Promises." Mal took his hand off the roof ready to pedal away but found his wrist caught and held, and gave in to Rob's pull. Ducking down to lean in through the window, Mal tilted his head until his lips could meet Rob's. Oh yes, that was so good. He groaned at the pleasure of his taste and the warmth of his tongue. "Oh God, I've missed you," he murmured against Rob's cheek."

"I missed you too – a lot – but you're dripping rain water into my crotch." Rob pushed Mal away firmly. "I best go. Got stuff to do for Mum. See you later, Mal."

"See you later, Rob," Mal said, and as he watched Rob drive away he felt a great lightening in his chest that was nothing to do with his cough and everything to do with feeling at least part of the way to being forgiven.

Sunday morning brought a much happier awakening for Mal. He stretched under warm covers and turned over to see that Rob, for once, was still sound asleep, dark lashes twitching as he dreamed, but his breathing deep and steady. Mal grinned and flopped back on his own pillow with a sigh of complete satisfaction.

He was forgiven. Uncomfortable though it had been they had talked it over and decided that honesty was the best policy and that it was best not to jump to conclusions. They both agreed that blaming Harvey was probably a good thing to do, also easiest because Harvey wouldn't care. While they had talked they had split a pack of no-alcohol beer – sacrilege, of course, but Mal wouldn't drink while Rob couldn't – and had eaten some pretty fine fish and chips, then they had shared the shower and gone to bed to make things up to each other in the best possible way.

But now the fake beer was making its presence felt, so Mal eased out of bed and grabbed his bathrobe to keep the shivers at bay on the short trip to the bathroom. Tea next, and he bunged a couple of slices in the toaster as well. Breakfast in bed could lead to crumbs in funny places but he didn't care, he was just so relieved.

The flush of the loo alerted him that Rob was on the move, and he carried the tray into the bedroom just in time to see Rob pulling the duvet back up to his shoulders.

"Hey," Rob said. He lay back with his head on the pillow and gave Mal a sleepy grin.

"Hey yourself." Mal put the tray on the bed side table then burrowed back under the covers to settle at Rob's side. "I have tea, and toast and marmalade."

"You're a star." Rob turned towards him and edged a bit closer, nuzzling Mal's shoulder, then reached to grab the mug he usually used. Mal smiled. It was a small thing, Rob having his 'own' mug, but very comforting. Mal took a sip of his own tea and balanced the plate of toast on his lap where they would both be able to reach it. They sipped tea and munched toast in mutual satisfaction for a few minutes, then Rob said, "I'm going to Glyn for Sunday lunch actually. Want to come with me? You've had a standing invitation ever since we, as Helen put it, started 'walking out' together."

"Which means staying in and shagging in modern idiom," Mal leaned to shoulder bump Rob. "I'd love to as long as you're sure. Had we better let them know?"

"I'll text," Rob promised. "I'd best check on Mum – and Dad – first. And bloody Kevin. Did I tell you he's moved back in with them? Julie moved out after that thing with the kids and he didn't want to stay in their flat on his own. Pick you up twelve thirty-ish? Lunch is one sharp."

"Great, that'll give me time to nip to Tesco and get a bottle. White or red?"

"Damned if I know. Third Sunday of the month so it'll be pork. What goes with that?"

"I'll find something," Mal promised and took another bite of toast. A small interested sound from Rob drew his attention. Rob was staring at his chest where, as predicted, Mal was developing a bit of a crumb problem. There was also a glistening drip of marmalade.

Rob reached over him to put his empty mug down. "Let me get that for you," he purred and lowered his head to lick.

Mal groaned as the lick turned into a gentle bite. "I don't think I had marmalade on my nipple, Rob."

"Mmm?" Rob sucked then pulled off the little morsel of flesh with a smack of the lips. "You had. In fact it's pretty much everywhere, you messy herbert. And the crumbs!"

He ducked down again, applying a series of little bites down Mal's chest and belly, throwing back the covers and almost causing Mal to drop his toast as he took him into his mouth. Mal put the toast on the plate and drove both hands into Rob's thick hair, not holding but definitely encouraging.

"Oh God, that's … oh yes … you're too good to me."

"Impossible," Rob said. At least that's what Mal thought he said. His voice was rather muffled.

It was brilliant. It was also brilliant in the shower when Mal returned the favour while Rob was washing the marmalade out of his hair. And the soap flavoured kisses as they slid and heaved against each other were pretty good too.

Dressed, Mal watched Rob pick through the clean laundry that had been in Mal's dresser drawer for the past week.

"You're the most fastidious person I know," Mal said, admiring the view as Rob stooped to pull on some boxers. "I really don't understand that stupid nickname?"

"Dirty Rob?" Rob grunted and perched on the end of the bed to put on clean socks. "It doesn't take long to pick up something like that," he said. "Mam was in hospital, Dad couldn't be arsed, I wore the same shirt to school for a week and someone noticed. That's all."

Mal leaned across the bed to press a kiss to the back of Rob's neck. "Well, as a professional person in reasonably good standing, and from up close and personal experience, I can affirm that you are spotless in every respect. Squeaky clean, in fact."

Rob snorted and grabbed Mal's collar to pull him into another proper kiss then reached for his jeans. "Where's my shoes? Ah, there's one."

Mal found the other for him, then followed him to the door.

"Twelve thirty," Rob said. "Not too smart but not scruffy."

"Rob, have you ever seen me look scruffy?"

"Glyn has. That night he came round with Harvey and Terry he said you looked rough as a badger's chuff. Also," Rob's smile turned sly, "I've seen you look wrecked a time or two."

"All your doing," Mal said, "and for a very good reason."

They kissed on the threshold, and Rob hurried down the stairs and away, leaving Mal with a wrecked bedroom and marmalade on the sheets. He couldn't stop smiling as he stripped the bed. Seeing Rob leave was quite a good thing because then he could look forward to all the fun of welcoming him back again.

Chapter 24

Monday was a busy day because Mal had a load of paperwork to catch up on. But on Tuesday morning, after getting up at silly o'clock to see Rob off for a job on the other side of the county, Mal opened up the museum early. By nine he had cleared a space in the ground floor stores where the heavier items from the museum collection were kept. Everything from a box of cannon balls to a plough had been stacked neatly on shelves, the pieces of the farm cart were propped securely against one wall and he had an area large enough to take the cist on its pallet. The room felt cool and dry, but not too dry. Just in case, Mal set a temp/humidity monitor on the nearest shelf, and added taking regular readings to his 'to do' list. Then he went to measure up the room he hoped to refurbish. When Betty came in with coffee for him, he was sitting with his back against one of the venerable cases with his laptop in his lap, pricing paint and sketching out a layout.

Betty plonked their mugs down on the floor beside him, seated herself and peered at his screen.

"Bad computer etiquette," he complained. "How did you know I wasn't looking at something private?"

Betty made a scornful noise. "You, look at porn during office hours? Leave it out. That's a thing to do furtively after dark, except you won't have to any more because a little bird tells me that you and Rob are knocking boots again, and you won't need the porn unless it's for inspiration."

"Excuse me," Mal tilted the laptop away from her again. "Why all this interest in my sex life? If I was interested in yours it would be wildly inappropriate."

"Well, yeah, because you aren't really interested, you'd be making a creepy and inappropriate point, which I totally know you wouldn't do, okay? But I'm making the point that I'm happy you and Rob are back together again but didn't want to just come out and say it."

"You're awful, Betty, but – um – thank you." Mal swivelled the laptop back towards her. "I'm doing pricings to make this room fit to see."

"Oh Christ, about bloody time. This exhibit is so boring." Betty rolled her eyes. "I don't think anyone under the age of sixty has ever said they liked it, unless it's to say 'my granny had cups like that'. What shall we have in here? Those creepy medical specimens?"

"I'm not sure Pemberland is ready for a tapeworm in a bottle."

"Pig foetus in alcohol?"

"Please God, not that. No, I'm going to use the room for the Early Peoples exhibition."

"Fantastic." Betty peered at the screen. "We've got masses of stuff. Enough to fill the cases."

"We'd need to get a grant. Have you any idea how horribly expensive the right type of paint is?"

"So a couple of coats of Dulux is out then. Pity because I know a bloke who could get it for you at trade."

"Really?" Mal considered. "I wonder if he'd know if there's a trade equivalent of Farrow and Ball paint?"

"I bet he would." Betty used his shoulder to push herself to her feet. "I'm going to get the desk sorted, and there's a package of shop stock to process, so I'll do that after. Also a message from Brian – PC Brian – asking you to get in touch when you have a minute."

"Oh? Any idea what he wanted?"

"He didn't say. Lots of engine noise, though, so I reckon he was in the car. Not driving, because, you know, *Brian*, but parked maybe."

"Are you sure he was as unconcerned as you made him sound, Bet?" Mal got up too, closing his laptop and tucking it under his arm. "You know Brian. He'd be moving people out of a burning building with a polite 'if you wouldn't mind, in your own time, no rush'."

"Well yeah," Betty led the way back to reception. "But I reckon if it was urgent he would have said. Like 'there's no rush but if he could, today, or this morning might be better, or, actually Betty could you go and fetch him now. I'll be by the phone' but he didn't say any of that."

"Okay. You make tea. I'll ring him from the office." Mal hurried upstairs and into his room, which was, he was pleased to note, looking much more like a place to get stuff done and a little less like a junk shop. Yes, it was still chaotic round the edges, and there was one corner he was a bit scared to address because everything was so tightly packed, but the desk was clear and he could see the carpet. It needed vaccing desperately but that was a problem for later.

With a mug of tea and two bits of shortbread from the tin – Sharon had evidently been baking again – Mal found the card that Brian had given him and picked up the phone. Landline or mobile? He plumped for the mobile number and listened to it ring. It rang twice and he heard Brian's voice, breathless, against a background of conversation and car noise.

"Hi, PC Farriner?" Mal decided that formality might be more appropriate because he wasn't sure in what capacity Brian had called him. "This is Malcolm Bright from the museum. I had a message to get in touch with you."

"Oh good, thanks for being so prompt." Brian's voice faded for moment against a back drop of engine noise. "I was wondering if you are free to come out. *Hey, no, you don't!* DI Cowper's anxious to get the cist back where it belongs."

"Oh, that's kind of him. Just as well I spent some time this morning making space for it." He winced at another shout. "Are you all right, Brian?"

"Just shooshing some bullocks off the road. *G'wan, hup!* To be honest, the cist is taking up a lot of floor space." Brian shouted over the sound of a heavy lorry driven very slowly. "We'd be doing formalities today, really. *Get over you bugger!* We need a formal identification of the goods and some paperwork filling in. You'll have to arrange your own transport, but I'm sure that won't be a problem. I know Glyn was really keen to help out. The thing is, I can come and pick you up and run you back after, if we can do it this morning." There was a squeak of metal and a clang. "There, that's got them. All right, Mal?"

Mal chuckled. "Well done. You do realise I'm sort of imagining you in Stetson and chaps now."

"Well, whatever blows your skirt up." Brian chuckled. "I'll pick you up in twenty minutes."

It amused Mal that 'behind the scenes' storage areas just about everywhere had the same slightly chaotic air about them. The place into which he was led by DI Cowper looked very much like a museum storage area – sensible flooring, Dexion shelves, and cardboard archive boxes alternating with bagged up bundles of stuff too bulky to box. The big difference was that most of the recognisable items were much more modern. Flat screen TVs, for instance, seemed popular. Likewise game consoles. But there was only one massive well-wrapped cist on a pallet.

"Okay then," Mal said in reply to Cowper's suggestion that he look the bulbous parcel over. "That's exactly the packaging as I remember it. There should be a packet taped to the side – yes, round here – that should have all the documentation. Exit forms, a description of contents with a CD of photos, and the signatures of Culmstock and the owner – er, of the putative owner."

Cowper made a soft sound in his throat that could have been a cough but that sounded to Mal far more like a startled laugh. "You've heard that, have you?"

"From Mrs Gaskell herself." Mal smiled. "Perhaps she's also been in touch with you?"

"Well, yes, as it happens. So you can formally state that this is the item taken from the High Rifles building site on the evening of fifth November."

"I can't believe that there'd be more than one, but, yes, I remember the pattern of tape on this side." Mal patted the top of the package, looking forward to having it safely in his stores. "Can I arrange for it to be collected now? You aren't still intending to press charges, are you?"

Cowper shook his head, his lips tight. "There seems to have been a genuine misunderstanding plus some drunken, knee jerk do-gooding and some petty vandalism. We could get them on charges of conspiracy to commit a crime except it turns out it wasn't actually a crime. Wasting police time is an offence but I had it pointed out to me that I'd have to arrest half the population of Pemberland to be sure of getting the right ones. The most serious charge would be unlawful imprisonment, for locking Rother in the Portaloo, but the same problems apply." DI Cowper scowled. "Frankly, I've got better things to do with my time than throw more man hours at this sorry business. Well, since you're satisfied it's the same package, you can make arrangements to collect it."

Dismissed, Mal went to fill in the necessary forms, then found Brian, but it wasn't until he was in the car and the engine was running that he let out his tension in a long sigh.

"Don't worry about Tim," Brian said. "His bark is worse than his bite – most of the time. It's pretty clear that you weren't involved with – um –

whatever happened."

"I wasn't worried about me," Mal said. "I can't help feeling that there could still be some trouble. Especially from Brian Rother."

"Oh Mal, I can't really discuss an open case," Brian's voice was serious but the look he shot at Mal was pure mischief, "but you can safely assume that DI Cowper feels much about Rother as we do. Nobody enjoys being told how to do their job."

Mal wanted to ask Brian how he coped, knowing that shenanigans had occurred, knowing whodunnit, knowing the aim of the conspirators, but never being able to speak up because of the way this odd little town regulated itself. Instead he said, "Well, that's a relief. I was worried I might end up in an orange jumpsuit somewhere."

Brian snorted. "Have you been watching too many US police dramas, or what? No, the boss would love to administer some good hard smacks on the wrist for wasting police time, up to and including jail last week, he was so annoyed. But we've got far too many other, more damaging, things on our plate to waste time gathering enough evidence to gain a conviction."

"I can't imagine what you're up against," Mal said. "Is crime very different in rural areas?"

"Not much. Same sort of nastiness you find everywhere. Car theft, drug dealing, loads of burglaries, plus your genuine sheep rustling is on the rise. Not big money, usually, but it all has to be policed."

"Define 'big money'," Mal said. "I'd imagine the theft of a pensioner's purse could be far more devastating. Or a kid sold rat bait instead of meow meow. Missing archaeology feels so trivial in comparison. To have never got the burial assemblage back would have been a huge disappointment, both personally and professionally. I had a lot of emotional investment in getting the best possible display made and seeing that those two men were –"

"Celebrated," Brian suggested. He was smiling, calm and a little bit wistful as he took the turn towards the old bridge.

"Yes, celebrated is the right word."

"I – er – never said how much I appreciated what you said in Lisa's bit in the paper, that thing about understanding priorities. We all have our own tragedies." Brian smiled and paused to let a woman with a milling bunch of spaniels cross the road. "But at least this turned out well. I'll look forward to your exhibition."

Chapter 25

As soon as Mal got back to the museum, he rang Zoë.

"Hello, bro'," she said. "So what's the news? It can't be bad. I can tell from your breathing."

"Well, actually," Mal beamed, "I think everything might be sorting itself out. First of all, Rob and I are a thing again."

"Thank fuck for that." He could hear that Zoë was smiling. "He's lovely, and doesn't take any of your nonsense. And what about the burial thing?"

"I can fetch it later in the week!"

"How?" She whooped laughing. "You'll never get that on your bike."

"Maybe I can hire a van?" Mal considered. "Or borrow one?"

"How about asking around?" Zoë suggested. "That lovely bloke of yours might know some good strong lads – ooh, I can just imagine them – who can give you a hand."

"Well," Mal smiled because he was using his imagination too, "asking can't hurt, can it?"

"You div." Rob laughed that night when Mal told him about it. "Of course we all want to help. Try and keep us away. Glyn's put a lorry aside for you, and if he's got spare guys they'll come and help. But if I were you, I'd ask Terry to find you some muscle."

Terry was absolutely willing, so on the Friday afternoon in the yard behind the museum Mal had a dozen visitors keeping him and Rob company while they waited for the lorry. Vanessa Gaskell was there with Leo Farriner, both expressing their intention to support the museum in any way they could. Harvey was there, arm in arm with Sharon, who had come in on her day off, and Terry had turned up with a tall bulky man in dungarees and wellies, and two of the Friday Nighters. Scruffy little Dai with his cap pulled down well against the cold wind gave Mal a taciturn nod, but Harry, equally scruffy, but so much grubbier, whooped a greeting to Mal then threatened the immaculately dressed Leo with a hug.

"Get off, brat," Leo said, but Vanessa giggled and offered her cheek for a kiss.

"Morning, Mal," Terry said and gestured to the big man. "This is my friend Alwyn Derry. I reckon he's maybe a cousin of yours a few times removed?"

"Really?" Mal grinned at his possible relative. "I'm so pleased to meet you."

Alwyn shook his hand. "Me too. We'd best compare family trees later, though. I got to get back for milking. Terry asked me to call up another matched pair of weight lifters so I brought Dai and Harry."

"Yeah," Terry grinned. "If you need something bulky shifted, call a farmer. They all have their own steel toe-capped boots and even the little ones can pick up a bullock with one hand and geld it with the other."

There was a rumble of agreement from the various men assembled.

"Thank you all so much for coming to help," Mal said.

"Absolutely our pleasure, darling." Harry offered a mud-smeared hand for Mal to shake. "Apologies for the smell. I've been cleaning out the hen house." He shot a sidelong glance at Rob. "Please don't hold it against me."

"He's not holding anything against you," Rob growled and Mal couldn't help but glow a bit at the possessive tone in Rob's voice.

"I say, here's the lorry." Harvey bounced on his toes. "Oh God, and the Press. Don't worry, Mal. I'll give them some sound bites."

Glyn reversed the vehicle close to the back door then organised the lifting crew according to height despite Mike the photographer's best effort to make them 'line up and point at it'. The power lift at the back of the lorry lowered the pallet, straps were passed under the bed of it then Terry and Alwyn, Rob and Mal, Dai and Harry manhandled the weighty pallet to the back door of the museum, heaved it up over the doorstep then shuffled through the old scullery and to the spot Mal had prepared for it. Gary met them there with Betty and grabbed the strap from Mal so Mal could direct operations.

"Mind your back, Gary," Betty instructed, and Mal stepped back to allow her to work. "You too, Harry. That way a bit, Alwyn."

It didn't take long to slide the pallet into position. Then Mal checked that the readings on the temperature and humidity monitor were holding steady, tweaked the dehumidifier, and shooed out his helpers before locking the door.

"Done," Mal said. "I'll check twice a day, but that should be fine for the time being. I'm so grateful, guys. To all of you."

"No probs." Alwyn grinned at him. "I got to go but we'll be in touch, yeah? Grandpa'll be interested to meet you. He's a great one for family history. Want a lift, Dai?"

Vanessa smiled her pretty, slightly vacuous smile and offered him signed copies of the forms that transferred ownership of the finds officially from her to the museum. "Selwyn told me to make sure that Gaskell Developments' name appears on all the publicity material." She grinned. "But I know that nothing'll be happening for a year or two. It takes money to set up something like that."

"Doesn't it, though?" Rob muttered. "I read something in the *Museums Journal* – what?" He glared as Gary burst into his deep rumbling chuckles. "I was at Mal's and he didn't have the *Beano*. I can read what I like, you div."

"Yes, he can." Mal pointed at Gary. "*Current Archaeology*, a couple of months back, there was an article about the history of domestic canids and there was a reconstruction painting of a man with a dog that looked just exactly like Morris."

"Really?" Gary's face lit up. "I gotta see that."

"You will, love." Betty gave his arm a gentle punch. "I'll be sure to remind, Mal. So, boss. What do we do now?"

"As Vanessa said – fund raising. There's so much I need to organise for this exhibition. Temperature and humidity control for a start."

"The right kind of paint," Betty chipped in.

"Display cases aren't cheap." Harvey smiled at Sharon. "And we need to make sure that everything is kept in tip top condition just to spite Culmstock!"

"I'm not normally one for spite," Glyn said, "But in this case, oh yes. As I said, Mal, Havard Plant Hire will give what it can."

"We'll all see what we can do," Vanessa said. "Have fun tonight. I presume you'll be going out to party."

"Too damn right." Betty beamed and punched Gary in the arm. "Seven o'clock in the Coach?"

"Friday night is White Horse night," Rob pointed out. "But you ladies are welcome to join us. And you too, Mr Farriner. No excuses. You can walk the dog before you come out."

"Oh well …" Leo's cheeks had pinkened a bit but Mal thought it was pleasure rather than embarrassment. "Seven o'clock it is then. But right now I'm due at the magistrates' court. I'll see you all later."

The party at the White Horse was a very satisfying end to the day and Mal, full of good food and feeling a pleasant little buzz from two pints of the excellent mild, was looking forward to getting home for another, more private but more energetic, celebration. The engine of Rob's car purred along the quiet lanes, Rob's thigh flexed slightly under Mal's hand as he changed gear. All was well with the world. So, Mal was a little surprised when Rob slowed the car and indicated to turn into High Rifles Lane.

"Let's just stop here for a while," he said.

"Rob, it's cold as a witch's tit." Mal peered out of the window at the moonlit development and the bright lights of Pemberland beyond. "There's no way I'm going to do anything too excitable tonight."

"Oh Em Gee, you don't trust me?" Rob parked the car in the shadow of the group of hawthorns he'd parked by back in October. "Naaah, it's perishing out there and I don't want icicles on my bits either. There's something I want to show you."

The moon was bright and they both had coats, so Mal didn't protest any further. He got out of the car and slung his arm around Rob's waist as they stumbled through the damp grass. Rob urged him on into the chilly dark, their lungs filled with the rich scent of the turned soil and just a hint of concrete and diesel, and followed the lane up to the top end of the development.

"Just here." Rob said. "I looked at the plans. It's gonna be a weird shaped plot, so a bit wider than the others and quiet because it's at the end of the row. Three bedrooms, though one's only about big enough for a cot – or a desk. It'd make a nice little study maybe. Going to have a tidy bit of garden. I've figured that if I really put in the hours I might have enough saved up to put a deposit on it by the time this end of the development goes on the market. About eighteen months to two years, it should be. Gaskell's doing the four bed houses with the big garages first."

As Rob had been speaking, his arm had tightened around Mal's shoulders, squeezing occasionally as though to add emphasis to *desk* and to *study*. Was there an implication there, or was Mal reading too much into it?

"It's good to have a goal," Mal agreed. "Two years. That's not very long to wait."

"Long time to stay at Dad's." Rob sighed. "But, I dunno. Two years is long enough to really get to know someone. Maybe enough time to figure out if you could share a house with someone?"

Oh, definitely there was an implication, both in the hopeful lilt in Rob's voice and the curl of the arm that urged Mal to turn and face him. Mal did, heart thumping, and held him close.

"And if you might decide to share the house with someone who was also working, maybe you could put a deposit down a bit earlier?" Mal suggested. "I guess you just need to find the right kind of person. Give them the right – um – incentive." Despite the cold and despite his good intentions he couldn't resist dropping a hand to cup one of Rob's firm buttocks under the hem of his coat.

"Well, yeah." Rob's grin might have been hidden by the dark but Mal could hear it in his voice. "So I thought I'd bring you up here and show you that." He pointed to the corner of the field where the hedge delineated the edge of the plot that would one day have a house, a home, on it. The low moon struck shadows across the rise of ground and Mal saw what he most probably would not have been able to see by day. A curving shadow that picked out a low mound, partly grown over by hedge.

"Oh dear God!" he said.

"That is what I think it is then?" Rob asked, beginning to snigger. Mal didn't reply. He clawed his phone from his pocket and took a couple of photos then sent the better one to Harvey with a message. "*Bloody hell there's another one!*"

"Harvey?" Rob asked. "Okay, but I think I'm going to insist we leave this one alone. I like the idea of it being there. Maybe we could turn it into a rockery?"

We. Rob had said 'we'. Mal grinned. Eighteen months to two years was a sensible amount of time in which to make decisions about, perhaps, living together, sharing bills, coming to terms with each other's parents. But there was something about Rob that made Mal feel very un-sensible indeed.

He gave Rob's arse another gentle squeeze. "Or a water feature? But for now, I don't suppose your digger's accessible, is it?"

"Oh aye? I thought you were too cold?"

"I've warmed up." Mal chuckled into Rob's kiss, leaning into his arms and kneading his handful with enthusiasm. Rob's hands slid up his back and icy air crept with them. "Oooh, ow."

"You wuss." Rob kissed him again.

In Mal's pocket his phone vibrated and began to play a specific ringtone, jolly Baroque music ringing out over the silent countryside. "Ah shut up, Harvey" Mal muttered and felt for Rob's mouth again, but Rob was pulling away shaking with laughter.

Down the hill a torch beam swung wildly and a familiar voice roared, "I'll get you, you little bastards."

"Or we could go back to yours?" Rob suggested.

"You'll be very welcome. Race you back to the car."

About the Author

Elin Gregory lives in South Wales and has been making stuff up since 1958. Writing has always had to take second place to work and family but now the kids are grown up it's possible she might finish one of the many novels on her hard drive and actually DO something useful with it.

Historical subjects predominate. She has written about ancient Greek sculptors, 18th century seafarers but also about modern men who change shape at will and how echoes of the past can be heard in the present. Heroes tend to be hard as nails but capable of tenderness when circumstances allow.

There are always new works on the go and she is currently writing about the Great War, editing a contemporary romance and doing background reading for a story set in Roman Britain.

Manifold Press

Life in all the colours of the rainbow

For **Readers**: LGBTQ+ fiction and romance with strong storylines from acclaimed authors. A variety of intriguing locations – set in the past, present or future – sometimes with a supernatural twist. Our focus is always on the characters and the story.

For **Authors**: We are always happy to consider high-quality new projects from aspiring and established writers.

Our 'regular' novels are now joined by the **Espresso Shots** imprint for novellas and our **New Adult** line. Visit our website to discover more!

ManifoldPress.co.uk

Made in the USA
Middletown, DE
31 August 2017